MAD ABOUT MIA

MILLIE CRISWELL

IVY BOOKS • NEW YORK

An Ivy Book
Published by The Random House Publishing Group
Copyright © 2004 by Millie Criswell

ISBN 0-7394-4018-7

Manufactured in the United States of America

To old friends and new:

Jesse, for thirteen years of unconditional love. I miss you!
Jake, for bringing joy back to my life.
Matt, for helping with all the legal stuff.
Leanne, for always being there when I need a shoulder to cry on.
Maggie, for use of the Wonderbra comment.
And to Larry, for everything!

ONE

Childhood is what you spend the rest of your
life overcoming.
Hope Floats

"Broke, busted, disgusted, parents can't be trusted
And Mia wants to go to the sea . . ."

Holding the firm banana that she'd brought for her
lunch like a microphone, Mia DeNero belted out "Creeque
Alley" at the top of her lungs, accompanying the Mamas
and the Papas, whose '60s song blared from the boom
box in the corner, while changing the lyrics slightly to
suit her miserable state.

Actually, her state wasn't really all that miserable, just
disappointing. The kind of disappointment that gives
you that funny little sick ache in the pit of your stomach
each time you think you might fail.

She'd finally opened her protective services business,
The Guardian Angel, despite major protests from her
parents, and had set up business in an old, smelly vacant
storefront on Eastern Avenue; the place used to be a fish-
and-chips restaurant and still reeked of old grease and
vinegar. But the rent was cheap, and right now she needed
cheap.

"Greasin' on American Express cards . . ."

Ha! Wasn't that the truth? Soon her credit cards

would be maxed, and then she'd be in major deep doo-doo. And she was determined not to borrow a cent from her parents, or from Angela, though her big sister had offered to help numerous times. But Mia was too proud to accept a handout, and determined to make it on her own.

Failure was not an option.

Been there, done that!

Surely there had to be someone who wanted to hire her. Being new to the area, and not having the advantage of referrals, she'd placed an ad in the local newspaper, *The Baltimore Sun,* more than two weeks ago, and had even passed out flyers to all of the local businesses in her area, hoping someone might need her services, or could recommend a friend who did.

Of course, Little Italy wasn't exactly the crime capital of the world. And there might not be too many people in need of protection. But she needed only one.

Plopping down in the rickety old swivel chair she had purchased at Carboni's Used Furniture, Mia propped her feet up on the equally battered gray metal desk and peeled her banana. No longer in the mood for singing, she took a bite out of her "microphone" and chewed.

Glancing around the small office, she grimaced at the badly dented metal filing cabinet, the ugly chair that fronted her desk, and the hideous bent-out-of-shape Venetian blinds covering the front window which she'd tried to clean before moving in and had ended up ruining in the process.

All in all, it was not a place to inspire prospective clients, unless, of course, they were Jack the Ripper. Though her diploma hanging on the wall behind her desk did certify that she had passed a bodyguard training course at the Serve and Protect Bodyguard School in Towson, Maryland. It was signed by Mike Hammersmith, her instructor, the man she'd nearly killed at the shooting range one day.

Mia had been a bit nearsighted—okay, a lot nearsighted—which made shooting a gun at any distance a bit problematic. But she wasn't about to let that little detail deter her. She now had contacts, though she didn't like to wear them.

Munching on her so-called lunch, which her mother would have found lacking—Rosalie DeNero was of the opinion that everyone should consume at least ten thousand calories per day—Mia focused all of her attention on the front door, willing someone to appear.

At this point, she didn't much care if it was a client. Sitting in her tiny office day after day, waiting for the phone to ring, or a living entity to visit, was not only lonely, it was damn boring, depressing, and totally disheartening.

Did she mention boring?

So when the front door opened, Mia was so startled that she shifted in her chair a little too quickly, trying to move her feet off the desk at the same time, hoping to present the best appearance to whomever it was that was calling. But she ended up pushing back on the old chair too hard, causing it to topple over backward.

Which was how Niccolò Caruso found her.

Nick leaned over the desk to make sure the woman who'd suddenly disappeared from sight was okay. One minute she was eating a banana and the next . . . *Boom!* Gone.

"Are you all right?" He pushed his glasses back up his nose and extended a hand, biting back a smile. Mia DeNero, with her Orphan Annie brown curly locks, was fifteen shades of red, but seemed otherwise unhurt.

"Yes, thanks. I was just daydreaming, and you caught me off guard. Let me assure you that I'm not usually so clumsy," she said, trying to right her chair and brush off her jeans at the same time. "How can I help you?"

Nick gazed at the pint-sized woman before him and wondered the same thing. She couldn't have been more than five feet, three inches in her stocking feet. His idea to hire Mia DeNero as a bodyguard might have been a little too rash.

Rash, hell! It was downright insane!

But he had a job to do, and she was going to help him do it.

"I'm in need of protection, Miss DeNero. I found one of your flyers and it was like an answer to my prayer." Nick hoped he sounded nerdy enough. He was certainly making himself sick.

Folding her hands atop the desk, Mia DeNero tried her damnedest to look professional and totally together. Unfortunately, there was a blob of banana clinging to the end of her pert little nose. Leaning toward her, he proffered his handkerchief. "Allow me. It seems you're still wearing your lunch."

"Oh, Jesus!" She shook her head, swiping her nose with the back of her hand, and then wiping the blob on her jeans.

Nick stared in amusement.

"I'm sure you think I'm a complete moron, but let me assure you that I'm a trained professional and very good in my field." Well, she was pretty sure that she would be good, if she just had a client to practice on.

Taking a seat, he arched a disbelieving brow and crossed muscular arms over his chest. "Really? And how many clients have you protected this past year, Miss DeNero? Can you provide references?"

She shook her head, her cheeks filling with color. "Well, no. You're my first one, actually. I've just opened for business, you see. But that means you're in luck, because I can give you our special introductory rate, and my complete attention." She hoped he was impressed. He didn't look very impressed. Maybe she should throw in a free pizza, or something.

He rubbed his chin. "I see."

Yanking a yellow legal pad across the desk, Mia picked up her pen, unwilling to let her first client slip away. "Let's start with your name, and the reason you need a bodyguard."

"My name is Niccolò Caruso. Perhaps you've heard of me? I'm an author."

An author! Now that was impressive. Mia should have guessed from the thick-framed glasses and ugly tweed jacket he wore. Tweed! She wrinkled her nose. Even the name was horrific, conjuring up old Sherlock Holmes movies.

"Afraid not. I don't have much time to read." A flaw she intended to correct. *Someday. Maybe.* Mia had made procrastination into an art form. "What kind of books do you write?"

"Mostly nonfiction. I've dabbled in true crime from time to time. And it's no wonder you haven't read any of my work. My books are out of print, unfortunately. But I'm presently working on an exposé of the Mafia, and I have great faith that it's going to recharge my career."

Mia's dark eyes widened. "Really? Aren't you afraid?"

"Well, yes, actually I am. I've had threats made on my life."

She gasped. "They're trying to silence you."

"That's right. But I won't be deterred. I intend to finish my book, and the consequences be damned. That's why I'm here, Miss DeNero. I'm hoping you'll be able to help me."

Mia's heart was beating so fast she felt like a hummingbird on speed. The Mafia was big-time stuff. If she could pull this off—okay, the odds were slim, but her motto had always been "no pain, no gain." "Of course, I'll help you. I can offer you twenty-four-hour protection; that's twenty-four/seven, until you finish your book. Do you live here in Baltimore?"

"Yes, I do. What's the usual procedure in these matters? I've never hired a bodyguard before."

"Normally, the way it works is that I move onto your premises and live with you."

"*Hmmm.* Well, that's fine, if you're willing to put up with my elderly aunt. She's rather a cantankerous old bird, and well . . . I'm embarrassed to say that the house smells a bit odd. Of course, you'll get used to the odor in time."

"Odd? How do you mean?"

"Aunt Bertrice is quite fond of Vick's VapoRub, and the house reeks of it. Then there's the other—"

Mia held up her hand, fearful she would barf if he continued. She had a feeling she knew what the "other" entailed. "Never mind. I get the picture."

Hell! What was she going to do now? No way was she moving into some smelly old lady's house. But she abhorred having a roommate. Her last two had been disastrous. No privacy, no food left in the fridge. No way!

"We could get adjoining hotel rooms? I'm sure that would work."

He shook his head. "Afraid not. I can't write in such an environment. I require total silence when I'm working. I don't like distractions of any kind."

Well, hell! It looked like she had no choice. Mia heard herself say, "I guess you could move in with me temporarily. But I should warn you, Mr. Caruso, that my apartment is small. I live above Mama Sophia's restaurant, here in Little Italy. It's not as quiet as you might like. And my landlady is a bit of a harridan." Major understatement. Donatella Foragi was a two-hundred-plus-pound walking, talking nightmare. She made the Bates Motel seem welcoming by comparison.

"Your offer is quite generous, Miss DeNero, and I'm happy to accept. I'm prepared to give you three thousand dollars per month, to cover the cost of your services, and for allowing me to live with you. I don't mind admitting that I'm scared of these hoodlums."

"Three thous—" She tried to catch her breath. Three thousand dollars a month would solve all of her pressing financial problems. The guy must be loaded. The most she would have charged him would have been a thousand, but she had no intention of letting him know that.

"That certainly seems fair. Do we need to go by your house to get your things?"

Are you insane, Mia? Are you really going to allow a total stranger you've just met to move in with you? A man you know nothing about? Caruso could be a serial rapist or killer.

Although, upon further reflection, she thought he looked more like a serial geek. He certainly had clothing issues, not that she should talk. But jeans were preferable to—was that corduroy he was wearing? My God! The man was a regular Howdy Doody. All he needed was a plaid shirt.

"Is there something the matter, Miss DeNero? You look distracted."

"How do I know you are who you say you are? Do you have identification? I need to be careful in my position, Mr. Caruso. I'm sure you understand."

"And I'd fault you if you weren't." Nick pulled out his wallet and showed Mia his driver's license. His wallet was bulging with hundred-dollar bills, which did not go unnoticed by the young woman, whose pupils were dilating rapidly.

"You'll have to sleep on the couch. I have only the one bedroom."

"That's not a problem."

Surprise, surprise! He probably doesn't get urges like normal men, she thought. After all, he still lived with his elderly aunt. What kind of man does that? Of course, to be fair, the older woman could be sick, which would make him a dutiful nephew. On the other hand—

"Miss DeNero?"

Smiling warmly, she stuck out her hand to seal their agreement. When he grasped hers in what felt like a pretty strong grip, a tiny shock of electricity raced up her arm, astounding her. "I'm certain our arrangement will work out quite nicely for both of us, Mr. Caruso. You're in good hands."

His thumb moved over the back of hers, and Mia swallowed with some difficulty. "I can see that. I think I'm going to like having my very own guardian angel."

"Oh, I'm sure you will. I can be very accommodating."

Nick's smile was almost wicked. "I'm counting on that, Miss DeNero."

* * *

"I can't believe you're going to allow a person you know nothing about to move in with you! Have you lost your mind? Wait till Mom hears. She's going to come unglued."

Like that was something new?

Rosalie DeNero gave new meaning to the term *hysteria*. Until recently, her mother believed that Armageddon was descending. Now, she just worried incessantly about every little thing.

Do you have enough toilet paper, Mia?

Are you bundling up when you go outside?

Did you remember to pay your electric bill?

Whoops! Well, two out of three wasn't bad.

Heaving a sigh, Mia's gaze fell on her older sister, who was in her office seated behind an impressive mahogany desk, so unlike Mia's used furniture. Angela was a lawyer, and partner in the firm Stefano, Franco, and Franco. She was married to John Franco, one of the senior partners.

An alarmist, Angela saw evil lurking behind every bush. She was also one of those women who actually looked good pregnant. Mia figured she'd look like Henrietta Hippo, if and when that day came. Not that it would come any time soon. The mere idea of having a baby gave Mia hives.

In eighth grade, her best friend Sarah Rafferty's mother had died giving birth. Mrs. Rafferty had only been thirty-one at the time—the same age Mia was now.

"I checked him out," Mia replied, but Angela remained skeptical.

"How, if you don't mind my asking?"

She shrugged, trying to sound confident. "The usual

methods—visual profile, driver's license . . . Did I tell you Caruso's a published author? The notoriety alone from this case could put my business on the map."

Rising to her feet, Angela tugged the hem of her green jersey maternity blouse, then rounded the desk to take a seat in the chair next to Mia. "Did you actually run his plates, check with the Maryland Department of Motor Vehicles, to see if his driver's license is real? It could be a fake, you know."

"Oh, for heaven's sake, Angela! Quit trying to tell me how to do my job. I've been trained, in case you've forgotten." Her sister rolled her eyes, prompting Mia to add, "I know you're a hotshot lawyer, and smarter than me, but give me some credit for knowing what I'm doing."

"I take it that means no."

"Niccolò Caruso is an author. If you saw the way he dressed, Angie, you'd know he poses no threat. Did I mention he wears corduroy pants?" Her sister's eyes widened, and Mia smiled smugly. "Caruso lives with his elderly aunt. He's not a sexual deviant"—*I should be so lucky*—"or a serial killer. My instincts tell me Niccolò Caruso is exactly who and what he says he is."

Geek. Nerd. Major nerd.

"I need this job. I've gone through most of my savings. And you know very well, having had Mrs. Foragi for a landlady, that she isn't going to wait much longer for the security deposit that's overdue."

"I can lend you—"

"No!" Mia shook her head emphatically, her curls bouncing every which way, like an out-of-control Slinky toy. "I'm going to do this on my own. I have to prove to myself that I can. And I have to prove to Dad, and everyone else who's ever doubted me, that I'm not the scatter-brained, impulsive woman they think I am."

Her expression softening, Angela reached for Mia's hand and squeezed. "Now, Mia, you know that's not what everyone thinks. We love you. Dad loves you. He doesn't think those things about you."

"Oh, really? That's news to me. Dad thinks I'm a flake, a complete moron, and just because I've made some rather unorthodox career choices over the years." Okay, so maybe driving a bulldozer on a highway construction crew hadn't been the greatest job she'd ever taken. But she'd stuck it out, had proven, if only to herself, that she could compete with men at their own level. Not an easy feat, when your on-the-job nickname was "Munchkin."

"I'm trying to be supportive, but I'm worried that you've bitten off more than you can chew. The Mafia is nothing to fool around with, Mia. These guys play for keeps. Be realistic. You don't pose much of an obstacle. If they want to get to this Caruso, they're going to find a way.

"Didn't you see *The Godfather*? Don't you remember how they took Sonny out in broad daylight, riddled him with bullets?"

"Of course, I remember. James Caan was so cute. Remember when he was banging— Never mind." She shook her head. "They're not going to get Caruso. Not if I have anything to say about it. I have a gun, don't forget."

"How could I? As I recall, I had to represent you in court when Mr. Hammersmith tried to have you thrown out of the bodyguard program. Not that I could blame him. You did almost kill the man."

"That wasn't my fault. How was I supposed to know that I needed glasses for distance?"

Angela crossed her arms over her chest. "Which brings me to the question—have you had your prescription filled yet?"

Mia nodded. "I have contacts." She'd never before considered herself vain, but every eyeglass frame she'd tried on at the optometrist's office had made her look like a bullfrog in the throes of death, so she had opted for contact lenses.

"Just be careful, okay? I don't want to read about your demise in the newspaper. Who would run interference for me with Mom and Dad if you disappeared?" Angela shuddered at the prospect.

"Now that you're married, you don't need my help anymore. Mom thinks the sun rises and sets on John. And Dad's been making a valiant effort to tone down his ensembles when you visit."

Angela laughed. "Quite a sacrifice, I must say."

Sam DeNero was a cross-dressing ex-cop, retired from the Boston Police Department and now living in Baltimore. His sense of fashion was a bit different from most men—he liked wearing women's clothing, which he bought from the Home Shopping Network. Sam had a real weakness for sequins and rhinestones. On his best day he was a Bob Mackie nightmare.

"Dad shouldn't criticize me when he's got his own problems."

"Dad doesn't think he has a problem."

"Well, I know I don't. From here on out all of my problems are solved, thanks to Niccolò Caruso and his generous retainer."

Angela looked as if she had more to say on the subject, but she smiled instead, saying, "I hope you're right."

Mia flashed a confident grin. "I know I am."

Staring at the heavyset, older man seated across the table from him at O'Grady's Irish Pub, Nick knew Burt Mulrooney was as close to a best friend as he was ever going to have.

They worked together at the FBI, and had been part of the Organized Crime Investigation Unit for the past nine years. Burt was his mentor, and the father he'd never had.

Mulrooney was a good guy, and a damn good agent. He hated to shave, always sported at least three days' growth of beard, now graying, and his belly confirmed his love for Guinness. He was Irish, through and through, down to the green articles of clothing he always wore.

"I bet Higgins ain't too pleased about this undercover op of yours, boyo. You'd better not screw up or he'll have your ass for dinner."

Nick popped a handful of peanuts into his mouth, then sipped his ice-cold beer. "Special Agent in Charge Higgins is the one who authorized this plan. My ass is covered, old man, so quit worrying. It's not good for your blood pressure." Burt had gained a considerable amount of weight since his last divorce over a year ago, and Nick was concerned that his friend was going to have a heart attack if he didn't pay more attention to his diet.

"How can I quit worrying? You're using an innocent civilian, Caruso, and if anything happens to that girl . . ."

"Relax. You're starting to sound like an old woman. Nothing's going to happen. Mia DeNero is thrilled to have a client to protect. She promises to be *'accommo-dating.'* " Nick flashed a grin. "I'm moving in with her later this afternoon, at her invitation, I might add."

"Jesus, Mary, and Joseph!" The older man's jaw dropped, and he shook his head of thinning red hair. "Not smart, boyo. Not smart, at all."

"It's perfect, Burt. Mia DeNero lives right above Mama Sophia's restaurant, eats there quite often, as a matter of fact. I'll be able to keep close tabs on the suspect, who frequents the establishment. Granted, it's not a perfect arrangement, but it's the best one I could come up with.

"Plus, Miss DeNero's sister, Angela Franco, married into the Russo family recently—her husband is Sophia Russo's nephew—which gives me another in. I'll be able to interview family members and obtain information that I wouldn't otherwise have access to."

Burt scoffed. "Can't believe those assholes at the Bureau think Alfredo Graziano knows anything about anything. I'd bet a month's supply of Guinness on that. He's strictly small potatoes, despite his claim to the contrary. He'd probably shit his pants if he ever got close to any mafioso."

"Probably, but he might be able to lead us to those who are involved. Money laundering is a very lucrative business, and our friend Alfredo has been flashing big bucks around lately. Legitimate car dealers don't make that kind of money, especially those splitting profits with a partner. Besides, Graziano has only himself to blame for raising everyone's suspicions. The man should have learned to keep his bragging to a minimum."

Reaching for the peanuts, Burt swallowed a handful,

then asked, "How come the woman asked you to move in with her? I realize you're God's gift and all, but . . ."

"I told her my elderly aunt lived with me, and I painted a rather disgusting picture of what life was like in the Caruso household. Plus, she needs the money. I made her an offer she couldn't pass up."

"You don't have an elderly aunt."

"Miss DeNero doesn't know that."

Burt's look was incredulous. "Is this woman stupid? She sounds stupid."

Nick shook his head. "Not at all. Just naïve, which is why I chose her. She's new to the bodyguard business, and as green as that ugly shirt you're wearing. I'm counting on her inexperience, and praying that she's not the inquisitive type."

Burt ignored the insult. He and Nick exchanged them on a regular basis, so he was used to his friend's biting comments. "I suppose she's a looker."

"Not exactly what you'd call beautiful, but cute as a button."

"I'm surprised you noticed, Caruso. You don't usually give women the time of day."

"Because I'm not looking to get involved with anyone, Burt, and certainly not with Miss DeNero. She's merely a means to an end."

"Yeah, that's what I said about wives one through three. Only the end stank." Burt motioned for the waitress to bring them another round.

"You can't blame your ex-wife for bailing on you, Burt. You're overweight, you drink too much, and you dress like shit. Plus, your hours suck. And you never took poor Gloria out anywhere. A woman will only stand for so many football games and poker parties."

The older man shook his head. "I realize now that Gloria was too young. As much as I hate to admit it, I should never have let Muriel go. She was the best of the lot."

Muriel was Burt's first wife. A homebody through and through, she had doted on her husband, waiting on him hand and foot. But Burt, being Burt, had never appreciated what he had until she was gone. He had tried to replace Muriel over the years with an assortment of women, but none of them had measured up to his first wife.

"So maybe you and your ex-wife should think about a reunion? Absence makes the heart grow fonder, they say."

Burt looked at Nick as if he'd lost his mind. "Are you nuts? The woman hates my guts. I cheated on her. Remember Vivian, wife number two? Besides, I heard Muriel remarried; he's a pharmaceutical salesman. Don't know what she sees in someone like that."

"You haven't spoken to Muriel in over ten years. For all you know, she may be widowed or divorced by now."

Burt thought a moment, looked hopeful, then a resigned expression settled on his face. "*Nah*. It's best to let sleeping dogs lie, too much muddy water under the bridge.

"And who are you to be giving me advice? You're the one known as the heartbreaker at the field office. Or have you forgotten the trail of disappointed females you've left in your wake?"

"I'm always up-front with the women I date. They're never under any illusions that our relationship is ever going beyond friendship and sex. That's just the way it is."

"You don't know much about women, Caruso. No matter how many times they tell you they understand, that it's fine with them, it's not. They're always thinking they can change your mind, turn you to the dark side."

"You been watching *Star Wars* again?"

"Best damn movie ever made. And don't change the subject. I'm on to you."

Nick shrugged. "I'm happy living the life I lead. If they can't deal with it, too bad."

"I think you're full of bullshit. So you had a rotten childhood. So what? Lots of people have. That doesn't mean you should push people away—women, in particular."

"Leave it go, old man. I'm not interested in hearing your opinions and psychological babble again. You're starting to sound like Dr. Phil. Pretty soon you'll be going on *Oprah*."

"Someday you'll be sorry for being such a callous bastard, Caruso."

"Maybe. But until that day comes I'm quite content to remain exactly as I am."

TWO

You aren't too bright, are you?
I like that in a man.
Body Heat

Nick Caruso looked as if he had just swallowed something utterly distasteful, like canned peas that mushed in your mouth when you ate them. Mia hated canned peas. Just the thought of them made her grimace.

"I tried to tell you the place was small. Guess you believe me now, huh? You can always change your mind, and we can go to a hotel instead." Mia was hopeful he would take the hint, but he looked like he was digging in for the duration.

Looking around for an inch of space where he could set his things, Nick finally settled on the arm of the sofa, the only part that wasn't strewn with Mia's clean underwear. Placing his suits carefully there, he tried not to stare at the lacy bras and teeny underpants, tried not to think about what she'd look like in them . . . *out of them.*

Heat rose up his neck, and he rubbed his sweating hands on his pants. "Uh, no, this will be fine. I'm just a bit surprised by the lack of . . ." He searched for just the right word as his gaze swept the room again, and he came up with "order," his nose wrinkling in distaste.

Nick was a firm believer in the old adage: a place for everything and everything in its place. Living most of his formative years in chaos and confusion had done that for him.

"Yeah, well, I live alone, or used to. And I wasn't expecting company, so I haven't folded my laundry and put it away yet. I take it you're one of those neatness fanatics."

"Guilty as charged, I'm afraid."

Mia swallowed a sigh. "Life's too short to worry about stuff like that, Nick. Hope I can call you Nick, because Niccolò is just too darn long to bother with." Plus, it sounded a bit effeminate, but she didn't want to insult him by saying so. Not that he minded one bit about insulting her lack of "order," as he so ungraciously put it.

So what if she wasn't Martha Stewart? The woman was a freak. It was unnatural for any human being to know so much about housework—*Who knew there were thirty-four ways to disinfect your toilet bowl?*—cooking— *So I don't have my own herb garden. Sue me!*—crafts— *Martha could probably sew curtains out of sanitary pads. Yuck!*

Mia pointed to the cranberry leather sofa. "You'll be sleeping there," she told Nick, then indicated the closed door leading to her bedroom. "That's my room, so if you need to use the bathroom, you're going to have to knock and let me know ahead of time. You've got to go through my bedroom to get to the bathroom," she explained. "Not the most convenient arrangement, but—"

"Understood. Where shall I set up my computer? I brought my laptop, so it wouldn't take up as much space.

But I'll need to spread out, with my research notes, books, and such, you understand?"

Mia scanned the small room, and was tempted to tell Nick Caruso exactly where he could stuff his computer and precious books, but then she thought about the three-thousand-dollar check that would soon be resting comfortably in her checking account, and opted to keep her comments to herself. This was a cushy arrangement, and she had no intention of blowing it. "I've got a card table you can use. It's pretty sturdy."

"A card table?" He tried not to show his dismay. Too late. Mia was glaring at him. "Fine. I'll go down to my car and get the rest of my sh . . . er . . . things. Have you had dinner yet?"

She shook her head. "I've got some frozen meals in the freezer. I was just going to pop a Stouffer's into the microwave. You're welcome to one of them."

"You eat frozen dinners?" He looked horrified at the prospect and made a face of disgust. "How about we go downstairs to that restaurant you mentioned? My treat. What did you call it, Mama Sophia's? It's Italian, right?"

"Uh, yeah." She refrained from rolling her eyes, but couldn't keep the sarcasm out of her voice. Maybe she should have charged him four thousand dollars. He was already starting to irritate her. "Little Italy. Italian. Get it? There's no shortage of Italian restaurants in this neighborhood, Nick. In fact, there are probably three or four on every block. That's why they call it Little Italy. *Capisce?*"

"I'll just go fetch my things."

"You do that, then we'll have dinner at Mama Sophia's, if that's what you want."

The look he gave her was filled with gratitude. She noticed how pretty his gray eyes were behind the hideous black Buddy Holly eyeglass frames he wore.

"I can't tell you how much better I feel now that I'm safely ensconced in your apartment, Miss DeNero."

Ensconced. Did people really talk like that? She had a college degree from Boston College and she didn't say words like "ensconced." "It's Mia, and I'm glad to help. I think this arrangement is going to suit both of us just fine."

"So do I, Mia." His smile was so dazzling and sweet that she grew momentarily flustered, until she remembered he wore corduroy and was a nerd. Well, it had been a long time since she'd—

"Shall I accompany you downstairs to get the rest of your things?" Mia asked quickly, horrified where her mind had traveled, and with whom. "I can keep a lookout, if you're worried or scared about going outside alone."

He shook his head. "No, I'll be fine. No one will think to look for me here; I'm positive of that."

She watched him walk out the door, and then shook her head. The poor man was frightened out of his wits, that was for certain. Mia had always been a sucker for stray animals and puppies, which was exactly what Nick Caruso reminded her of—a lost soul in need of protection.

She'd have to utilize a bit more patience where he was concerned. After all, he didn't seem very worldly, despite the fact he was an author. And he was paying for her services. Which brought up the nagging question: why?

Why had Nick Caruso chosen her as a bodyguard? He seemed to have plenty of money. He could have hired someone with more experience, not to mention a bigger apartment. So why did he choose to go with a wet-behind-the-ears female?

Don't ask, Mia! You need the money.

The man obviously had issues. Maybe he felt more relaxed and less intimidated having a female bodyguard. After all, he lived with his aunt. How normal could he be?

Mia's gaze locked on the clothing he had left on the couch and made a face of disgust. More corduroy and tweed. *Ugh*. And there was even a herringbone jacket.

Good God! She was having a Sir Arthur Conan Doyle moment. All that was missing was the deerstalker cap.

Do all authors dress so hideously?

She didn't think so.

John Grisham always wore jeans and a cool-looking sports coat. And he had that three-day growth of beard thing going for him. Kinda sexy. She didn't think Grisham, or even Tom Clancy, who was no looker by any stretch of the imagination, would be caught dead in tweed or herringbone. She wasn't sure about Stephen King; he was rather . . . different.

Clothes definitely made the man.

Poor Nick.

At the moment, poor Nick was crouched low in his car seat, talking on his cell phone to SAC Higgins—a man he considered arrogant, borderline incompetent, but who was still his boss and commanded respect, if only for that reason.

"Yes, sir, I've moved in. I'll start surveillance tonight. We're having dinner at Mama Sophia's. According to my source, Graziano eats there almost every night of the week."

Nick held the phone away from his ear, murmuring agreement at the appropriate times, as Higgins went on, ad nauseum, about the cost of the operation, how the Bureau couldn't afford any lawsuits, since they were already facing budget cuts, and warning Nick, much as Burt had told him he would, not to screw up.

Higgins didn't come right out and say his job was on the line, but Nick had been with the FBI long enough to know that his future depended on getting the goods on Graziano, or whomever was involved with the money-laundering scheme going on in Little Italy.

There'd been a screw-up on the last operation, and he had shouldered the blame, though it hadn't been entirely his fault. Crime boss Johnny Malcuso had walked away from a racketeering charge because the evidence seized had been the result of an improper search—a violation of the Fourth Amendment. The agents he'd sent in had neglected to obtain the proper warrant that sufficiently described the premises to be searched, and the judge had thrown out the case as a result.

Higgins had been furious. And since it had been Nick's operation, and his call to send in relatively inexperienced agents, he'd accepted the blame.

Disconnecting, Nick leaned back against the headrest and sighed. His new role as Dork of the Year was already beginning to grate, and it was only the first day.

Mia thought he was the complete geek from hell, and that he was afraid of his own shadow, a pathetic excuse for a man. Of course, if this charade was going to work, that's exactly what she must continue to believe, no matter how painful it was to have her look at him as if he were truly pathetic.

If he had any ego left after this operation it would be a miracle.

Nick hadn't made up his mind about what he thought of Mia. Aside from being cute and very naïve, she had guts, and he liked that about her. Facing the Mafia, if only because she believed she had to, wasn't an easy prospect, even for a seasoned and experienced agent like himself. She seemed intelligent and pretty damn calm and collected for a woman who probably knew very little about being a bodyguard. He wondered if she had ever fired a gun outside of training class. He doubted it.

Still, despite her lack of experience, she had grit. Spunk, Burt would call it. And she was pretty easygoing, far more so than he. Though she wasn't the tidiest person he'd ever come across.

Nick liked things orderly. Orphaned as a small child, and raised in a succession of foster homes, he hadn't had many personal possessions while growing up. He'd worn hand-me-down clothing and underwear that often came from the Goodwill store, and his shoes had more often than not been too small for his growing feet.

Some of the families with whom he'd resided hadn't been too awful, but there'd been others who'd lived like animals, in homes that were filthy and unkempt, and who had forced the children in their care to live the same way.

Nick had sworn an oath that if he ever got a home of his own, and had enough money to buy nice clothes and furnishings, he would take care of them, treasure them.

You had to go without, before you could appreciate what you had.

And Nick had gone without for a very long time.

He thought of Mia, her frilly underwear, the way she

smelled, all clean and fresh, like the great outdoors, not cloying and overdone like some of the other women he knew, and he cursed a blue streak, steaming up the windows.

And himself.

This charade wasn't going to be easy to pull off. He had to keep his perspective, keep his mind on the matter at hand. He had a job to do; he couldn't afford any distractions.

And dammit! Mia DeNero was definitely a distraction.

"How come you keep glancing over your shoulder like you're looking for someone? Don't you like the manicotti? Do you want me to call Mary over? She owns the place. I'm sure she'll be happy to bring you something else, if you're not happy with it."

Noting Mia's too inquisitive stare, her eagerness to accommodate, Nick shook his head and cursed inwardly his stupidity in being so obvious. "It's great. Really."

Graziano hadn't put in an appearance this evening as yet, and Nick hoped the alleged suspect would arrive before he and Mia finished their meal and had to leave. He hadn't spotted anyone else who looked remotely suspicious and was counting on Graziano's arrival, hoping the older man would bring some of his acquaintances with him—someone Nick might recognize from FBI file photos.

"I'm sure you've heard how nosy we authors are, Mia," he said in an effort to cover his error. "I take great interest in my surroundings. I love studying people. I find it's quite useful for creating interesting and believable characters and settings."

Jesus! He was starting to sound like he knew what he was talking about. Scary.

"Writing must be hard work. I could never fill up one page, let alone hundreds. Don't know how you do it."

"You seem to be an intelligent woman. I'm sure you wouldn't have any trouble with the creative process. It's just a matter of keeping your bu . . . behind in the chair and remaining disciplined."

Disciplined! Yikes! Mia shook her head, knowing that wasn't one of her strong suits, either.

Sipping her wine, she said, "My sister's the smart one in the family. Angela's a lawyer. She always got the best grades in school, and ended up marrying a really nice man, who's just as smart as she is. Angela's made quite a success of her life." Unlike me, she could have added.

Mia had been into shortcuts, and taking the easy way out for most of her adult life. She'd stuck it out in college, earned her bachelor's degree, but had had no desire to further her education. The truth was she hadn't known what she wanted to do with her life. Law had never interested her, as it had Angela, teaching was out—she wasn't that fond of kids—and she had no desire to work for someone else in a boring nine-to-five job.

She hadn't been any more successful in her relationships with men. At twenty, she'd fallen madly in love with one of her professors, who'd professed to love her back. They'd spoken of marriage, children, and traveling to exotic places. He had painted a rosy picture, laying out their futures before her, like a magic carpet. And she'd believed him. Believed every word that poured out of Greg Farris's mouth, until the day the professor's wife had shown up at her apartment.

The young, attractive woman had been residing in Los

Angeles with her two young children, taking care of her dying mother, while Mrs. Farris's husband had been taking care of Mia.

Mia had been humiliated, devastated, and hurt beyond belief. She'd experienced every emotion known to a woman who'd been played for a fool, and then she'd gotten angry. And she'd stayed angry for the last eleven years, vowing never to let any man use her so shamelessly again.

"Is it too much to hope that this sister of yours has a large wart on the end of her nose and weighs three hundred pounds?" Nick asked, interrupting her disturbing reverie.

His eyes twinkled with merriment, and Mia forced a smile. "Angela's a babe. She's gorgeous. Of course, now that she's married and pregnant she probably wouldn't like me saying that."

"Sounds like you suffer from second-child syndrome. Do you have other brothers and sisters?"

"Nope, just the one sister. And you're right. Angela is the eldest, and the apple of my father's eye. How about you? Do you have any brothers or sisters?"

He masked the pain her question elicited, then shook his head. "No, just my aunt. I was an only child." A *lonely* child. "My parents are both dead. I went to live with my aunt when I was quite small; she raised me." If only he'd been that lucky, he thought, as the lies rolled off his tongue.

"I'm sorry. That must have been tough. It's really a shame you don't have any siblings. Angela and I are very close and always have been. I can't imagine not having her in my life. My parents are kinda weird, so we've always run interference for each other. Not that I don't love them, because I do. It's just that they're . . . well, parents."

"I'd like to meet them." Horror flashed across her face, and Nick smiled, asking, "Do you eat here often? I hope so, because I'd like to come back again. I'm really enjoying the food."

"Great. I'll call Mary over and let her know. She's really sweet, and would love to hear your opinion."

"Oh, that's not necess—" But it was too late. Mia was already motioning the dark-haired woman over. Nick, who'd been trying not to draw unnecessary attention to himself, knew Mia had now made that impossible; he plastered on a smile.

"Mary Gallagher, this is my client, Nick Caruso. Nick's staying with me temporarily, so I guess you'll be seeing a lot of us. Nick loves the food at Mama Sophia's."

"What's not to like?" Mary replied with a wink, smiling warmly at Nick as she held out her hand to him.

"Excellent cuisine, Mrs. Gallagher," he said to the pregnant woman. "I'll be back often, you can be sure of that."

"Thanks!" Mary rubbed the small of her back, then plopped down in the chair next to Mia. "We try."

"Mary's married to a former food critic—the same one who trashed this very restaurant in the newspaper when it first opened. I wasn't living here then, but everyone in Little Italy loves to talk about it."

Nick's eyes widened. "You must be the forgiving sort, Mrs. Gallagher. I'm not very fond of reviewers, and I doubt I would have been as gracious."

"You haven't seen Dan," Mia told him. "The guy's hot."

Mary laughed. "You've probably already discovered

that Mia speaks her mind, Nick. Welcome to the neighborhood. I've got to get back to the kitchen to make sure Mario—that's my chef—isn't throwing knives again. Damn Italian is so temperamental he makes me crazy. Dessert's on me tonight, by the way. Try the tiramisu. It's *molto bene*."

Nick watched Mary Gallagher make her way through the swinging doors of the kitchen, then disappear. "I like your friend. She's very nice."

"Yeah, Mary's a good sort. Wait till you meet her mother, and the rest of the Russos. They're neat people. Weird, like my parents, but nice."

"I'm looking forward to meeting everyone. The Russos sound interesting. Anyone in particular stand out?" He was fishing and hoped he didn't sound overly interested.

"You mean, besides Sophia?" Mia grinned. "She's the matriarch of the family—if you don't count Grandma Flora, that is—and quite opinionated. I don't think she likes me very much."

"I find that hard to believe."

Mia shrugged. "Sophia's a hard nut to crack, if you get my drift. My sister is married to Sophia's nephew, John Franco. I'm not really sure she's accepted Angela into the family yet, though they seem to get along okay. Of course, Angela hasn't crossed her yet."

"Fierce, is she?"

Mia nodded. "Wait till you meet Sophia's brother, Alfredo. The guy thinks he's connected to the mob. Nobody believes him, of course. But we all go along with the fantasy since it's harmless enough."

Nick forced a laugh. "Sounds like he'd be a good person to interview for my book."

She waved off the idea as preposterous. "Nah. Uncle

Alfredo is just a bunch of hot air. Nice man, and he's got hundreds of funny stories, but I doubt he knows much about the Mafia. You, being a writer and all, probably know a lot more." Disappointment crossed Nick's face, and Mia added quickly, "But I'll certainly be happy to introduce you, if the opportunity presents itself."

"Thanks. I'd appreciate that."

"Don't mention it. I told you I'm very accommodating."

"Yes, you did, and I can't tell you how grateful I am. Having my normal routine interrupted is going to be very difficult. I'm rather structured, as you've probably noticed."

You mean, because you've got that stick up your . . . ?

"No, I hadn't," she lied, and Nick swallowed his smile.

"I don't make friends too easily."

Mia patted his hand, and Nick felt a frisson of heat race up his arm. "Well, we're going to have to do something about that. Just because you're in a tight spot at the moment doesn't mean you can't enjoy yourself. I'm a firm believer in having a good time, and I'm making it my goal to loosen you up a bit, show you how to have a good time. You'll be making new friends in no time at all."

Nick's smile froze. "Great!" he choked out, wishing he'd kept his big mouth shut.

The fried calamari, as good as it had tasted, had made Mia thirsty, and she was dying for a Coke. Okay, so maybe she was addicted to the stuff. But that didn't mean she wasn't thirsty, because she was. Parched, even.

The problem was Nick. He was between her and the

kitchen—she could hear him banging away on his computer—and she was already dressed in her short nightie. Mia didn't use a bathrobe very often, and she didn't plan to change her ways now. Especially now. She might have to put up with Nick's intrusion into her life, but she was determined to remain in control.

The Coke can, all red and frosted with ice, loomed before her eyes as her imagination and thirst swelled to gigantic proportions. She swallowed with great difficulty, clutching her throat, and was pretty sure she'd die of dehydration if she didn't get something to drink.

And why shouldn't she just march out there and get whatever she wanted? This was her apartment, after all. Nick was merely a guest—a paying guest, true—but still a guest. And it was his idea, not hers, that they live together.

So what if she disturbed his nerdy sensibilities? So what if the sight of a half-naked woman sent him screaming into the night?

He'd better get used to seeing her half-dressed if they were going to continue living together. Mia wasn't much for modesty. Her mother usually referred to her as a shameless exhibitionist, and all because Mia used to run around naked in front of the relatives. Well, hell! She'd only been four at the time.

Glancing at the bed, Mia wondered if she should pull the comforter off to cover herself, then opted not to. Certain things needed to be set straight right from the beginning, if this bodyguard/client thing was going to work.

Cracking the door open, she peered out. Nick was staring at his computer screen, intent on whatever it was he was reading, so she doubted he'd notice her presence anyway.

On tiptoe, she silently made her way into the kitchen,

not bothering to turn on the light as she reached for the refrigerator handle. The interior bulb sent a shaft of illumination into the small room. As quietly as she could, she reached inside to grab the soft drink. Which promptly slipped out of her hand and onto her right big toe.

"Holy shit!" She screamed as her toe started throbbing, jumping up and down on one foot. "Holy, shit, shit, shit!"

"Is everything okay?"

"No! Everything is not okay!" *Was the man dense?* She turned to find Nick standing right behind her and nearly jumped again.

Switching on the light, Nick's eyes widened appreciatively as he took in her scanty attire, and very pretty legs.

"I was thirsty. The Coke can fell on my foot," Mia explained, her eyes starting to water.

"Shall I take a look at your toe, make sure it's not broken?"

"No! Thanks." Mia couldn't take her eyes off Nick Caruso's chest. His shirt was unbuttoned, and she could see that he had major pectorals, and a nice sprinkling of chest hair, sort of a Tom Selleck kind of chest.

Whoosh! Who would have ever guessed what was hiding beneath that tweed? No author she'd ever seen looked like that.

Noting where Mia's gaze had fallen, Nick drew the edges of his shirt together and quickly began buttoning it. "I was getting a bit warm," he said, by way of explanation. "Guess you were, too."

Mia's face flushed an unbecoming beet color. "I don't use my robe much, and I was thirsty. You'll just have to get used to seeing me undressed, because I'm not going to change my habits, just because you're here."

Nick's eyes were presently riveted on the two pert nipples poking through the thin cotton of her nightgown. He forced himself not to look below her waist, fearful of what else he might see. "I . . . That's fine. I wouldn't want you to feel uncomfortable around me."

She smiled sweetly. "That's good, otherwise I'd have to blame you for my throbbing toe."

Yeah? And who was he going to blame for his throbbing—?

"Uh, do you think I could use the bathroom before you go back to bed? I'd like to take a shower." *An ice-cold one.*

"Help yourself. I'll just sit on the couch and wait for you to finish. Take your time. There are clean towels in the cabinet below the sink."

Nick disappeared into the bedroom, and Mia couldn't contain her grin. She'd noticed the bulge in his pants—how could she not? It was hardly a small matter—and it made her feel good to know she had the power to excite someone as reserved as Nick.

Poor Nick. He probably didn't get many erections, unless he was into watching porn movies or reading dirty magazines. And even if he did get one, she wondered if he'd know what to do with it.

The man seemed inexperienced when it came to women. You could always tell the innocent ones; they were shy and somewhat backward in their relationships with the opposite sex. Nick might even be a virgin. *Hmmm.* Wouldn't that be something? A virginal male. One could call that an oxymoron, if one actually said words like oxymoron, that is.

Living with Nick was certainly going to be interesting, not to mention challenging. He was a man in need of a great deal of improvement, especially as uptight and conservative as he was.

It might be fun to loosen him up a bit, let him see how the other half lived. Maybe even fix him up with a few girls. Donna Wiseman was single, though Mia suspected the woman still had the hots for Lou Santini, the butcher with the abs and buns of steel.

Well, it was definitely worth considering. And Nick would no doubt be very grateful for her help.

After all, a man couldn't go through life in a state of permanent unrequited arousal, now could he?

THREE

Fate! There is fate.
But it only takes you so far.
After that, it's up to you to make it happen!
Can't Hardly Wait

"Here's the money for my cleaning deposit, Mrs. Foragi." Mia handed her landlady the check she'd been unable to pay her the previous month, when she'd rented the apartment.

The older woman studied it to make sure it was real, and not something Mia had just printed out on her computer that morning. "About time you brought it," she said, looking none too happy about the delay. But then, Mrs. Foragi wasn't happy about most things, including having Mia as a tenant. It was Angela who'd been instrumental in convincing Mrs. Foragi that her baby sister would be a good rental risk.

"Thanks for being so understanding." *Not!* Her landlady had made it a point to hound Mia incessantly about the money owed, as if she didn't believe that Mia would actually pay her; this, after she'd promised the woman on a stack of Bibles and had even given the Girl Scouts' honor sign.

Well, what could you expect from someone who

35

wore a red plaid flannel shirt and a tool belt as a fashion accessory?

"Who's that man living in your apartment?" Donatella Foragi wanted to know, eyeing Mia suspiciously. "You didn't say anything about a boyfriend when you rented the place. I don't want any hanky-panky going on under my roof. I got a good reputation in this community, I'll have you know."

Mia fought the urge to roll her eyes. Everyone in Little Italy knew that for the past umpteen years Mrs. Foragi had been having an illicit affair with the local undertaker—the local *married* undertaker—Benny Buffano.

"Oh, you mean Nick," she replied, trying her damnedest to sound innocent. Lying had never been her forte, though she was definitely getting better at it. Necessity being the mother of ... *Right!* "He's my ... cousin. Nick needed a place to crash for a few weeks. I didn't think you'd mind. You know how it is with family. I just didn't have the heart to say no."

Mrs. Foragi looked far from convinced. "What's he do, this cousin of yours? Does he have a job? Or is he a bum? We got enough bums living in this neighborhood already." She didn't elaborate on who they might be.

"Nick's an author. He's writing a book about ... about Little Italy. Isn't that exciting? But you mustn't mention it to anyone. He's a very private person and would be upset if he knew I told."

Interest sparked in the woman's dark eyes. "An author? Maybe I should speak to him about writing my life story. It would make a good book, probably even sell to the movies. I've led a very interesting life, you know. You think Jackie Collins knows hot. I've lived hot. She has nothing on me."

"No, actually, I didn't. And I don't think you should talk to Nick about it. But I'll be sure to let him know. He's always looking for good story ideas."

Glancing down at the check again, Donatella asked, "Your business is doing better, no? You have clients, now?"

Smiling, Mia nodded enthusiastically, hoping she wouldn't be struck down for exaggerating. "Yes, a few. The Guardian Angel has spread her wings, and is finally taking off. It was only a matter of time, just as I promised. Good things come to those who wait, as they say."

"Hmph! Just be sure you get next month's rent to me on time. I don't like waiting. Your sister, Angela, was never late. You should follow her example." With that, Mia's landlady shut the door in her face.

"Witch!" Mia mumbled under her breath, crossing the short distance to her own apartment, then slámming the door loudly behind her, remembering too late that Nick was working at his computer.

"Would you mind keeping the noise down?" He swiveled about in his chair, annoyance masking his face as he confronted her. "I'm trying to write, and I'm having a hard enough time as it is." Actually, he'd been online with the FBI's mainframe computer, trying to get more information on Alfredo Graziano's car dealership. So far nothing useful had turned up, which served to put him in a rather foul mood.

"Oh, bite me."

"What did you say?" Nick heard exactly what she'd said, and he felt like laughing out loud, but knew that he couldn't. Instead, he kept his mock indignation firmly in place.

"I said, sorry. I forgot you were working. I just had my ass chewed out by my landlady, for paying my security deposit late."

Nick's brows rose to his hairline. "Looks like she didn't take all of it."

Mia glanced around at her flat butt, which looked a little too boyish for her liking, then back at Nick, who was grinning. "Did you make a joke? I'm impressed. Oh, by the way, Mrs. Foragi thinks you should write her life story. She says it's hot."

"I'm not into science fiction, but thanks." Mia's land-lady looked like a Paul Bunyan clone. The woman gave Nick the willies.

Mia giggled uncontrollably, then said, "Hey, I didn't know you had a sense of humor."

"Why? Don't you think nerds can be fun?" Nick shut down his computer, so Mia couldn't see what he'd been working on.

"I hadn't really thought about it," she replied, vault-ing over the back of the couch, and then plopping down on the leather cushions. "You're the only one I've met so far." Her previous job had been in highway construc-tion, and nerds had been few and far between. Now, ma-cho jerks—that was a whole other matter.

Frowning at Mia's behavior, Nick debated whether or not he should comment on her tomboyish ways. Since she never withheld her opinions, especially when it came to his clothing choices, he decided not to hold back. "Don't you ever wear anything besides jeans and T-shirts?"

"I'm fresh out of herringbone," she replied, feeling somewhat satisfied when his eyes narrowed slightly.

"Women should dress like women, in my opinion."

Her brow arched. "Really? I wasn't aware that you were acquainted with that many women," she said, and his lips puckered like two tart lemons.

"My life is rather solitary, it's true. But that doesn't mean I don't appreciate the opposite sex. I just don't have time to date when I'm working on a book."

"And you're always working on a book, right?" She'd heard some lame excuses in her time, but that one took the cake. Maybe he was gay. But what about the bulge? There was no denying that bulge.

"Something like that."

"Don't you ever want to get married and have children?" she asked.

He shrugged. "I haven't given it much thought. I'm content to live the life I have."

"Me too. I think that whole relationship business is a crock. And for what? You invest a lot of time and effort and it rarely pays off. I haven't met a man yet that I'd be interested in tying myself to for the rest of my life. Men are more trouble than they're worth."

Of course she was lying. She would have married Greg in a heartbeat, had his children, if he'd asked. But his wife had beaten her to the punch. Mia would never forget how gullible she'd been, how stupid and naïve. And she'd vowed that no man would ever take advantage of her like that again.

Mia's unexpected proclamation had Nick rocking back on his heels. Mia was certainly different from most of the women he knew, and he found that refreshing. "What about children? Don't most women want children?"

"They might, but I'm not most women, and I'm not sure I do. Children are a lot of work. Plus, that whole childbirth thing seems pretty risky. I had a good friend in junior high whose mother died giving birth. And recently I went to the hospital with Angela when she had some tests done, and it grossed me out. All those needles poking and prodding." *Not to mention the gloved hand exam.* She gagged silently at the memory of what her last exam had been like. She was not a fan of the whole OB-GYN thing. "I'm not ready for that just yet."

"You don't want to face the pain and danger of childbirth, but you don't have a problem facing bullets from organized crime thugs? That seems odd."

"Taking a bullet for a client is my job. Besides, if I do my job right, things don't get that serious. I try to avoid confrontation, if at all possible.

"Having a baby is a different story. It's like having one of those *Alien* creatures popping out of you. They pop out, they scream, then they scamper around the place." She couldn't repress her shudder.

Brow wrinkling, Nick played dumb. "Alien creatures? You mean, from outer space?"

"Don't tell me you haven't watched *Alien*, one of the best science fiction movies ever made."

Another movie nut, Nick thought, heaving a sigh. Putting up with Burt's addiction was bad enough. No doubt Burt and Mia would get along well—too well. It was a horrifying thought. "I don't have a television at the moment; it's broken. I read to relax."

That wasn't entirely true. He had a TV—a big-screen number. In fact, he loved watching movies, but he rarely got the chance. His job took precedence over just about everything else, leaving little time for pleasurable pursuits.

Mia's mouth dropped open, then, recovering quickly,

she declared, "We'll rectify that this evening, Nick. I've got a huge video collection, and *Alien* is one of my favorite movies. Of course, my all-time favorite is *In the Line of Fire* with Clint Eastwood. He plays this cool Secret Service agent. I bet you've seen it."

Shaking his head, Nick bit the inside of his cheek when Mia flashed him an annoyed look and threw up her hands. "You haven't seen that one, either? Where have you been living, in a cave?"

"No, with my aunt. She likes opera and classical music. On those few occasions when we watch TV, it's usually PBS. The programming is far superior to what's on the networks."

"*PBS!*" Clearly disgusted, she stuck a finger down her throat and made a gagging sound. "I see I've got my work cut out for me."

"What do you mean?"

"Oh, nothing. It's just an expression I use. So, what else do you like to do besides read and listen to Mozart?"

"Well, I have a real weakness for playing the stock market. I find it absolutely fascinating."

"Get out!" It was the first exciting thing he'd said since she'd met him. "Me too. Though I don't use real money or anything. Can't afford it. But I'm getting quite good at playing my hunches and picking winners. I made twenty-two thousand dollars last month."

His eyes widened. "You're shi . . . kidding me!"

She shook her head. "It's true. Of course, I didn't actually invest any money, but if I had, that's what I would have made."

The wheels in Nick's head began turning. The stock market was the one weakness he indulged. "Do you have a computer that's connected to the Internet?"

"Yes, why? Is yours broken? Because I just saw you using it, so it can't be."

The woman was too sharp for her own good. Nick realized he'd have to be more careful. "Ah, no. But I don't like to access the net while I'm working on a book. I'm afraid I might get a virus that will infect my computer and destroy my files."

She rolled her eyes, looking at him as if he were a simpleton. "Nick, they've got virus protection for that. It's like condoms for computers."

Mia figured she must have shocked him, because he didn't say anything in response. "I suppose we can use my computer, if you want me to prove that I can do what I say."

"Let's do a trial run, using no money," he suggested. "If by the end of next week you've made a profit, I'll consider investing some money."

Mia smiled so widely two charming dimples appeared. "Oooh! I'd love to do this for real. Okay, we'll do a trial run. But I can assure you that you won't be disappointed. I always pick winners. I have a sixth sense about things. I'm good at judging people, at playing hunches, and I'm rarely wrong. Just call it woman's intuition, if you want."

Nick smiled warmly. Mia was absolutely adorable when she was excited about something. "Ah, the perfect woman. It's been so long since I've met one." *Like never!*

But that was probably his fault. He'd never allowed himself to get close enough to any woman, to see beyond the flaws every human being exhibited, at one time or another. Perhaps in seeking perfection, which was obviously unattainable, he was seeking excuses to keep his distance.

She grinned again. "I'm a woman of many facets, Nick. You're going to find that out if you stick around here long enough. Now come on. Let's go play the market. But I'm warning you: prepare to be dazzled."

Problem was: Nick already was.

"Was it really necessary to drag me down to the market?" Nick asked, frowning deeply. "I could have stayed at the apartment and worked on my book."

Mia shook her head at the absurdity of the question. "By yourself? What kind of bodyguard would I be if I'd left you, my client, to fend for himself? You hired me to look out for you, and that's exactly what I'm doing. Now grab a basket. The quicker we get the groceries, the sooner you can go back to work."

Nick swallowed a smile. "Are you always this bossy?"

"Yep. By the way, I checked on Amazon last evening and couldn't find any of your books. I was hoping to read one."

Startled by the comment, Nick crashed the cart into a display of cereal boxes, knocking several to the ground. Mia eyed him strangely. Bending over to pick them up, he replied, "I told you—my earlier books are out of print. They had a very small print run and aren't available any longer."

"Don't you have any copies I could read?" Mia asked, tossing a head of lettuce into a plastic bag then dumping it into the cart. "Maybe I could borrow one."

Nick shook his head, wishing she'd quit pushing. As he'd feared, Mia had an inquisitive streak. "They're packed away in my basement. Sorry."

"Why don't you write fiction, something steamy and full of sex? I bet you'd sell a lot more copies."

Tossing a couple of porterhouse steaks into the cart, Nick did his best to look aghast. "I'll keep it in mind."

"I don't usually buy my meat here. I shop at Santini's. But I guess it'll be okay this time."

Santini. Nick did a mental rundown of the names. Lou Santini, the butcher. Apparently the mother was something of a nightmare. He'd checked them out previous to beginning the operation. There didn't seem to be any irregularities where they were concerned.

Mia pushed the cart around the next corner. Out of the corner of her eye she spotted something that looked like a gun. "Gun. Get down!" she ordered, letting loose of the cart and pushing Nick out of the way.

"Mommy! Mommy! The lady's yelling at me."

Mia looked up to find a toothless five-year-old kid with a plastic gun, and breathed a sigh of relief. "Sorry, kid. I thought you were someone else."

Mia's reflexes impressed Nick, still seated on the floor. She'd acted quickly and without hesitation. If he had been in actual danger, she would have saved his life. "Thank you, Mia. You acted without hesitation."

The young boy's mother, who'd been farther down the aisle, arrived to drag her child off, but not before giving Mia and Nick a nasty look.

"Apparently she wasn't quite as grateful as you," Mia replied, holding out her hand to Nick to help him to his feet. "Sorry I knocked you down. I thought you might be in danger."

"Don't be sorry. It's the reason I hired you, after all. If you don't protect me, who will?"

Mia smiled, feeling good about her actions, for a change. "Exactly. And now that I've saved you from a wetting by a plastic water pistol, what do you say we go home. I'm starving. All this excitement has worked up an enormous appetite."

"I've never met anyone so anxious to meet other people's relatives. Man, you weren't lying when you said you've led a solitary life," Mia told Nick two days later, unable to believe he actually wanted to go to a family gathering that wasn't his own.

But she'd had no trouble convincing him to attend the belated honeymoon party that Sophia and Frank Russo were hosting at Mama Sophia's for their nephew John Franco and Mia's sister, Angela.

In fact, he seemed almost eager to meet the parents—a lot more eager than Ben Stiller, at any rate.

Nick made great pretense of picking imaginary lint off his dark blue sports jacket—the third he'd tried on, and the first Mia had approved of. It had been easier to accommodate Mia's nagging than balk at her wardrobe suggestions.

I may as well be married, he thought, blanching at the thought.

"You look nice in that jacket, by the way." She smiled up at him and with another wifely gesture adjusted his burgundy pin-striped tie. "You should dress normal more often."

Nick tried to ignore her smile, the twinkle in her eye, the way his gut twisted into a tight knot at the tantalizing fragrance of her perfume. He never allowed himself to get too close, to attach himself to another human being— Burt was about as close as he'd gotten to anyone—and he wasn't making an exception for a cute, curly-headed bodyguard, no matter how intriguing he found her.

That path led to heartache, and he'd had enough of that to last him a lifetime. It was the orphan in him, he guessed, the fear of being abandoned. Too many broken promises, too many foster homes, too many excuses for why he hadn't been wanted. He had no intention of opening himself up to rejection again.

Gazing down at Mia's gamine face made him realize that he needed to keep his focus on the operation, and not on the woman. At any rate, it went against his professional ethics to get involved with anyone while working on a case. And he would never compromise an investigation.

It had been less than a week since he'd met Mia. What the hell was wrong with him?

"Earth to Nick. Are you ready to leave for the party, or do you have a spacecraft waiting to take you there?"

You have a very big mouth for such a little person, he was tempted to say, but instead smiled apologetically. "Oh, was I woolgathering again? Sorry. I tend to do that a lot when I'm absorbed in a book."

"Woolgathering! Never mind." Mia sighed. "Anyway, you don't want to be late for one of Sophia's parties, or you'll never hear the end of it. She makes Conan the Barbarian look tame by comparison."

"I'm looking forward to meeting her. She sounds like a colorful character."

Mia laughed. "Why don't you tell that to Annie Russo, and see what she has to say about it. I don't think colorful is the word she would use to describe her mother-in-law."

They entered the party to find that only a handful of people had arrived. A tall, decorated, artificial Christmas

tree stood by the front window, its colored lights twinkling prettily, lending a festive air to the large room.
Overhead, tiny white lights threaded throughout the lat-
ticework covering the ceiling, adding even more of a
holiday touch.

Mia waved when she spotted her sister and new
brother-in-law. "Come on, Nick. I'll introduce you to
Angela and John."

Nick's gaze flitted across the room to the attractive
couple standing by the tree, holding hands and looking
very much in love. The word "newlywed" radiated from
them like a pulsating beacon. "I'd love to meet your
family."

"Dad will be the one in sequins. He's a cross-dresser,"
she said matter-of-factly, and Nick did his best to mask
his surprise. He'd missed that tidbit when performing
Mia's background check.

As soon as the words left her mouth, Nick noted a tall,
heavyset man crossing the room in their direction. He
was garbed in an emerald sequined gown with a red
feather boa draped around his neck, looking very . . .
well, Christmassy. Next to him stood a conservatively
dressed woman in black chiffon, who seemed nonplussed
by the fact that her husband was dressed up like Cher.

The DeNeros. Well, Mia did say they were weird.

"Here come Mom and Dad," she announced. "You
may as well meet them first and get it over with. Dad's an
ex-cop, so he may try to grill you. Just remain calm. He
can be a bit overbearing, but he's really just a big teddy
bear."

An ex-cop! Nick knew he'd have to be careful not to
arouse the man's suspicion. Cops had a sixth sense and

could smell a lie a mile off. "I'll try," he said, plastering on a smile as Mia's parents approached, and thinking that her father looked more gorilla than teddy bear.

Kissing both her parents, Mia made the introductions.

"You're not a pervert, are you, son?" Sam DeNero asked Nick, his eyes narrowing as he sized him up. "I won't allow anyone to take advantage of my daughter."

"No, sir! I'm an author," Nick replied with a straight face, amused that Sam DeNero would have the gall to call anyone else perverted.

"What? Authors can't be perverts?" Rosalie wanted to know, giving her daughter a chastising look. "I don't like that my daughter is living with a man she's not married to. In my day that was considered a sin."

"Stop it, both of you! Nick is my client. He's not a pervert, as far as I can tell." Mia smiled up at him and winked. "He's under my protection, and our relationship is strictly platonic, so leave him alone."

"My daughter, the bodyguard." Sam reached out to shake Nick's hand. "Strong grip. You work out or something? I didn't think authors had such strong grips."

"When I can," Nick replied. "How about you?"

"Hell, no! I had enough of that crap when I was walking the beat back in Boston. I'm retired now. I don't exercise at all." He said it proudly, daring his wife to make a remark.

And Rosalie was only too happy to accommodate. "Your father will be sorry when he drops dead of a heart attack," she told Mia, glaring at her husband. "Or when he can't wear those sequined dresses anymore.

"Have you seen how awful Diana Ross looks in her gowns now, Sam? She's gained weight, just like you."

"Mrs. DeNero is correct, if you don't mind my saying so, sir. I have a friend who doesn't watch his diet and doesn't exercise, and I'm worried that he's going to keel over dead one of these days."

Rosalie's face split into a smile. "Ah, an intelligent man, I see. You must be, if you chose my daughter to help you. Mia's very good at everything she does, Mr. Caruso."

Nick's gaze strayed to study Mia. She was wearing hunter green slacks and a white turtleneck sweater. It was an understated outfit, though dressier than what she usually wore, making her look pretty, soft, and very female. It wasn't often that he got a peek at her feminine side, but every once in a while, like now, he got to see the woman behind the tomboy facade. And he found that he liked that woman.

"Men should stick together, Nick. Why don't you and I go and have ourselves a drink, get a few things straightened out." Without waiting for an answer, Sam grabbed hold of the unresisting federal agent and pulled him toward the bar.

Laughing at Nick's startled expression, Mia decided that he'd better get used to it. If they were going to be living together twenty-four/seven, he'd be exposed to the entire family, warts and all, on a regular basis. And the DeNeros had a whole lot of warts.

"I hope Dad isn't going to scare Nick too badly, Mom. I need this client in order to survive."

"Oh, you know your father's bark is worse than his bite, dear. He probably just wanted an excuse to get a beer. You know how Sam loves beer."

"So how are things between you and Dad?" Mia

asked, noting the soft blush that covered her mother's cheeks.

"Very good. I have no complaints at the moment. How about you? Are you happy doing what you're doing?"

Mia nodded, smiling happily. "I think I'm going to love this job. I'm getting paid good money, and it's not unlike baby-sitting. Nick works on his book most of the day, and I just sit around and watch TV, or do crossword puzzles. It's really more boring than I thought it would be."

"So it hasn't been dangerous?" Rosalie looked relieved. "I've been worried."

"I told you not to worry, Mom. This bodyguard thing is a piece of cake."

"But your sister told me that the Mafia was involved. That sounds very dangerous. They kill people. I've watched *The Sopranos*."

"That's what Nick says. But he was probably worrying for nothing, overreacting. I haven't detected anything that could be remotely construed as dangerous." She'd made it a point to study the patrons at Mama Sophia's, whenever they came here for dinner. But most of the faces were familiar, and those who weren't had been introduced as friends of friends.

"It hasn't been that long," Rosalie was quick to point out. "Something could still happen."

"True. But I don't think those Mafia types would wait long to strike, if they intended to. It's not their style." Of course, Mia was basing most of this on the *Godfather* trilogy, *Goodfellas*, and *The Sopranos*, one of her favorite shows on HBO.

Though her mother nodded, Mia could tell she wasn't quite convinced by her reassurances. "Your father's been worried," she said.

"Because he doesn't think I can handle myself, doesn't believe I know what I'm doing. Nothing ever changes. Dad always compares me to Angela, and I always come up short."

Rosalie patted her daughter's hand. "It's because he loves you, Mia. He's your father. Parents worry about their children. Plus, his being a former cop makes him more concerned and afraid than most fathers. He's seen too much evil in the world."

Mia's gaze drifted to the bar, where Nick and her father were engaged in what seemed like a friendly conversation. Nick was laughing, her father slapping him on the back. They looked like long-lost buddies.

All seemed right with the world until her mother said, "I like your young man. Mr. Caruso seems very nice. And I bet he makes a lot of money as an author."

"Don't start, Mom. I told you, Nick's not my young man; he's a client. Big difference. And he is nice, but terribly backward. He's led an insular life, living with an elderly aunt. I'm hoping to bring him out of his shell a bit, let him see how other people live."

"You're taking him under your wing, then. That's nice, dear. And who knows, maybe something good will come of it. You never know. Love often comes from friendship. And you're getting to that age where you need to start thinking about settling down, especially now that Angela is married and expecting a baby, my first grandchild." Her face glowed at the thought.

"You're consistent, Mom, I'll give you that. But you're starting to give me a headache." Mia reached out to a passing waiter and snagged a glass of champagne off his tray. It was going to be a long night, she decided.

Rosalie shook her head. "Women of your generation think you don't need a man in your life, but you do. Men give women purpose. Not to mention . . ."

"Sex?" Mia grinned, and her mother frowned deeply.

"I was going to say that they also provide stability and creature comforts. Not to mention, children."

"Like I said, sex." That's all men really wanted. Everything else was part of the big lie.

"One has nothing to do with the other."

"No? Then how do you get children, if you don't have sex?"

"There's more to a relationship than sex. God knows I would have left your father years ago if that wasn't the case."

"I thought you said things were good between you and Dad."

"They are now. But if you recall, it hasn't always been that way. Thank goodness your sister . . . Well, never mind about that. Water under the bridge, as they say."

"I'm not looking for marriage and family. I like my freedom, my ability to come and go as I please, without having to answer to anyone." And she was never going to allow another man to play her for a fool.

"I'm not like Angela, Mom, so you shouldn't expect me to follow in her footsteps. Besides, there aren't too many John Francos hanging around, ready to rescue damsels in distress."

"He's a handsome man, your sister's husband. But then, so is Nick Caruso."

Mia's mouth fell open. "Nick's not handsome. He's—" She turned to look toward the bar again. Well, he wasn't ugly, but he definitely wasn't Brad Pitt handsome. "—interesting."

Rosalie's smile filled with pleasure. "Interesting is good, no?"

Mia gulped down her champagne. "No!"

FOUR

For some moments in life
there are no words.
Willy Wonka and the Chocolate Factory

Nick had just stuffed a ham-filled deviled egg into his mouth when a short, generously rounded redhead, whose bright hair color could only have come from a bottle of Clairol, came up to him, clasped both sides of his head between her hands in a death grip, and said, "I can't believe how much you look like my Joe. You are taller and have more muscle, but you look just like him." She kissed him smack on the mouth, much to his astonishment.

Nick choked on the egg he was eating, then swallowed with some difficulty, before saying, "I . . . uh . . . my name's Nick Caruso. I'm a friend of Mia's."

With a great deal of impatience, she waved away his introduction with a flick of her wrist. "I know that. I've heard all about you. Joe Perillo was the man I fell in love with, before I married Frank Russo. He was my first love.

"I hope you don't mind that I kissed you—I'm married, so don't get any ideas—but, when I look at your handsome face, I am taken back so many years to my youth." Pulling a handkerchief from her sleeve, she dabbed her eyes with it.

54

"You must be Sophia Russo," Nick said. "I've heard a lot about you, too."

The woman's eyes narrowed. "From who? You can't believe everything you hear. There are those who are jealous of me. I have attained a measure of stature in this neighborhood. You know how it is?"

Nick swallowed his smile. "All good things, Mrs. Russo, I assure you. I'm staying temporarily with Mia DeNero, who has mentioned you quite often."

Sophia pulled a face, shaking her head. "Oh, that one. Mia's a trial to her mother, that's for sure. Though nothing like the father, of course." She crossed herself and glanced heavenward. "That girl hasn't decided whether she wants to be a boy or a girl, if you ask me. Always with the jeans and sneakers. But she's the sister to my nephew's new wife, so I don't want to speak badly about her. I'm still getting used to Angela."

Nick opened his mouth to comment, but she rolled right over him, not giving him the chance.

"All these marriages in such a short time make my head spin. It's hard to adjust. And then I've got my mother-in-law. *Madonna mia, discratzia.*" She clutched the gold cross around her neck, praying to the Almighty to lift the terrible burden that had been placed upon her shoulders. "Why me, dear Lord? Why me?

"The old woman drives me nuts. She's not only a thief, she's crazy in the head. But will anyone listen? They all sing her praises because she's an old woman. My husband, Frank, dotes on her. In his eyes, she can do no wrong. It's Mama this and Mama that. I am cursed among women. Cursed, I tell you."

"It sounds like you have your hands full." He pulled out a chair at a nearby table so they could sit down.

Sophia's connection to her brother, Alfredo Graziano, could prove useful, and Nick wasn't about to alienate her by refusing to listen to her diatribe. Besides, he rather liked the woman.

"You don't know the half of it, Nick. I can call you Nick, no? I feel like we've known each other a very long time, because of your resemblance to Joe, I guess.

"I'm a woman who has known her share of pain. You met my daughter, Mary?" When he nodded, she added, "Well, she's married to an Irishman—they drink a lot, those Irish—not like my other daughter, Connie, who had the good sense to listen to her mother and marry a proctologist, who's Italian, thank the good Lord. Mary calls Eddie a butt doctor. But, so what? He gets paid good money for doing what he does.

"Both Mary and Connie are expecting, and they'll want me to baby-sit, like I have nothing else to do. Not that I'm complaining, mind you. But I'm not as young as I used to be." She patted her chest. "My heart, you know.

"Then Joe, that's my son, Joe, not the other one I mentioned before. He was a priest, a man of God, but he left the church." She crossed herself again. "And do you know why?" Nick did, but he shook his head to the contrary. "To marry a wild woman who dresses like a *puttana*, a woman of the streets. He broke his mother's heart, which is why I have chest pains, from time to time.

"I'm telling you this, Nick, because you seem nice. Caruso is an Italian name, so you must be a *paisan*, and you look just like my Joe Perillo. I should have married Joe. I can see that now."

Feeling as if he'd just gotten off a high-speed, upside-down roller coaster, Nick waited for the dizziness to pass, taking several deep breaths before speaking. "I'm sorry things have been so difficult for you, Mrs. Russo."

"I'm a mother, and these are my burdens in life. I try not to complain. Like most mothers, I don't get the appreciation I deserve for the sacrifices I'm asked to make. My brother, Alfredo, is the only one who really understands what I go through. We're very close."

Nick leaned closer, knowing this was the opportunity he'd been waiting for. "It's nice you and your brother have each other. Tell me about him."

"Alfredo is a good man. He's—"

"There you are, Sophia Graziano. You sit with this handsome man and leave me alone in the bathroom. *Vaffunculo*." The old woman flipped off her daughter-in-law, much to Nick's surprise. "I coulda have fallen and broken my neck."

"I should be so lucky," Sophia muttered before saying, "Nick, this is my mother-in-law, Flora Russo. My husband's mother lives with us. You see? You see what I'm talking about?"

Nick cursed under his breath. Damn! Why couldn't Flora have waited just one more minute before interrupting their conversation? He felt certain Sophia was about to say something important about her brother.

Pasting on a smile, he took the old woman's wrinkled hand. "It's very nice to meet you, Mrs. Russo."

"Nick is the spitting image of Joe Perillo, Flora, the man I should have married, instead of Frank."

The old woman's lips slashed into a thin line. "You don'ta deserve my son. He'sa too good for you." Flora cast her daughter-in-law the evil eye. "*Sie la figlia del diavalo*. The devil is in this woman," she told Nick, pointing an accusing finger at Sophia. "*Del diavalo*."

"Be quiet, old woman! Joe Perillo owns a very successful olive export business in Sicily. He makes a lot of money. I could have been living the sweet life, *la dolce vita*."

"Bah! My Frank is a saint. He makes tings with his hands. He'sa very smart, my Frank. Have you sat on a heated toilet seat, Nick? My son invented that."

The agent's eyes widened. He'd heard of the Bun Warmer, had almost bought one, in fact. "Your son invented the Bun Warmer? I'm very impressed."

"You see, Sophia. Nick isa impressed. Anyone can grow olives. Bah!"

Ignoring her mother-in-law, Sophia turned her attention back to Nick. "What do you do for a living, Nick? Are you married? I don't see a ring," she said, examining his left hand and smiling slyly.

Sophia's goddaughter, Gabriella Perillo, would be coming from Rome to visit soon. Perhaps Sophia would introduce her to Nick. They would make a very handsome couple. And it was time Gabriella got married.

"I'm an author. I'm writing a book on organized crime."

Flora crossed herself. "*La Cosa Nostra*. We know about that, don'ta we, Sophia?"

"Really?" Nick arched a questioning brow, excitement building in his breast.

Sophia shot her mother-in-law a lethal look. "Be quiet, old woman! You don't know what you're talking about."

"You're always saying that sainted brother of yours isa connected, Sophia. Maybe Nick shoulda talk to him. Alfredo mighta be able to tell him a few tings. Her brother says he isa connected to the Gotti family." Flora made a cutting motion to her throat. "They kill people."

"My brother has never killed anyone. I'm sure of that," Sophia said, though Nick thought he detected a hint of doubt in her eyes. "And we promised Alfredo that we wouldn't talk about this anymore. Lenore doesn't like it, and my brother is keeping company with her."

Nick made a mental note to check out Alfredo's girl-friend, Lenore.

"Well, you certainly have my attention, Mrs. Russo. I'd love to hear all about your brother. Do you think he would allow me to interview him for my book?"

"You want to put Alfredo in your book?" Sophia asked, her face effusing with pleasure as she warmed to the idea. "He would become famous, like Eddie Fisher."

"He woulda become dead, if he spills hisa guts about the Mafia," Flora pointed out. "You know whatta they do to the ones who squeal likea pigs?" She pointed to Nick's crotch. "They cut off their you-know-whats. No more rooster to crow loudly."

Nick winced, shifting restlessly in his chair, but didn't comment because he knew the old lady spoke the truth.

"We don't know for sure that Alfredo is even con-nected," Sophia said, more to herself than anyone else. "I'd have to think about it, ask him if he's interested."

"If he wants to speak on a condition of anonymity, I'm willing to do that. Someone who has firsthand knowl-edge of the inner workings of the mob would be invalu-able to me. I would be forever in your debt, if you could arrange it, Mrs. Russo." He gave her the most charming smile he could muster.

An image of Nick and Gabriella walking down the aisle suddenly flashed before Sophia's eyes, and she smiled with satisfaction, patting Nick's hand. "I will see what I can do. Alfredo is a very private man, but he usually denies me nothing."

"That's because you nag him, like you nag my son," Flora said, crossing her arms over her chest with a loud harrumph.

Sophia glared at her mother-in-law. "Who asked you?"

Nick leaned back in his chair and smiled to himself. He liked the two battling old ladies. In fact, he liked everyone he had met at the party. Oh, they were different, there was no denying that—Sam DeNero in sequins came to mind—but they were a family, something Nick had never had the good fortune to experience.

He'd always told himself he needed no one, didn't want to take the risk of opening himself up to hurt, but deep down he yearned for that kind of closeness, and wondered if he'd ever have it.

"I can't believe how my mother is doting on your friend Nick," Mary said to Mia as she stared across the room to where the duo sat engrossed in conversation. "Ma usually doesn't take to strangers like that, and she's been talking to that man nonstop."

Mia's gaze followed her friend's, and she shrugged. "Nick's a nonthreatening male. He's not at all macho, so Sophia probably feels safe around him, or maybe even protective. He affects women that way."

"How come you don't think he's macho?" Annie asked. Mary's best friend and sister-in-law was standing on Mia's other side. "I think he's kind of cute. Without those hideous glasses, he might even be handsome. Not as good-looking as Joe, of course, but still handsome. And he's got a pair of shoulders on him. I bet he's got nice pecs, too. Have you checked him out, seen him naked yet?"

"Annie Russo!" Mia looked at her friend as if she'd lost her mind. "Married life has definitely warped you." Of all the new friends she'd made since coming to Baltimore, Annie was definitely the most outrageous and fun. Mia liked her a great deal.

"Annie's always been warped," Mary tossed out with a grin, which prompted her sister-in-law to flip her off.

"Nick is about as boring as they come," Mia said. "I don't find him the least bit attractive." *Liar!* "And I haven't checked him out." *Liar! Liar!* "He's my client, not my lover. Although I did catch a glimpse of his chest once; it was muscular and somewhat hairy." *Mmmm. Nice.* "But that was strictly accidental. We are living together, you know. Accidents are bound to happen."

Annie and Mary exchanged knowing looks.

"Who's not attractive?" Sidling up next to Mia, Angela wrapped her arm about her sister's waist, kissing her cheek. "I've been waiting to meet this famous author client of yours. I thought you were bringing Nick Caruso over to introduce him."

Mia smiled apologetically. "We got ambushed by Mom and Dad. And then, by the time all the well-wishers had finally left you and John alone, Nick was deep in discussion with Sophia and Flora, and I didn't want to interrupt them. He's probably trying to talk Sophia into introducing him to Alfredo, for the book he's writing."

Mary laughed. "Because my uncle claims to be connected? Didn't you tell him that the man is insane, that he wants everyone to kiss his ring and call him *Don*? Trust me. My uncle is no Marlon Brando."

"I wasn't quite that blunt, but I did let Nick know that

Alfredo is just wrapped up in an innocent fantasy and nothing more."

"Your dad is looking particularly stunning tonight, Mia," Annie remarked, gazing toward the dance floor where Sam and Rosalie were dancing cheek-to-cheek to a Frank Sinatra standard by the same name. Though it was hard to tell who was leading whom.

"I would kill for that dress. I know for a fact that he didn't buy it at Goldman's."

Sid Goldman came up just then, and having heard what his daughter had said, replied, "Because you're not pushing hard enough, Annie." He patted her cheek affectionately. "You'll learn in time. Those gowns have a tremendous mark-up. We could be making a big profit on Sam DeNero's purchases.

"If he's going to shop for ladies' dresses, he should be shopping at Goldman's Department Store. We got quality, and I can order whatever he wants. I'll give him a ten percent discount, too. Sam DeNero won't find that on the Home Shopping Network. Not to mention that we at Goldman's pride ourselves on being very discreet. What?" he asked his daughter when her brows lifted.

Angela and Mia exchanged grins.

"Hello, Mr. Goldman," Mia said. "It's nice to see you again. I'll talk to my dad, suggest that he try shopping at your store."

Mollified by the offer, Sid nodded, saying, "Good," then beating his chest with his fist, he belched as silently as he could. "I got gas. Those meatballs are spicy, and my stomach is no damn good. I gotta go take my antacid." He kissed Annie's cheek and walked away.

All four women looked at each other, and then burst out laughing.

"Do you think it's just our families, or is everyone's weird?" Mary wanted to know. "I think it might have something to do with living in Little Italy."

"You're probably right, but I love it here," Mia admitted. "It's such a tight-knit community, where everyone seems to care about everyone else. I feel as if I've come home."

"Where everyone seems to care about everyone else's business, you mean," Mary corrected.

"How are you getting along with Mrs. F, Mia?" Annie asked. "Has she been giving you a hard time?"

When Mia made a face of disgust, Mary said, "That's just her way. She wouldn't harass you if she didn't like you."

"Well, I wish she would like me a little bit less." Mia glanced around the room, now crowded with people. "Where's Donna Wiseman? I was hoping to introduce her to Nick tonight. I thought they might hit it off." Donna was Annie's cousin, though not by choice. They had what some might call a love/hate relationship. Annie loved hating Donna.

"She'll be along later," Annie replied. "The prima Donna likes to make an entrance."

"Is she still mooning over Lou Santini? I really don't know what she sees in that man," Mia stated. "His mother is a witch. Can you imagine having her for a mother-in-law?"

"Yeah, well there are no guarantees about in-laws when you decide to fall in love."

"Now, Annie," Mary said, clasping her friend's hand. "My mother's been better lately, you have to admit that."

"Sophia tolerates me because of Joe, but she's never going to forgive me. She still blames me for Joe leaving the priesthood; she mentions it every time we talk. 'My son, my son, he could have been Pope,' " Annie mimicked.

Mary laughed. "Stop! You're giving me goose bumps." Then her baby kicked and her eyes widened. "Oh!"

"Let's go collect your client, Mia," Angela said, "and introduce him around. I think he must need saving from Sophia and Flora by now. No offense, Mary."

"None taken. After what you did for Dan and me, getting custody of Matthew and everything, you have my permission to say anything you want about my mother."

Angela smiled softly. "Believe it or not, I'm actually growing quite fond of Sophia. She has a good heart beneath all the bluster."

"Really?" Annie's face fell. "Then what am I doing wrong? I've been bending over backward to please that woman, and nothing works."

Angela patted the distraught woman's arm. "You've got to give it time, Annie. Try to remember that it was you who took Sophia's son from her. Priest or not, Joe was her first-born, not to mention the light of her life. It'll take time for Sophia to come to grips with the fact that he loves another woman more than he loves his mother."

"I think you made Annie feel better about her situation with Sophia," Mia said to her sister when they were out of earshot.

"Yeah, well, I think I can speak from experience. Adele Franco isn't exactly thrilled that I married her son, or that John's going to be raising another man's child." Angela's ex-fiancé was the biological father of her child. He was a cheating, conniving womanizer and the biggest mistake of her life. Next to the baby, John was the best thing that had ever happened to her. "Although she does seem excited about being a grandmother again, so maybe in time she'll come around."

"This just convinces me more than ever that I'm never getting married. What a hassle. Not only do you have to put up with a husband telling you what to do, and how to do it, you've got to contend with all those other family members, like disgruntled mothers-in-law. It's not worth it. I'm just going to live in sin."

"And is this Nick Caruso the candidate with whom you'll be sinning?" Angela asked.

"Ha, ha, ha." Mia noticed how Nick's jacket stretched taut across his back as he leaned over the table to talk to Sophia and Flora. He was gesturing with his hands, and she saw that his fingers were long, the nails manicured nicely—nicer than hers—and that his dark hair fell across his brow in an engaging fashion.

Stop it, Mia! Are you insane? The man is your client.

But he's so cute. She wondered why she'd thought otherwise. And any man who spent as much time talking to two old ladies, who argued at the drop of a hat, had to be rather nice, didn't he?

Or dumb as a stump.

But for some reason, she didn't think Nick Caruso was dumb. On the contrary, he seemed altogether more interesting and intelligent than she'd first thought.

Interesting, intelligent, and handsome.

You're in big trouble, Mia.

FIVE

Life moves pretty fast.
If you don't stop and look around once in a while,
you could miss it.
Ferris Bueller's Day Off

"I'm bored! Don't you ever do anything besides read or play on the computer? I'm getting jungle fever."

Nick smiled at Mia's obvious impatience. She'd been sitting on the sofa for hours, working crossword puzzles and humming Christmas carols to herself, while he accessed the FBI's mainframe computer again, looking for a connection between Alfredo Graziano and the money-laundering scheme. He'd come up with a half dozen names he intended to check out.

He'd also done some research on Lenore Gallagher, who was, as it turned out, Dan Gallagher's mother—the same Dan Gallagher Mia had waxed poetic over.

It seemed Graziano and Lenore Gallagher were a couple, which made Nick wonder if the woman knew anything about her boyfriend's alleged illegal activities. He hoped not. He'd met Dan at the Russos' party and liked him, though he didn't think him as handsome as Mia did. That was probably a good thing, Nick decided.

"Are you zoning out again, Nick? It seems you do that a lot when you're around me. I'm starting to develop a complex. I'm not that boring, am I?"

66

With an apologetic smile, he shook his head. "I think you meant to say cabin fever, not jungle, Mia."

"Yeah, whatever, that, too. You know, it's almost Christmas, and I haven't put up a tree, bought a single present, or baked cookies." Not that she baked all that well, but she had no problem eating her mistakes.

"What is it you're trying to tell me?" As if he didn't know. When it came right down to it, women were all made from the same mold. Shopping loomed large among the species, and he doubted Mia, even with her lack of fashion sense, was any different. It was an inherent gene in females. Nick liked to shop, but he wasn't fanatical about it.

Looking somewhat like a caged kitten, Mia jumped up from the sofa, hands flying wide. "I need to go out. *We* need to go out. I'm stagnating in this apartment, suffocating to death. I need fresh air, sunshine, or whatever is waiting on the other side of that door." She pointed at said door, a pleading look on her face.

"But it's been less than a week since we went to the Russos' party. How can you be bored so soon? Sometimes when I'm working on a book I don't emerge from the house for months. Everything I need is delivered. It's so much easier that way, and it keeps me from getting distracted."

Distractions were hard on a man, Nick knew. Mia stood before him in tight jeans, her perfume as teasing and provocative as her pert nipples almost poking through the fabric of her knit sweater. The close confinement was taking a toll on his resistance. He tried his best to keep a professional distance, but the longer he stayed the harder—poor choice of words!—it got.

Mia made a face of disgust. "I'm not used to sitting

around all day, like you. I'm an active person. All this watching you work is making me fat. I need to walk, get some exercise."

"I seriously doubt that you're getting fat. I'd be surprised to learn that you weighed a hundred pounds, soaking wet." Mia ate like a bird. But, of course, it was said that birds ate their own weight every day, which pretty much described her appetite. Last night she'd devoured six slices of mushroom and pepperoni pizza and four cans of beer; he'd only had three each. For a petite woman, she could pack it in. As thin as she was, he wondered where it all went.

Folding her arms across her chest, Mia glared defiantly, chin tilted ever so slightly. "I'll have you know that I weigh one hundred and ten pounds." *After meals.* Normally, she weighed one hundred and eight, but she wasn't going to let Mr. Know-it-all think he was right. Nick was difficult enough to live with, as it was.

"Shouldn't you have considered this boredom aspect of the bodyguard business before becoming one? It's rather like a cop being on stakeout, isn't it? You wait around for something to happen, and sometimes nothing does. Surely your father must have told you what it was going to be like."

Mia shrugged. Her father had gone ballistic when he'd heard her plan to become a bodyguard, and had railed at her for days on end about what a dumb decision she had made. There'd been no discussion of stakeouts. But she wasn't going to tell Nick that, either.

"I'm not complaining, exactly. I just thought being a bodyguard would be a little more exciting than it has been. I haven't even had a chance to shoot my gun."

"What kind do you own?"

"A Glock 9mm. Want to see it? I have a license to carry concealed, and I keep it in my purse, just in case. You know the old Boy Scout motto?"

He shook his head. A 9mm was much too big for a woman her size. Why hadn't her instructor told her that? "Actually I don't. I was never a Boy Scout. I don't like guns. And I'm happy it's been dull around here. The alternative is not something I care to contemplate. After all, it's my life on the line. I don't look upon our present situation as an adventure."

Mia was reflective for a moment. "Are you positive about the threats on your life? You've never shown me the threatening notes you said you received. Can I see them?"

"I tossed them out. Why?"

"It's just that I haven't sensed that you're in any danger, aside from water pistols, that is." She grinned, adding, "True, we haven't gone out much, but surely by now the Mafia would know where you are. I think they would have made a move, if they were going to."

"I hope you're right. But until I'm convinced that there's no danger I'm staying put."

Staying put was not something Mia had any intention of doing.

"Is your aunt going to be okay by herself? Maybe we should go over to your house and check up on her. I'd think you'd be worried."

Nice try, Mia, very nice try. He had to give her points for creativity. And persistence. She reminded him of a scrappy bull terrier in search of a bone, and not about to give up until she got her way. "Aunt Bertrice is not alone. A close friend is staying with her. I didn't want to leave her alone in the house. I spoke to my aunt just this morning, while you were at Fiorelli's Bakery, picking up the bagels. She's doing just fine; thanks for asking."

Eyes narrowing ever so slightly, Mia was not about to give up. She'd argued her case with tougher opponents than Nick Caruso, having cut her teeth as a teenager on Sam and Rosalie's constant denials. "I don't suppose you'd like to go Christmas shopping, then? The mall is having a huge sale. You do Christmas shop, don't you? I mean, don't you have an editor, agent, or somebody to buy for? And there's your aunt. Surely, you want to get her a nice present. I mean, unless it's against your religion, or something."

Nick had only Burt to buy for, and he usually ended up taking his friend out to dinner and a Baltimore Ravens' football game, then knocking back a few beers at O'Grady's. But noting Mia's pathetically hopeful expression, and not wanting to raise her suspicions, he finally relented. "All right. Let's go shopping. But I'm warning you I don't have a lot of patience when it comes to this sort of thing. Are you going to change first? You look a bit disheveled, if you don't mind my saying so."

"Even if I minded, you'd still say it, so what's the point of qualifying?" Mia glanced down at her blue jeans and sneakers, and then shook her head, wondering why he was being so critical. Her clothes might not be the height of fashion, but so what? They were clean. "I'm dressed fine for shopping. You, on the other hand, might consider putting on something other than corduroy pants."

Considering her present attire, she probably shouldn't have picked on Nick's wardrobe. But corduroy! A person of good conscience had to draw the line somewhere.

He stiffened. "What's wrong with my pants? I bought these not long ago from the L. L. Bean catalogue."

She heaved a suffering sigh. "It would take too long to explain. And I doubt you'd understand, even then."

"I don't like shopping. And I still have a great deal of work to do, so I hope we won't be gone too long."

"You don't like shopping because you've never been with someone who can make it fun." She crossed the room and peered out the double-hung window, breaking into a smile. "Oh, look! It's clouding over. We might get some snow before this day is through. Wouldn't that be festive?"

As hell, he thought, trying his best to sound enthusiastic. "It sounds terribly seasonal."

Mia couldn't contain her excitement, which was shining brightly in her eyes. "Oh, it will be. And we can sing Christmas carols all the way over to the mall."

Oh goody. This day just keeps getting better and better.

What was it about Christmas that made people giddy? It was just another day, as far as Nick was concerned. *Bah! Humbug!*

"Shall we take your car or mine?" he asked.

"It might be better if you drive," she suggested, "so I can keep a lookout, just in case."

After performing a quick mental inventory of his Volvo, Nick decided there was nothing incriminating that Mia would find to link him to the Bureau. "Excellent thinking. I've been a bit nervous about venturing out, but I can see I'll be in good hands."

"Just like Allstate."

"Pardon?"

Mia rolled her eyes. "Never mind."

*　　*　　*

The parking garage at the mall was packed with holiday shoppers, eager to spend their hard-earned money. Nick and Mia finally managed to find a parking space on the third level, in the far reaches of the garage. But only after circling through five times, and only after Nick had finally lost his temper and blurted, "Son of a bitch!" without thinking.

"Tsk, tsk, Niccolò. Mustn't curse. It never solves anything, now does it?" Mia teased.

Nick glared. "I suppose not, but it sure made me feel better. Did you see that moronic asshole? He . . ." Noting the woman's puzzled frown, Nick caught himself. "Sorry. I shouldn't have lost my temper. I really do try to keep it in check. My aunt would be very disappointed."

"Oh, lighten up, will you. I was only kidding. There are times when a body just has to curse, and this was one of them. That guy shouldn't have cut you off. He really was an asshole. And quite frankly, it makes you seem a bit more . . . well, human, if you don't mind my saying so."

Touché! "Really?"

"Of course. How do you write characters who curse, if you've never cursed yourself? The same goes for lovemaking. I'd think you'd have to know a thing or two about that sort of thing"—*Well, do you?* she wanted to ask—"before you actually put it down on paper. I mean writers have to know which end is which, and what goes where, don't they?"

He swallowed his grin, intrigued by the topic she'd chosen. "I suppose so."

"Of course, they do. Now let's go find you some decent pants."

"My pants are perfectly fine."

"Only if you're entering a Howdy Doody look-alike contest. Now, come on."

Nick allowed Mia to drag him from store to store through the very large mall. He noticed her vigilance in surveying the surrounding area, looking constantly over her shoulder, noting the various passersby, and he was impressed that she'd taken her responsibility of protecting him to heart. It seemed he had underestimated her.

Thus far, Mia had bought a black lace negligee for her sister that would have looked dynamite on Mia, cookbooks for her mother, along with a few romance novels, and for Dan, three CDs of Irish tunes that he could play at his restaurant, Danny Boy's. Mia had also purchased a pair of dangly rhinestone earrings for her dad, which, Nick thought, would be most appropriate, considering Sam's present wardrobe choices.

They paused outside of the Earring Shack, while Mia decided on her next destination. "You've certainly made a dent in your Christmas shopping," Nick said. "Are you ready to go?"

With "Jingle Bells" playing in the background, and fifty screaming, crying kids lined up to tell Santa their innermost desires, Mia stared at Nick as if he'd just committed blasphemy. "Go? To paraphrase John Paul Jones: I have barely begun to shop, thank you very much. And I remind you that you haven't found anything for your aunt yet. What do you think she'd like? I'll help you pick out something."

He rubbed his chin, provocative thoughts about that black lace nightgown still swirling. "How about something from . . ." He paused, hoping he looked confused enough. Playing dumb was a lot harder than being dumb, he'd decided. "I think it's called Victoria's Secret? My aunt likes frilly things."

Her brows shot up. "You're joking, right? I would have thought at her age she'd be into flannel."

"Aunt Bertrice is a bit eccentric when it comes to nightwear. I've heard her order from the Victoria's Secret catalogue on several occasions." He put his tongue in his cheek. "She once bought something called a teddy bear."

Mia's mouth hung open, before she said, "You mean a teddy? Your elderly aunt wears a teddy?" The woman must be in fabulous shape, because Mia didn't think her own body was good enough for a teddy. Of course, she'd always hated her body, which she thought was all angles and planes, fine if you were a building or an airplane, but a woman needed curves and bumps, like Angela had.

He shrugged, an innocent smile firmly in place. "That's what I heard. And I do want to get her something she would enjoy. That's what Christmas is all about, isn't it?"

Still extremely skeptical, Mia replied, "Well, all right, if you're sure. It's your money."

"Oh, I'm very sure."

They entered the store, and in that exact moment, a loud popping noise went off. Mia threw herself in front of Nick, reaching into her purse for the gun she kept there.

"It's all right," he told her, placing his hand over hers, so she couldn't draw her weapon. "It's just a balloon."

Breathing a sigh of relief, she smiled. "I seem to be getting quite good at defending you from unruly children. Let's finish our shopping."

In less than a minute, Mia found exactly what they were looking for. She held up a sheer peach teddy that had Nick holding his breath as his imagination charged into overtime. "That's a teddy? Well, my goodness. Um, do you think you could hold it up in front of you, so I can get an idea of how it will look . . . on my aunt, I mean."

She hesitated a moment, then did as he requested. "It's hard to imagine anything while you're wearing that bulky sweater and baggy blue jeans," he told her.

"If you think I'm going to put this little number on and model it for you, Nick, you're nuts. I'd have to take off my clothes, and this teddy is about as sheer as they come. I'd be exposing all of my assets."

"Which are considerable . . . I'm sure."

She stared suspiciously, her eyes narrowing slightly. "Thanks, I think. Are you positive that your aunt wears this type of garment?"

"Positive. She also wears something called a strap . . ." He shook his head. "Or maybe it's a rope. Ah, a thong, that's it. Do you know what a thong is?"

"I should. I wear them myself, but not often." They were too masochistic for her taste. "But I really don't think—"

"I told you," Nick interrupted before she could object, "my aunt is an eccentric woman. And what's wrong with a thong? You look horrified."

Mia turned around and rummaged on the table behind her, pulling forth a red lace thong that made his heartbeat quicken and his palms start to sweat.

"You wear these?" he asked, finding his voice again. "But how do they work?"

"The narrow part goes in the back. There's not much to them. And they're not very comfortable. But they are sexy as hell. And men like them, so . . ." Her face was heating to the boiling point, matching the panty exactly.

"Never you mind. I just hope your aunt doesn't have hemorrhoids."

Nick's eyes twinkled. "Would you please pick out three teddies and three thongs, in various colors, for me?"

"What size?"

Nick studied Mia so thoroughly from top to bottom that she began shuffling her feet nervously. The heat of his gaze made her whole body quiver. "My aunt isn't a very big woman. She's about your size, I'd guess, so whatever you wear should be fine."

"You're absolutely sure about this?"

He nodded. "Absolutely."

After paying for the purchases, they made their way across the mall to Wilson's Leather.

"Are you buying a purse?" Nick inquired, inhaling the distinctive odor of tanned hides. He owned three leather jackets, which he loved and wore, when he wasn't playing the nerd from hell. He didn't think Niccolò Caruso, the author, would be caught dead in an animal skin.

"No, I don't need a new purse. I thought it might be fun if you tried on a pair of leather pants, just for the heck of it."

Grinding to a halt, he stared at Mia as if she'd lost her mind. *No way! No damn way!* "Leather pants! You're joking, right?" Jackets were one thing—very cool—but leather pants . . . well, they were the stuff of rock stars, male prostitutes, and gay men on the make.

Mia smiled in that impish way he found so incredibly appealing. "Don't you want to look hot for women, Nick? You are never going to look sexy in those god-awful corduroys, I can promise you that."

"I don't need to look sexy. I'm comfortable with my masculinity." *What was left of it, anyway.* It was quite apparent that Mia didn't think he was the least bit sexy, or "hot," and for some reason he didn't care to contemplate at the moment, that rubbed him the wrong way.

He was a man used to being chased after and fawned over by females, not someone who had his ego pounded into the dirt by a pint-sized bodyguard with a penchant for speaking her mind.

An opinionated woman is a dangerous thing.

"Good. Then you won't mind trying on these pants." She thrust them at him, and he blanched.

A woman with a one-track mind is diabolical.

If anyone at the Bureau caught him dressed in black leather, like some dominatrix, he'd never live it down. A few years back, he had gone undercover as a pimp with a penchant for puce silk, and Burt and the others had teased him unmercifully for weeks, calling him "Puce, The Pussy Hunter."

Nick evaluated the situation for a moment, deciding how he could use it to his advantage. "I'll consider the pants, if you're willing to try on a leather dress. Something feminine. And different from what you usually wear."

Cheeks aflame, Mia shook her head. "That's not my style."

It should be, Nick thought, *you're a beautiful woman.* "Mine, neither. Guess we've reached an impasse. Let's go home."

Mia weighed the alternatives, then said, "Oh, all right. I'll go see if I can find something suitably feminine and meet you in front of the dressing rooms."

Nick's ego raised a notch. Mia might think him homely, but she couldn't think of him as dumb; he'd very effectively bested her at her own game.

When Mia appeared a few minutes later, wearing a thigh-high red-leather dress, with plunging back and neckline that fit like a second skin, Nick could barely draw a breath, or form a coherent thought. His reaction was instantaneous, obvious, and borderline painful in the tight leather pants.

"You look"—*yummy, delicious, good enough to eat*—"lovely," he said when she finished her pirouette.

"I feel like a hooker." Mia studied her reflection in the mirror and made a face. "Well, maybe an expensive call girl, judging by the price of this dress. I don't think your average streetwalker could afford an outfit like this, unless, of course, business was good, really, really good. Though I doubt I could clear fifty bucks on a good night working the streets."

"In that dress you could clear five hundred easy," Nick blurted without thinking.

Smiling at the rare compliment, Mia's gaze was drawn to Nick's tight leather pants and silver silk shirt. He looked hot. Or as hot as Nick could look wearing those horrible glasses. "If you ditched the specs, you'd look like Val Kilmer playing Jim Morrison."

Just as he'd thought: rock star.

Nick feigned ignorance. "Sorry?"

"Never mind. I like those pants on you. They make you look like a different person, sort of dangerous." *And sexy as hell.*

Where had that thought come from? Mia wondered, touching her palm to her forehead. *No fever, dammit!*

"I like that dress on you, too. I'm not usually in the company of call girls, so it's a nice change of pace." He grinned, and so did she, and then they burst out laughing.

"I'd like to buy that dress for you, Mia, if you'll allow

me. It looks wonderful on you. Really. And I don't think you look at all like a prostitute."

Mia contemplated the offer, and then decided to accept it as part of her fee, since Nick was getting her services so cheaply. She'd done a bit more research, and discovered that she could have charged him at least five thousand a month, plus expenses, for their arrangement. But a deal was a deal, and it was only a dress. "I'll agree to the dress if you buy those pants," she told him.

"But they're three hundred dollars! I'll never wear them again."

"Never say never, Nick. Life is much more interesting when you don't plan everything out. You need to live in the moment, stop to smell the roses; something wonderful could be lurking right around the corner. No pain, no gain has always been my motto."

What the hell! It was only money, Nick thought, and he was having a good time, too good a time. He'd been enjoying Mia's company, enjoyed the sound of her voice, her laughter—she laughed a lot—the kooky way she had of looking at life and everyday situations, her willingness to try new things. She wasn't the least bit closed off.

He liked her.

And he sure as hell liked her body.

He couldn't help wondering what she'd be like in bed.

But why did she try to hide her feminine side? Under the baggy jeans and sweater lurked a dynamite figure that was rarely on display. Why? What was she afraid of?

"I'll change and meet you at the cash register," he said.

"Please wear the pants home, Nick. You can ditch the shirt and put on your own shirt and sports coat. But please keep on the pants. Pretty please. I really love how they look."

Was he out of his mind? Nick felt himself weakening, knew he was going to give in. Something Nick rarely did . . . for anyone. "Oh, all right. As long as we go straight home and don't make any stops along the way. I wouldn't want anyone else to see me dressed this way." The mere thought was too hideous to even entertain.

"Okay. I'll go change and be back in a sec."

While he waited for Mia to return, Nick changed his shirt, grabbed the rest of his stuff out of the dressing room, and headed to the checkout counter, feeling like a conspicuous fool.

He was waiting in a rather long line when someone tapped him on the shoulder. Thinking it was Mia with another outrageous request, he turned, about to say something scathing when the words froze on his tongue.

Burt Mulrooney stood right behind him, a shocked look on his face.

Oh, shit! Now he was in for it.

"Jesus, Mary, and Joseph! I thought that was you, boyo. Where the hell did you get those pants? And why are you wearing them? Wait till I tell the guys back at the office."

Nick brazened it out. "It's a long story. One I can't go into right now. Suffice it to say that it's part of the ongoing operation, and leave it at that. And if you breathe a word of this to anyone, Burt, I'll reveal that you wear a toupee."

"You know damn well I don't wear it all the time." Burt reached up to clasp his rug, his frown deepening. Self-conscious of his thinning hair, the older agent had purchased the toupee in the hopes of looking younger, and he sure as hell didn't want anyone to know about it, especially anyone at the Bureau. Of course, that didn't stop him from busting on Nick.

"I came here to buy a new wallet, and instead I find you parading around like some—" He shook his head in disgust. "You look positively gay in those pants, Nick. Why, that handsome lad across the store is staring at your ass. I think he likes you."

"Shut the hell up, Burt! And wipe that stupid grin off your face. I told you—"

"I'm back," Mia said, nodding politely at the man Nick was talking to. "Aren't you going to introduce me to your friend, Nick?" She didn't wait for him to comply, just stuck out her hand toward Burt and grinned. "Hi! I'm Mia. Nice to meet you."

Instantly smitten, Burt returned her grin with a puppy-dog smile of affection, making Nick sigh. It was quite obvious Mia had a new champion. "This is Burt Mulrooney. Burt and I used to work together."

"Oh? Where?"

Burt and Nick exchanged worried glances.

"I was Nick's editor, years ago. We worked for a now defunct magazine called *Gay Men's World*," Burt said, making Nick choke.

Mia's eyes widened. She'd heard of the magazine. When *Gay Men's World* had first hit newsstands, her father had been appalled, going on and on about how disgusting it was that gay men were allowed to have their own magazine. She'd tried to point out that it was no different than the appeal *Playboy* or *Playgirl* had for straight men and women, but Sam DeNero would not be convinced by anything she had to say.

No surprise there.

Mia had always found it strange that her father could

be judgmental of other peoples' lifestyles when his own proclivity to dress like a woman marked him as different.

Really different!

"I was only freelancing," Nick was quick to point out, glaring at a grinning Burt, whose eyes were twinkling mischievously, and who was enjoying every moment of his friend's discomfort.

"As I recall, Nick was very popular with the lads at the magazine, Mia. I think it was his wardrobe." He stared meaningfully at the pants, and Nick's face reddened.

Mia picked up on Burt's teasing and winked at the older man in conspiratorial fashion. "Well, as a woman, I think those pants make him look hot."

"Oh, I don't doubt for a minute that our Nick here is hot. I don't doubt that at all."

SIX

I laugh in the face of danger!
Then I hide until it goes away.
Buffy the Vampire Slayer

"I don't know why you were so upset with your friend, Nick. Burt seems like a very nice man. And you were quite rude to him. I think you may have hurt his feelings. I'm going to invite him to dinner, to make it up to him."

Nick fought the urge to roll his eyes. Hurt Burt's feelings? Ha! That was a joke. The man's hide was Teflon-coated. Insults bounced off him, like bullets off Superman.

"Burt rubs me the wrong way, that's all." He assumed a priggish air. "He's rather rough around the edges." She opened her mouth to dispute his opinion, but he cut her off. "I really don't care to discuss Burt Mulrooney. And we're not inviting him to dinner."

"But he told me he liked to watch movies. I know we'd have a good time. Burt loves *Star Wars*, and—"

"No!"

Heaving a sigh, Mia decided to let the matter drop for now. Nick could be so darn stubborn when he wanted to be. But so could she. Timing was everything, however, and now was not the right time to argue.

"Do you remember where we parked the car?" She cranked her head from side to side, perusing every aisle they walked passed. "I know it was somewhere on this level." Level three was relatively deserted. They'd stayed at the mall and eaten an early dinner. Now, dusk had fallen, darkening not only the sky, but the parking garage as well.

"This place isn't well lighted, which isn't very safe, if you ask me. I should complain to the mall manager about it. Women who aren't trained in the martial arts, as I am, might feel afraid. And who could blame them? There are a lot of weirdos out there."

Noting the glass lightbulb fragments littering the ground, Nick opened his mouth to respond. Just then, two men jumped out from behind a parked car, catching both of them by surprise. Mia let loose a startled cry.

"Stop, or we'll blow your heads off!" The taller one, who looked to be about nineteen, was holding a gun on them. His hand was shaking a bit, making Nick think that he wasn't very experienced at armed robbery. Still, dead was dead if the gun went off, even by accident.

"My God, Nick! It's the Mafia," Mia whispered, eyes wide and tugging his coat sleeve. "They've sent hit men to kill you. Don't worry. I'll protect you with my life, if need be." She paled slightly at the thought, but then her resolve hardened. Mia never backed down from a challenge.

"Don't do anything rash, Mia." Obviously Nick knew the pair weren't hit men, but they were both armed and looked scared—a dangerous combination. It wasn't a good idea to provoke them, and Mia was an expert at provocation, he'd discovered.

"We've been shopping," he tried to explain in a meek

and mild manner, so they wouldn't feel threatened by his larger size. "I'm afraid we don't have any money to give you. We've spent it all."

"Don't give me that shit, man!" the shorter one with the Orioles baseball cap said. "Empty your pockets and wallet. And you, lady," he indicated with a nod toward Mia, "let me see what's in the purse."

Mia wasn't about to let these two gangsters get hold of her client. She'd been paid to protect Nick Caruso, and that's exactly what she intended to do. "All right," she agreed timidly. "Please don't shoot. It'll just take me a minute to open my purse."

"Leave the lady alone," Nick warned, trying not to sound too macho, but needing to convey his warning. He had to protect Mia at all costs.

"Hurry up! We don't have all day," Baseball Cap ordered.

"You," the larger of the two men said, and pointed his gun at Nick. "Shut the fuck up and take a step back. That's right. Now lean your hands against the hood of the car behind you. And don't try to be a hero. This will be painless, if you don't fight."

Mia gasped. They were going to shoot Nick in the back, just like she'd seen on that episode of *The Sopranos*. Oh, God! Nick was probably more terrified than she; somehow she had to save him.

Nick did as instructed, watching Mia out of the corner of his eye, begging her silently not to do anything rash. "Mia, please be careful," he said. "This is not—" Before he could add "what you think," the impulsive woman had pulled the Glock from her purse and fired.

The shot went wild, reverberating loudly off a steel girder, the gun's powerful thrust knocking Mia on her butt. She fell back, hitting her head on the car door behind her, and was rendered unconscious.

"Jesus! Mia!" Nick glanced down at the prone woman, praying she was all right and cursing a blue streak. Enraged by the sight of her, and fearing for her safety, he turned his wrath upon the two robbers.

Startled by the fact that the petite woman had fired a gun at them, the two assailants let their guard down momentarily. It was the opening Nick needed. Rushing them, he head-butted the taller one, then landed a blow to his jaw.

Frightened at the sight of his unconscious friend, the other perp took off running, but Nick tackled him to the ground, subduing him with a well-placed knee to the chest.

"Lie still, you creep. Your friend's out cold; he can't help you now."

Fear glittered in the boy's dark eyes. "Hey, bro! We didn't mean anything. We were only funning with you."

"Tell it to the judge, *bro*. And you'd better find yourself another line of work, if you know what's good for you. As lousy as you are at armed robbery, you're gonna end up dead." Maybe the kid could turn himself around with the proper guidance. Nick hoped so. It would be a waste of a life—a life that in all likelihood hadn't had any worthwhile experiences yet—and there was already so much waste in the world.

Nick might have ended up the same way if it hadn't been for the organization Big Brothers of America. His big brother, Roland Keyes, had turned his life around by taking him under his wing and teaching him about football, basketball, and how important getting a good education was for his future. He owed the man a great deal.

And he'd tried to give back, by being a Big Brother when he could find the time, which wasn't as often as he liked.

A few minutes later mall security arrived. Assessing the situation, the two guards briefly interrogated Nick, who had made up a suitable story to keep his cover intact, called the incident into the police, then hauled the two men to their squad car and drove off toward police headquarters.

Nick rushed over to an unconscious Mia, who was lying still as death on the ground; she was pasty, her skin clammy to the touch. Taking the gun out of her hand, which she still held in a death grip, he placed it on the pavement next to her, and then felt for bumps and bruises. She had a doozy of a lump on the back of her head, where she'd knocked it against the car door.

"Mia, you are a brave but foolish woman." And he was responsible for her injuries. Dammit! This was his fault. If she had been seriously injured, Nick would never have forgiven himself.

With gentle hands, he probed her arms and legs, then her rib cage, to satisfy himself that nothing was broken. His knuckles grazed against the underside of her breasts, and he heard her moan softly in response, which made it difficult to keep his mind on the matter at hand.

Focus, Caruso. Focus!

Mia's eyes fluttered open. At first, she smiled absently, thinking she was having a very pleasant dream. It wasn't every day that a man fondled her breasts. But then, recognizing Nick, and remembering what had happened, and who was feeling her up in such a memorable fashion, that smile melted into a frown, and Mia filled with indignation.

"I don't think we've known each other long enough to

play touchy-feely, buster!" The worst part was that she had actually liked his attentions, a little too well for her comfort zone.

Nick was the last person Mia wanted to feel attracted to. Not only was he her client, they weren't at all suited for each other. The man was too structured, too uptight, too well read. She liked playing things by ear, so to speak, doing stuff on the spur of the moment. And they were definitely not compatible in the neatness department. Nope. She and Nick didn't suit at all.

Not that she was contemplating a relationship. She'd flunked that course back in college. But there was no denying that he sent her pulse racing.

Nick's cheeks flushed. "I was trying to determine if you have any broken bones. You don't, I'm happy to say. I assure you, I wasn't taking liberties."

Liberties! Was this guy old-fashioned, or what?

"That's good. What happened to the two hit men? Did I scare them off?"

He nodded, letting loose a smile. "You were brilliant. The sight and sound of your gun had them fleeing the scene. I don't think I've seen two people run faster. You saved my life."

Her smile didn't quite reach her eyes, which filled with suspicion. "Really? Are you sure about that? Those two guys didn't seem easily intimidated."

He didn't answer her question, but said instead, "You shouldn't have taken such a chance, Mia. I don't know what I would have done if you had been injured."

"That's so sweet."

"Those men might have taken me hostage, after they killed you, of course. Then what would I have done?"

Reminding herself that this was Nick who was speaking, Mia tried not to feel disappointed at his self-serving remarks. "I'll try to remember not to let it happen again."

"Good. Now, I think we'd better go home. I've had enough adventure for one day, haven't you?"

Mia nodded, then wished she hadn't. Her head was pounding like a kettledrum being played by a masochistic school marching band. "Adventure is highly overrated, in my opinion. I think I'll stick to crossword puzzles from now on. Who knew shopping could be so dangerous?"

This episode had been far worse than her last visit to Filene's Basement in Boston. The women who shopped there were vicious, but they didn't carry guns, at least none that had been pointed at her.

And hadn't that been scary as shit!

"Do you need to see a doctor? I don't mind taking you."

"No, I'll be fine. I just want to go home and lie down for a bit. Maybe take two dozen aspirins."

"How about if I cook dinner tonight, so you can rest?"

"You can cook?" Her eyes widened at the revelation. She just assumed he didn't know how. Nick had never offered to prepare a meal before. Mostly, he just criticized her efforts.

So she'd burned a few dishes. So what? She'd never pretended to be Martha freakin' Stewart.

"It won't be anything fancy, but I make a pretty good meat loaf, if I do say so myself."

"You know, I really can't figure you out sometimes."

Nick held open the car door and helped Mia inside. "How's that?"

"Sometimes it's almost as if you're two different men. You have a lot of sides to you, Nick Caruso."

Nick paled slightly, wondering if Mia somehow suspected the truth. *But how could she?* Unless she hadn't really been unconscious and had seen him apprehend those two men. Shit! If that was the case, his whole operation was blown. "I—"

"But then, I guess most people do. You just haven't let your caring side show before now. It took me by surprise. I rather like it."

He smiled in relief. "Making dinner is just my way of thanking you for what you did today."

"So, you are grateful? I wasn't sure. You often give off mixed signals."

"Of course I am. Why wouldn't I be? I'm still alive, aren't I? We shall live to fight another day, as they say."

Mia smiled with contentment, thinking how much she liked that idea, before closing her eyes and drifting off to sleep.

"The meat loaf is delicious. Thank you for cooking dinner tonight. You really are a man of many talents."

Nick held up his wine glass in a toast. "I could say the same for you. You saved my life tonight."

"It seemed like a worthwhile one to save." Mia sipped her milk; Nick wouldn't allow her to drink wine because of her head injury. "You've never told me much about yourself, Nick, except that your aunt raised you," Mia said, stifling a yawn, then smiling in embarrassment. She was determined to find out more about Nick. "Were you very lonely as a child? I'd think being raised by an elderly person would have had some drawbacks. I mean, I doubt your aunt was into Little League and other boyish activities."

Swallowing his forkful of mashed potatoes, Nick felt that old familiar yearning churning inside him, and knew that no matter how much time passed, how much success he had achieved career-wise, he couldn't let go of his unhappy childhood.

He had missed what other children had while growing up—a close-knit family, someone to share achievements and failures with, a hug before going off to school and a story at bedtime. It didn't sound like much, but to a small, love-starved boy, it was everything.

Nick chose his words carefully, mixing fact with fiction; something he'd been doing since the day he met Mia. "My parents were killed in an automobile accident when I was a baby, so I never really knew them. I spent time at an orphanage, and in foster homes, until my aunt came forward to claim me.

"I stayed with my aunt until I was seventeen, then I ran away to join the army." There he'd learned discipline, a sense of belonging, and gotten a good education. The army had paid for his college, and he'd worked his way through law school, finally obtaining the degree that allowed him to pursue his career with the FBI.

Mia's face softened, as her heart went out to that parentless little boy, who'd had to rely on the kindness of relatives for love and comfort. "Was it difficult for you being raised without siblings, or not having parents come to school functions, and things of that nature? As much as I complain about mine, I'm not sure I could live without Sam and Rosalie. Even though they make me nuts, interfering and making suggestions on how I should live my life, I know they only do it because they care about me."

"I guess I was luckier than some." He hadn't been beaten or sexually molested. Not everyone in foster care could say as much. He'd heard the nightmarish stories while growing up, and had lived in fear that the same fate would befall him. "But it was a lonely way to grow up. And you're right—I did miss what the other kids had. I would have loved having a family, brothers and sisters. But we end up with whatever fate deals us."

"I'm sure I'd be even more neurotic than I am, if the same thing had happened to me."

Mia gulped down the remainder of her milk, wiping her face with the back of her hand, and Nick smiled at the childish gesture. "What made you decide to become a writer?" she asked.

Nick shifted in his chair, unable to look Mia in the eye and see the concern he knew would be reflected there. Mia cared about people. It was one of the things he admired about her. "It was my aunt's idea. She's the one who inspired me to read and try my hand at writing. I probably wouldn't have considered it for myself, if it hadn't been for her. I didn't have a lot of self-confidence while growing up." That much was true, at any rate.

"Me, either. I was always in Angela's shadow. I guess that's why I decided to become a bodyguard. It was something I could make totally my own. And I wanted to make my dad proud of me. I always felt that I came in second best, after Angela, at least as far as my dad was concerned."

"I'm sure Sam is very proud of you, Mia. You should have seen his face when he told me about you opening up your own business. I thought he was going to burst his buttons."

"No doubt they were rhinestone buttons and he didn't want to ruin them. Sam's very fussy about stuff like that." Grinning, she reached out to touch his hand. "Thank you for telling me that. Dad and I have always had a rather uneasy relationship. For years he thought of me as a loser. At least, that was my impression. And I couldn't really blame him. I took jobs I knew would piss him off. But they were good learning experiences. And I'm not sorry for trying my hand at different professions. I thought about going into police work at one time, but then decided against it."

"Why? I'm sure you would have been good at it." He couldn't think of anyone, except maybe Burt, that he'd rather have guarding his back. The woman was fearless.

"I saw how worried my mom got every time my father left the house to go to work. There was always that fear in her eyes that she would never see him again. I didn't want to put her through that. And to be perfectly honest, I'm not sure I wanted to put myself through it, either."

Reaching for the milk carton, Nick refilled their glasses. "Law enforcement has always fascinated me," he admitted, choosing his words carefully, lest he reveal too much. "When I was twelve I was caught shoplifting at a sporting goods store. My foster father at the time of the incident didn't punish me in the usual way. Instead, he took me down to the police station and showed me what happened to those who stole from others.

"The experience left a lasting impression, to the point where I couldn't think about anything but law enforcement." Admiration for his Big Brother, Roland, who had happened to be a cop, only reinforced that desire.

"Wow! Sounds like your foster father was a pretty smart guy. So why didn't you pursue that career?"

As a youth, Nick had been fascinated with the movie *The FBI Story* and had watched it countless times, even fantasizing that Jimmy Stewart and Vera Miles were his real parents. When he graduated college, then law school, he knew the FBI was the place he wanted to be. Becoming an agent seemed a natural progression, and the fulfillment of a lifelong dream.

The only regret he had is that his work had kept him from forming any significant relationships, although that could also be blamed on his unwillingness to open himself up to hurt and abandonment. He'd played it safe.

"I'm sorry. Did you ask me something? My mind was wandering again."

"Was your interest in law enforcement the reason why you decided to write about crime?"

"Something like that," Nick said, deciding it was time to change the subject. He'd shared enough confidences for one day. Soon he'd be spilling his guts to Mia about the whole operation, and he couldn't let that happen.

Paul Buttoni and Vincent Palumbo were huddled inside Vincent's office at the car dealership that Vincent owned jointly with Alfredo Graziano.

Named after Alfredo's deceased father, Lucky Louie's Auto World had been his brainchild. The name hadn't mattered to Vincent, who was only concerned about the bottom line and making money, lots of money. If Alfredo was considered the brawn of the business, then Vinnie was definitely the brains.

Paul, Vincent, and Alfredo had been friends since childhood. They'd served together as altar boys, and had even lost their virginity to the same prostitute they'd pooled their money to buy when they were fourteen. After graduating high school, Pauley and Alfredo had joined the army, while Vinnie stayed behind to marry his high school sweetheart, whom he later divorced.

But none of that seemed to matter now that Pauley and Vinnie had decided that skimming profits and chopping cars was a whole lot more lucrative and satisfying than their friendship with Alfredo.

"You sure Al don't suspect anything?" Pauley wanted to know, looking over his shoulder nervously, even though his friend was at lunch and wouldn't be back for at least another hour. "I don't mind cheating him, but I don't want to hurt him. You know, me and Al, we go back a long way, Vinnie."

"Fuck, Pauley! It's a hell of a time for you to be getting a conscience. We've been cheating the poor bastard for months, and now you're worried about how he's going to feel?" Vinnie shook his head and laughed, his double chins bouncing. "You're a stupid bastard, you know that? This scheme was your idea. You're the one with the mob connections. Little Larry Calzone is your *goombah*, not mine."

The shorter man shrugged, pulling a comb out of his back pocket to smooth his slick, dyed black hair straight back. If Alec Baldwin had been five feet, six inches tall, wore lifts in his shoes, and looked like a pygmy, he would have resembled Pauley Buttoni. Fortunately, Alec had been spared that fate.

"We've been friends a long time. I don't want him finding out, that's all."

"I'm keeping two sets of books. Alfredo's not smart

enough to know about the second set. He can't even operate a computer, for chrissake! He sells the cars, I keep the books, and dole out his commissions.

"The arrangement is perfect, especially for us, Pauley. Al don't suspect a thing, and he never will. The man's always been too trusting. It's the reason we couldn't cut him in on the deal in the first place. Sad to say, but he's not the criminal sort. Doesn't have the balls for it. And he likes the extra money he's been making. I doubt he'll ask any questions. In fact, I can almost guarantee he won't."

"And now that he's set on marrying that Gallagher woman he won't want to jeopardize his reputation, right?"

"No more than he has already. Al set himself up as the perfect patsy, with all that mafioso talk about being part of the Gotti crime family, as if they would have the dumb bastard. If ever there was a fall guy born, it's Al. We couldn't have invented anyone better if we'd tried."

Pauley's brow wrinkled in confusion. "I thought you liked Al. He's godfather to your youngest daughter."

Vinnie shrugged. "I like him fine. But what's that got to do with business? Business is business. I keep telling you, Pauley, we got to keep sentiment out of it."

"If Al finds out that he's been selling stolen autos, and that Calzone's been laundering his money through the business, he's going to be pissed. He's always bragging about doing an honest day's work and getting paid well for it. I almost feel sorry for him."

Vincent's love for pasta was well documented by the size of the belly hanging over the alligator belt around his waist; his frown deepened as he caressed the manicotti resting within, thinking that, like Al, Pauley was becoming a real liability. "Having Al pissed at us is the least of our worries. We just gotta make sure that if this deal goes south, he's around to take the fall.

"I've covered our tracks pretty well, so I'm not that worried. Still, there's always a risk. The good news is that if the feds get suspicious, they'll look at Al first. He's the one who's been flashing around a lot of money, trying to impress that girlfriend of his."

Smiling widely to reveal a large gap where his two front teeth had been—the result of having pissed off an associate—Pauley reached into his inside coat pocket to extract two cigars, handing his friend one. "You're smart, Vinnie, that's why I decided to cut you in on this deal. I knew you'd be perfect for it."

Vincent Palumbo smiled, but the smile never reached his eyes. He lit the Cuban, puffing hard to encourage it to life. "Not to mention that I'm part owner of a car dealership, which makes things a hell of a lot easier for everyone concerned, no?"

"I'm not saying that wasn't a consideration when I was approached by the boss to put this thing together, Vinnie. But I wanted someone I could trust."

"So far, we've cleared over three hundred thousand, Pauley. We're going all the way with this. It's a sweet deal, so nobody better get in the way and ruin things."

The mobster's brow furrowed. "What are you saying? That you might do something to Al if he finds out? I don't think I'd like that, Vinnie. It's one thing to use Al; it's another to snuff him out."

Vincent wrapped his arm about the shorter man and smiled. "Not to worry. Al's our ticket to the pot of gold. You don't cut off the hand that feeds you."

"That's right, you don't. Just remember that Al's our friend."

Vincent smiled secretively, and said nothing more.

"What, may I ask, do you think you're doing? I have work to do tonight and you've moved my chair."

In fact, Mia had moved back all of the furniture in the living room, leaving a large, cleared space in the center.

"Four days ago we were attacked in a parking garage. It's time you learned how to defend yourself, Nick. I should have apprehended those men, and I apologize for not doing so. But if you'd been a little more knowledge-able about the martial arts, you might have been able to do more to protect yourself. It's a precaution we need to take."

"I thought that's why I hired you."

"I might end up incapacitated, like the other day, and be unable to help you. You were lucky those hit men de-cided to run." The timely arrival of mall security, accord-ing to Nick, had aided their decision to make the big skedaddle. She'd taken him at his word, but doubts still remained.

"*You* are going to teach *me* how to defend myself?" Nick's mouth dropped open, and he stared at the petite woman before him. Hell, he could pick Mia up with one hand tied behind his back. And that meant he could hurt her, something he wasn't willing to do, charade or no charade.

Shaking his head, he added, "May I remind you that you've just recovered from a minor concussion. I'm not going to allow you to get physical and hurt yourself further."

"The doctor said it wasn't a concussion, not really. Well, maybe just a teensy one. But I'm fully recovered, and he told me I could resume all of my normal activities."

"Does he know you play Rambo in your spare time?"

Mia grinned. "You're getting to be more fun with every day that passes, you know that, Nick? I like this new you. Now, we've just got to whip you into shape.

"Trust me, women are wild about guys who know karate and can wrestle." She placed a hand on his stomach and gave it a pat. "You're getting a bit soft around the middle. Not good. I don't want to have to refer to you as the Pillsbury Dough Boy."

Nick's frown deepened as he sucked in his gut. "I'm in excellent shape." Placing his hand where hers had just been, he felt only muscle and breathed a sigh of relief. Nick did three hundred sit-ups and two hundred push-ups every night after Mia went to bed. Fat around his middle was not an acceptable option. A flabby agent was a dead one, which is why he worried about Burt.

"I'm not the least bit interested—"

"Can it, Nick. You're going to learn how to defend yourself, and I'm going to teach you. Every evening after dinner, we'll put on our sweats, and—"

"I don't own any sweats."

Rolling her eyes, Mia heaved an exasperated sigh. "So you'll buy some. Go to Goldman's and get a ten percent discount from Annie. In the meantime, I guess you can just wear whatever it is you're wearing."

"These are chinos. You said you didn't like the corduroy so I changed."

"Do you own a pair of jeans?"

He nodded. "Yes, one pair. I use them to work out in

the garden. My aunt is very fond of roses, but they take a lot of care."

"It's nice that you take such good care of your aunt, Nick. I admire that about you."

"Thank you. I don't find it a hardship at all."

"Why don't you go change into your jeans and a T-shirt. You do own a T-shirt, don't you?" When he nodded, almost cautiously, she added, "Please hurry and change. I'd like to get started."

"Oh, all right. But don't blame me if you get hurt. I weigh a lot more than you do."

Mia smiled slyly. "I'm not the least bit worried."

"I think you may have broken my collarbone."

Hands on hips, Mia stared down at Nick and smiled. He was red-faced, mostly from embarrassment, she thought. He didn't appear to be injured, unless you counted his pride, which he was sitting on at the moment. "I told you to brace yourself, that I was going to flip you over my shoulder. I gave you plenty of advance warning, something an attacker isn't going to do."

"You caught me off guard, that's all."

She held out her hand. "Shall we try it again?"

Nodding, Nick took Mia's hand. When she started to help him up, he yanked her off balance, pulling her down to the rug, and then rolling over to cover her body with his own. "Is this a good move?" he asked, innocence dripping out of his mouth like sweet honey.

Mia could feel his hardness pressing into her belly, and her mouth went dry. Yes, Nick, she wanted to say, it's a very good move!

His lips were only inches from her own, and she had the sudden urge to kiss him, to see if they were as soft as they appeared. But sanity suddenly returned with a vengeance, and she ordered, "Take off your glasses, Nick. I'm going to get rough, and I don't want to break them."

"Uh, I don't see very well without them. I'd better keep them on."

"You don't have to see well, you just have to pay attention. Besides, you'll be too busy eating dirt or, in this case, carpet nap, to worry about it."

Nick smiled inwardly at Mia's feistiness and self-confidence. There was a whole lot of woman packed into that pint-sized package. He removed his glasses, and her shocked expression told him far better than words that he really did look bad in the heavy frames he'd chosen.

Which was the idea, after all. But he couldn't help feeling an ego boost by the admiring way she was looking at him.

"You have such pretty eyes. Why don't you get contacts, instead of hiding them?"

To indicate his own displeasure, he tugged on her sweatshirt. "You have a very nice bod . . . figure. Why do you hide beneath baggy, unattractive clothing?"

She pushed to her feet. "My body isn't attractive at all. It's too boyish. Angela not only got the brains, she got the fabulous body and big boobs. I got the leftovers, which wasn't very much." She'd never admitted those feelings to a man before, but this was Nick. And he was easy to talk to, rather like a best girlfriend, though she certainly hadn't been thinking "girlfriend" when he'd been lying on top of her.

"Your sister is a very attractive woman, but she's not as pretty as you," he said, taking a seat next to her on the sofa.

Mia was pleased by the compliment, and grateful to

Nick for saying it, though she didn't believe one word. "Look, Nick, I realize you're not all that experienced when it comes to women, so I'm just going to tell you how it is.

"You got a bit excited while you were lying on top of me. I could feel your . . . well, you know, and I firmly believe that men oftentimes think with that particular appendage rather than their brains. It's nothing to be ashamed of," she added at his horrified look. "It's just colored your perception a bit, made you see things that aren't really there."

He picked up his glasses and put them back on. "I have twenty-twenty vision with these on, and I see perfectly fine. You just don't know how to take a compliment when it's handed out. Why do you hide your femininity? What are you afraid of?"

Nick's remarks were hitting too close for comfort, and Mia stiffened. "If there's one thing I can't abide, it's being lied to. And if I had any femininity, I'd know it. I look in the mirror every day, and the mirror doesn't lie, like some people I could name."

Mia had always been a tomboy. It was easier just being one of the guys. Rejections were kept to a minimum. And if she didn't take herself too seriously, didn't allow herself to get her expectations too high, didn't put any credence in sweet words and lovemaking, she had a lot shorter fall when the time came to be dumped. And the time always came.

Lasting relationships had always eluded Mia. She'd been dumped so many times, and for such a variety of creative reasons—*my mother is dying, I'm gay, I'm becoming a missionary*—she'd actually started to enjoy the excuses and considered handing out an award for the best one.

Nick thought for a moment. "I might not always tell the truth about everything," he admitted cautiously, "but I'm being perfectly honest when I say that you, Mia DeNero, are an attractive woman with a dynamite b . . . personality.

"And where did you get the impression that I'm not experienced with the opposite sex?" That notion had wounded, though he wasn't the least bit surprised by the conclusion she'd drawn. After all, she had him pegged as the geek from hell from the get-go. And who could blame her? He certainly looked and acted the part, and it was beginning to wear thin. A man's ego could only be stretched so far.

"You're a virgin, am I right?" she blurted.

Nick was so stunned that he couldn't speak for a moment, which Mia took as an assent. "I knew it."

Annoyed by her presumption, Nick grabbed hold of Mia's shoulders and pulled her to him before she could protest, covering her mouth in a soul-searing, tonsil-tickling kiss that had her growing light-headed and breathless.

His lips moved over hers in masterful persuasion, as he nibbled playfully on her bottom lip, then drew it in and sucked. Mia's reaction was instantaneous: her stomach twisted into a tight knot of wanting. And she felt herself growing hot.

Mia moaned loudly, and Nick drew back, a satisfied smile on his face. Rising to his feet, he said, "I've got work to do."

Somewhat dazed, she leaned back against the cushion of the sofa, touched her lips gingerly, and heaved a satisfied sigh, watching as Nick placed his chair in front of the computer and sat down to work.

Just goes to show you, you really can't judge a book by its cover.

Niccolò Caruso, author at large, had just turned from G to X-rated in a matter of moments.

And oh, my, what a good kisser!

SEVEN

*Why should I live up to other people's expectations
rather than my own?*
10 Things I Hate About You

Mia had thought of little else since the previous night
but *that* kiss, that exquisite, heart-thumping, mind-
blowing, whopper of a toe-tapping kiss.

She'd thought about it while lying in bed—*alone,
dammit!*—thought about it while showering this
morning—her skin felt taut and tingly—and she thought
about it now, while peering over her crossword puzzle
book to observe Nick, who seemed oblivious to her turmoil and didn't seem to have a turmoil of his own, as he
tickled the computer keyboard in pursuit of the perfect
paragraph.

Mia knew she had to face facts. She was hopelessly
enamored of Nick. He wasn't her type—not that she
had a specific type, mind you—but if she did, she was
pretty sure that it wouldn't be someone like fastidious,
anal, quiet, conservative, brussels-sprouts-are-good-for-
you Nick.

Besides, she had to keep reminding herself that Nick
was a client. And she had no business having lecherous,
sexual thoughts about a client. It wasn't professional.
Not to mention good for her health.

But he did have a nice butt. She'd never noticed that before.

A bodyguard did not swap spit with a man she had sworn to protect. Yes, she was offering her body, but not in the carnal sense. Okay, so Patty Hearst had married her bodyguard, but she'd been a little messed up by the kidnapping and those SLA people.

Mia was messed up, too, mostly due to lack of sex, which probably accounted for the attraction she was feeling. It had been a while. It had been so long, in fact, that she couldn't remember with whom she had last done the deed. Obviously it hadn't been anything to write home about.

Not that she would. Her father would lock her up in a chastity belt for sure. Sam DeNero was protective to a fault.

Mia needed to get laid, for lack of a better word. Well there was the "F" word, but that seemed a bit crass, and not at all politically correct, in this day and age. Unfortunately there were no candidates on the horizon—no one except Nick, that is, and he was hands off.

He did have nice hands—strong and tender, with long fingers that could—

Mia needed to find a man; Nick needed to find a woman.

Just not each other.

There'd been a lot of pent-up longing and emotion in last night's kiss. Heat—sizzling, sweet, hormones-into-overdrive heat. Desire had ripped through her body like a knife through butter. His lips had been so soft and tender. And when his tongue had entered her mouth and played tickle tag with her own. Oh my! Firework city.

A man with an erection was like a time bomb waiting to explode. He could blow at any time, and she couldn't afford to allow him to . . . well, erupt anywhere near her.

Uh, uh. No matter how interesting that idea might be, Nick needed a woman. And fast. It was the best form of protection for her . . . heart.

And she knew just where to find one.

"How much longer are you going to be, Nick? We need to go to the butcher shop and pick up something for tonight's dinner. I was thinking pork chops might be good."

"Fine, fine. Whatever. I'm busy."

She sighed. "I'm kinda hungry. I thought we could go out for a burger or something. My treat."

Swiveling around in his seat, Nick heaved a sigh. It had been difficult facing Mia today; he couldn't stop remembering how it had felt to kiss her.

And how foolish it had been.

He couldn't afford to jeopardize his entire operation because of some horny, teenage-like attraction.

Damn his stupidity!

And damn her for being so . . . so . . . Mia!

He'd broken the first rule of undercover work: Never get involved, romantically or otherwise, with a civilian, especially if that civilian was . . . is a woman.

"All right. I'm almost finished. Go do whatever it is you do before you go out, and I'll be right there."

Mia headed to the bathroom, not to put on makeup— she rarely wore any—but to use the facilities. Emptying one's bladder always made more room for french fries and Coke.

Someday she intended to write a book on the subject.

She would list all those famous little hints that could help people cope with the stresses of life.

Voiding your bladder was just one of many. There was also hiding inessential items, like books and magazines, in your grocery cart, so you wouldn't feel guilty about spending money unnecessarily. And if you were on a strict diet, the kind that counted exchanges, you could list a strawberry daiquiri as one of your fruits, and not feel the least bit guilty.

Unlike Nick's book, which would probably appeal to a limited audience, hers would be a blockbuster. There were a lot of people in the world looking for excuses.

She couldn't be the only one, right?

Suppressing the urge to burp—she'd eaten onions with her cheeseburger at lunch—Mia entered Santini's Butcher Shop a short time later, Nick close on her rear . . . um . . . heels.

Lou Santini, the owner's son, was standing behind the refrigerated case, a side of beef slung over his shoulder, looking like one of those "Me Tarzan, you Jane" types, giving new meaning to the song "A Hunka, Hunka Burning Love." Not that she was interested in him as anything other than a friend. As nice as he was, he just didn't ring her chimes.

Mia couldn't help but admire his strong, bodybuilder physique. The man had major pecs and abs. And his arms . . . tree trunks should be so lucky. There was no doubt about it; next to Donatella Foragi, Lou Santini was the Paul Bunyan of Little Italy.

And resident stud of the neighborhood, much to Donna Wiseman's dismay. It was clear Donna coveted her employer, though if asked, she would deny it vehemently. And Lou was smitten with Donna, Mia was certain. The looks that passed between the two stubborn people were hot enough to melt steel.

So what was keeping them apart?

Not what, but who?

Lou's dragon-lady mother, Nina, couldn't stand the sight of Donna. She thought the young woman was a brainless piece of fluff, not to mention a gold digger, and made no bones about the fact that Donna wasn't good enough for her only son. Not that anyone would be.

Mrs. Santini was a widow, and Mia had figured out shortly after arriving in town and meeting the Santinis that Lou was having a difficult time trying to fill his dead father's shoes, and the obligation of taking care of his overbearing mother. There was also the matter of Nina's expectations of Lou, which weren't reasonable, by anyone's standards.

Italians! They really were absurdly old-fashioned when it came to family matters.

Mia knew that firsthand.

"Hey, Mia!" Lou tossed out the greeting with a wide grin, proving the claim that orthodontia worked. Mia had straight teeth, too, but only by the grace of God, and good DeNero genes.

"Good to see you," he said. "What can I do for you today? I've got some dynamite veal that I just cut up."

"Lou, I'd like you to meet my client. This is Nick Caruso, multi-published author."

"No kidding? Anything I might have read?" the butcher asked. "I'm a sucker for a good thriller."

Mia shook her head. "Nick's books are out of print, or so he tells me. Isn't that right, Nick?"

"Right." Nick didn't like the hungry look Lou was tossing Mia's way, as if he were about to devour her, so he had a difficult time mustering up a pleasant smile. "We're here to buy pork chops," he announced, and Mia cast him a curious glance.

"Is Donna here?" Mia asked the butcher, who was also staring strangely at Nick. "I'd like to talk to her about something."

"Donna will be right back. She went to Moressi's Pharmacy to pick up a prescription for my mother. Ma's been feeling under the weather lately."

"Oh, I'm sorry to hear that. I hope it's nothing serious."

Lou shrugged, worry filling his eyes, but didn't elaborate further, and Mia thought it best not to press.

The bell over the door tinkled just then, and Mia and Nick turned to find Sophia Russo entering. The older woman, whose hair resembled Lucille Ball's or Bozo's, depending on how you looked at it, smiled when she saw Nick, then rushed up to greet him, as if he were some long lost friend or relative. As was her practice, she ignored Mia, who was disappointed that it hadn't been Donna who'd arrived instead of the annoying woman.

"*Bona sera,* Nick. I have such good news for you. My brother is willing to be interviewed. Alfredo said that I should arrange the time and place, and he will come and meet with you. I had to convince him, of course, but I didn't mind. I told him you reminded me of Joe Perillo. Alfredo always liked Joe."

Trying not to look as excited as he felt, Nick held out his hand to clasp the woman's, and Sophia's cheeks filled with color. "Thank you so much, Mrs. Russo. I really appreciate your help. Interviewing your brother, Alfredo, is going to add so much texture and authenticity to my book. I can't begin to tell you how grateful I am."

"Then perhaps someday you will return the favor to me, yes?"

Mia knew a loaded question when she heard one, and wondered what the woman was up to. Nothing good, she was certain. Sophia was a natural born trouble-maker, and she was damn good at stirring things up, in-terfering where she didn't belong, and offering advice that no one wanted.

"Of course, Mrs. Russo. I'd be happy to assist you in whatever way I can." At this point, Nick would do just about anything if it meant furthering his investigation, which at the moment was at a standstill.

Neither he nor Burt had been able to find any concrete evidence tying Graziano or his partner, Palumbo, to the money-laundering scheme. Whoever was cooking the books was doing a damn good job of it.

"Doesn't he talk nice, Lou? Nick is an educated man, so refined, a real gentleman. The woman who gets him is going to be very lucky." She turned to give Mia a look that said, *It won't be you, Mia DeNero, not if I have any-thing to say about it.*

"You're too kind, Mrs. Russo."

Grunting in agreement, Sophia turned to place her meat and poultry order with Lou, then headed upstairs to the family apartment to visit with Lou's mother. She and Nina barely tolerated each other on most occasions, but when someone was ill, as in Mrs. Santini's case, you were duty bound to put aside grievances and offer what comfort you could.

The old ways were not ignored in Little Italy.

"So, Nick, do you play poker?" Lou asked, handing Mia a wrapped package of pork chops, and taking her money in exchange. "Me and some of the other guys in the neighborhood get together once a week for a friendly game of five-card stud. Would you like to come over this Friday night? We're playing at Eddie Falcone's house, and could use another player."

Nick, who adored playing poker almost as much as the stock market, opened his mouth to accept the invitation, but Mia didn't give him the chance.

"Nick's not going to be playing poker with you and your card-shark friends, Lou Santini, so don't even think about inviting him." She turned to Nick and explained, "The last time I played poker with Lou and his friends I almost lost my underwear. They didn't bother to tell me it was a game of strip poker."

An unreasonable anger settled in the pit of Nick's stomach. "You took your clothes off in front of strange men? I must say, Mia, that I'm surprised by that." Actually, the idea pissed him off royally, but he didn't pause to consider why. He didn't dare.

"Hey, watch who you're calling strange!" Lou said, but his eyes were smiling.

Mia laughed. "Don't worry, Nick. I had on plenty of jewelry, sweaters, and such. Lou here looks damn good in his skivvies, I can tell you that." She winked at the butcher, and then the two shared a conspiratorial laugh that Nick didn't appreciate.

"How nice for Lou. Sounds like you two are very well acquainted."

"No need to be jealous," Lou stated. "Mia won't give me the time of day, not that I haven't tried."

"You haven't tried very hard," she said, almost flirtatiously, in Nick's opinion.

Did Mia have the hots for the butcher? Is that what this visit was all about?

"So you wanna go out tonight and get a bite to eat?"

Mia was saved from answering Lou when the door opened again and Donna strolled in. The attractive redhead was dressed in a green designer suit that clearly cost a fortune, and matching heels. She held a prescription bag in her right hand.

When Nick saw the striking woman, his eyes widened appreciatively, which made Mia unreasonably annoyed. After all, the whole point of their visit to Santini's was to introduce him to Donna, which Mia finally did, before reminding herself that she was doing everyone concerned an enormous favor. However painful that might be.

"Did you watch *The Sopranos* the other night, Mia?" Donna asked. "James Gandolfini is getting so fat. Carmella should divorce Tony; he looks like a pig."

"Donna is quite the expert on all things relating to television and movies," Mia explained to Nick. "My knowledge is minuscule by comparison."

"It's a worthless pursuit and a waste of time, if you ask me," Lou said, and Donna flashed him a hurt look, masked by annoyance.

"Nobody did. Here." She thrust the prescription bag at the butcher's chest. "Go and give this to your mother. If she knows I went to get it, she'll think it's poisoned."

Lou's eyes filled with gratitude before he nodded, made his farewells, and headed up the stairs.

"How do you like our little community, Nick?" Donna asked. "I've grown used to it, but my mother hates it when she comes to visit, thinks it's too conventional and boring. But then, Lola's used to the excitement of Atlantic City. Did Mia tell you that my mom used to be a lounge singer?"

And her father was a blackjack dealer at one of the casinos. Nick had done his homework. He'd also made sure that there was no Atlantic City connection to the ongoing illegal operation here in Baltimore.

"No. She didn't mention it. And to answer your question, I like it here very much. The neighborhood is friendly, and the food's terrific. What more could anyone ask for?"

"Yeah, I wouldn't mind staying here permanently, but . . ." Donna shrugged, looking toward the stairs and the man who had disappeared up them, heaving a disappointed sigh. "I'm not sure what I'm going to do."

The following afternoon, while seated at Mama Sophia's waiting for Alfredo Graziano to appear so Nick could interview him, Mia took the opportunity to grill Nick about Donna.

"What did you think of Donna Wiseman? She's pretty, isn't she, with all that red hair and that fabulous figure? A man would have to be nuts, or gay, not to want to go out with her."

So that was Mia's motivation in going to Santini's. She wanted him to meet the attractive redhead. Mia was trying to set him up with a woman. No doubt so he could lose his virginity, Nick thought with no small measure of disgust.

Jesus! If that passionate kiss they'd shared didn't prove that he knew what the hell he was doing, that he could satisfy a woman, had satisfied many, in fact, there was only one other thing that would.

Don't even think about it, Caruso.

"Why isn't Lou dating Donna? They're two attractive people who seem to work well together. Surely he's thought about it."

"Well, he's not gay, I'm sure of that."

Arching a brow, Nick's lips thinned ever so slightly. "Really? I wasn't aware that you two had dated, aside from your strip poker parties, that is."

"Word gets around. I haven't been with Lou in the biblical sense, if that's what you're asking." And why was he asking? Nick seemed almost jealous, which was quite an interesting notion in itself.

He shrugged. "It's none of my business."

"If you'd like to go out with Donna, I can probably arrange it. I sense she's lonely and frustrated."

Or was she speaking about herself?

"Thanks for thinking of me, but I'm quite content as I am. As I explained, I don't have time to get involved with anyone right now. Besides it's clear Donna's heart is already engaged."

Mia heaved a dispirited sigh. "You saw it, too, huh? I know Donna's crazy about Lou, and vice versa. But they're never going to get together." She explained about Nina's unreasonable dislike of Donna and the mean way she treated the younger woman.

"If Lou was any kind of a man, he wouldn't let that stand in his way. He's an adult. Or maybe he's just a mama's boy and can't make up his own mind, or stand up to his mother."

Mia flashed Nick an angry look, and he realized

immediately that he'd made a mistake. "I would think, seeing as how you are in a similar position with your elderly aunt, that you would understand Lou's situation. He has responsibilities to his mother. Italian men take that kind of thing very seriously. You're Italian; you should know that."

Nick nodded quickly. "Of course, you're right. I do understand, totally. It's just that Lou and Donna seem so well suited. I'd hate to think that he would let his mother come between him and a woman he obviously cares about."

"Well, you could be in the same position one day. If your Aunt Bertrice is as healthy as you say, she could live for years. You might meet someone and want to get married, and she might not like the woman you've chosen."

"Of course Aunt Bertrice would like her. I have excellent taste, in all things, and . . ."

"Except clothing," Mia interrupted with a grin. "Oh, look," she added before Nick could spew the angry retort she was sure teetered on the tip of his tongue. "Here comes Uncle Alfredo. And doesn't he look the part of dapper mafioso?"

Nick eyed the man walking toward them. Alfredo Graziano looked every bit the Italian gentleman, from the tips of his shiny black wingtips, to his head of dark graying hair, which had been pomaded into place and looked as stiff as a two-week-old corpse. His suit was dark gray, pin-striped and double-breasted, his overcoat, lambs wool and expensive, and on his head he wore a black felt fedora.

"Ah, my little Mia," Alfredo said, removing his hat and gloves and setting them on a nearby chair. "You look prettier every time I see you." The older man kissed Mia's cheeks, then held out his hand to Nick.

"I'm Alfredo Graziano. I think you are expecting me."

Nick stared at the gold pinky ring and thought the wannabe don might be expecting him to kiss it, like Don Corleone or something. He grasped the man's hand and shook it. "I'm so pleased to meet you, Mr. Graziano. Thank you for coming and agreeing to talk to me."

"You may call me Don Alfredo or Fredo, if you like. Whatever suits you best is okay with me."

With eyebrows raised, Nick replied, "Thank you, but I think we should remain on formal terms, if you don't mind. I've brought my tape recorder along, and I think formality would be best for the record, you understand."

"Nick's a stickler about his work," Mia explained, hoping the older man hadn't taken offense.

Like a pope giving dispensation, Alfredo waved his hand and dismissed her concerns. "As you like."

Removing a yellow legal pad and pen from his brief-case, Nick prepared to take notes. Though he was taping Graziano's responses, he wanted to record his impressions of the man as they talked. "It's my understanding that you admit to knowing individuals who might be connected to organized crime. Is that correct, Mr. Graziano?" Nick held his breath, praying the man would admit it and make his job easier. But instead he evaded the question.

"Why are you writing a book on the Mafia?" Alfredo wanted to know. "There's been so many written, by Puzo, and that snitch Sammy 'The Bull' Gravano, who ratted out Gotti. What else is there to say on the subject? I think you might be beating a dead horse, as the saying goes."

Nick had his answer memorized and replied smoothly. "I've always been interested in the subject matter and have been wanting to tackle a book on organized crime. I still think there's room for new interpretations. And I'd like to do an honest portrayal of what life inside the Mafia is really like, less Hollywood, more true to life."

"My sister says you have hired Mia to protect you from some bad elements," the older man stated, his disgust at the idea, and with Nick, evident.

"A few threats were made. I thought it best to take precautions."

"Mia," Alfredo asked, "would you please go to the bar and buy me a soda? I'm very thirsty." He pulled out his wallet, pressing a dollar bill into her hand, and Nick noted the hundred-dollar bills it contained were numerous.

Business at Lucky Louie's Auto World had to be booming. But he'd bet his season tickets to the Ravens' football games that the money wasn't being earned legally.

Disappointed by the request, for she didn't want to miss a word of what was being said, Mia nodded and took the money. "I'll be right back. Don't say anything good while I'm gone, okay? This is really interesting stuff."

After she was out of earshot, Alfredo leaned toward Nick. "How come you picked a woman to do a man's job? It doesn't seem right that you would ask a woman to protect you. Men are supposed to take care of women, not the other way around. Women have babies and supervise their families. They don't play bodyguard. I cannot give respect to a man who hides behind a woman's skirts."

Since Mia rarely wore skirts, Nick knew that would have been difficult. But he was embarrassed, nevertheless, that the old man had called him on it, and felt heat rise up his neck. "I saw Mia's advertisement and decided to give her a call. It's not legal to discriminate based on gender, Mr. Graziano. Surely you know that. And I'm of a mind that women are quite capable of handling just about anything that's thrown at them."

"I almost didn't come because of this." The older man shook his head. "I don't like such things. But my sister, Sophia, she says you're a nice man, so I come. I like to please my sister, or else she makes my life hell. The woman should have been a capo."

Nick smiled, quite able to believe that about Sophia. "Speaking of which, do you know any?"

"You know the term *omerta*? It is not wise to speak of such things outside the family. Otherwise, it might not be good for my health. *Capisce?*"

"So you took a death oath? With whom, the Gotti family?"

"If you want to ask general type questions, I will try to answer them for you, but I cannot be specific about anything. It is important that I stay alive because I am getting married."

Though disappointed, Nick forced a smile. "Congratulations!" He held out his hand to shake the older man's. "I hope you'll be very happy. Who's the lucky woman?"

"Lenore Gallagher. She's a good woman, so I know I will be very content. We are having an engagement party here at the restaurant next week. You must come, and bring Mia. I like her. She's a smart girl. And she has heart. You can't say that about every woman, only the good ones."

"Are you bragging on me again, Uncle Alfredo?" Mia placed the Coke before him and kissed his cheek. The restaurant was relatively empty and quiet, and she had heard every word of Alfredo and Nick's conversation.

Mia was pleased that Nick had defended his decision to hire her. Though she wasn't mad at Alfredo for his archaic opinions. He was from the old school that believed that a woman's place was in the home, on the bed, having babies. *Ugh*.

"You are a good girl, little Mia, but you shouldn't be doing such a dangerous thing. You could get hurt. Let me know if you need help finding a new line of work. Maybe I can talk to some people. Or better yet, you could come work for Vinnie and me. We could use some part-time help at the dealership."

"Nick can attest to the fact that we don't get out much, and things have been pretty quiet lately. But thanks for the offer, Uncle Alfredo."

"And what about what happened at the mall? Was that quiet, too?" Alfredo's gaze bore into her, and Mia's eyes widened in surprise.

"You know about that? But we haven't spoken to anyone about what happened." She and Nick had agreed that it wouldn't be wise to alarm friends and family unnecessarily and decided to keep the matter between them.

"I have friends who supply me with information," Alfredo replied.

"God, I hope my mother doesn't know. She hasn't mentioned it."

"Well, don't be surprised if your father does," Alfredo warned. "Ex-cops know everything. Sam's probably as well connected as I am. Your father might wear a dress, but he's no old woman."

"Nick and I are going to my parents' house for dinner tonight, so I guess we'll find out soon enough."

Nick flashed Mia a look of annoyance, and she smiled apologetically, sat down, and said, "Okay, I'll shut up now so you two can talk some more."

"Thank you." Nick turned his attention back to Alfredo, who he was pretty sure didn't know shit from shinola about the Mafia. It was just a gut feeling he had, an instinct for bullshit that blared loudly whenever he heard it, and he was fairly certain that he was hearing it now. He hoped he was proved right, because he liked the old guy. And he wanted Dan's mother to be happy, something she wouldn't be if her fiancé ended up in prison.

Nick and Alfredo talked for another thirty minutes, then the older man made his excuses and left. Nick was disappointed by the interview. Alfredo hadn't imparted any useful information, other than the time of the engagement party, what Nick should wear, and what type of wine he should bring to the DeNeros' house for dinner this evening—Italian, naturally.

"So is your mother a good cook?" Nick gathered up his notes and made ready to leave. If Rosalie DeNero was anything like Mia in the kitchen, he'd better take an antacid pill before going over, maybe two.

Mia nodded enthusiastically. "The best. She's making lasagna for dinner. It's my favorite."

At the mention of the pasta dish, which Nick adored, his stomach grumbled. "Sounds good. I'm sure it'll be much better than the Stouffer's we had the other night."

Mia let the remark pass. "Are you pleased with the way the interview went? Did you learn anything?"

"Not really. Which is rather disappointing. Most of what Alfredo told me were things I already knew."

"Well, that's a lot, isn't it? I mean, you've been on your computer researching for days. You must be an expert on organized crime by now."

"I need more, a lot more. This is only the tip of the iceberg. Supporting evidence is essential to any good . . . book."

"Maybe I can help. You know, look over your notes and make suggestions, that sort of thing."

He shook his head emphatically. "No! I mean, I do all of my own research. And I'm very superstitious about anyone reading my work before it's finished. I'm used to working alone."

"And used to being alone, from what you've told me. Careful you don't end up that way."

EIGHT

Like a midget at a urinal,
I was going to have to stay on my toes.
Naked Gun 33⅓

"It's about time you brought that handsome man home for dinner, Mia. Your father and I were beginning to think you were ashamed of us. You're not, are you?"

Ignoring one of the hurt looks her mother imparted with routine regularity, Mia handed over the hunk of Parmesan cheese she had retrieved from the new GE side-by-side refrigerator—Rosalie's early Christmas present from Sam—wrinkling her nose at the pungent odor.

"Why would you think a silly thing like that? I've always brought my friends home."

"You know . . ." Rosalie nodded her head toward the living room, where Sam was entertaining Nick, and rolled her eyes meaningfully. "Because of your father, and the way he dresses. Not everyone is comfortable with it."

Mia thought that Sam DeNero as drag queen was far preferable to Rosalie DeNero as drama queen. And at any rate, her father's bizarre dress didn't bother her that much, not anymore. Not like it had when she'd been an adolescent and was left to wonder why Daddy liked

123

dressing up in Mommy's nightgown and bathrobe, and why he sometimes wore lipstick and panty hose. Eventually, she had come to think of him as a full-size, real-life Barbie, which sort of lessened the strangeness.

Tonight Sam was garbed in fire-engine red stretch pants, a green, jeweled sweater that had been adorned with a large Santa's head, whose beard was trimmed in white rabbit's fur—quite festive for the holidays, really—and tiny gold bell earrings that tinkled whenever he moved. On his feet he wore red velvet slippers, his, not her mother's.

The sight was enough to keep Santa at the North Pole for the rest of his life.

"Don we now our gay apparel, fa, la, la, la, la, la, la, la, la."

Nick hadn't flinched, gasped, or said anything untoward upon greeting her father this evening, and as a result had racked up major brownie points for his sensitivity and tolerance.

Okay, so he wasn't always that understanding of her, especially when it came to her inexpertise in the kitchen. But if he was nice to her parents, Mia could put up with the other. Though she didn't have to like it.

"Nick thinks Dad's a nice guy. And he likes you, too, Mom, so I wouldn't worry. But as I've told you before, Nick and I are not a couple, so it doesn't really matter if he likes you guys or not."

"The man is very refined, as well as handsome. Nick Caruso would make a good catch. Those authors make lots of money. I read somewhere that John Grisham owns a huge house in Virginia, with horses and everything."

"Puleeze! I won't bring Nick over here again if you

keep this up. You must promise not to say anything in front of him that remotely smacks of matchmaking. It would be very unprofessional." Not to mention embarrassing, though she should be used to that by now. You didn't grow up a DeNero without developing a hide as thick as an elephant's.

"And kissing him isn't?"

Mia nearly dropped the plate of mozzarella she was about to place on the kitchen table. "Damn that Angela! She's got a big mouth. And for your information, I didn't kiss Nick, he kissed me. There's a big difference."

She should have never confided in her sister; Mia could see that now. But why would Angela have told their mother? It didn't make any sense. They'd always kept each other's confidences.

Rosalie's smile filled with gratification, and just a hint of mischief. "Your sister didn't tell me. I was fishing. You just have that look about you that says you like Nick more than you're letting on."

Fishing? Mia should have known. "I can see that you have a one-track mind, and I refuse to discuss this with you one minute longer. I'm going into the living room to see what Dad and Nick are up to. Perhaps the conversation will be saner."

"I doubt it."

Unfortunately, Rosalie was right.

"You ever think about trying on your aunt's clothes, Nick?" was the question Mia heard when she entered the living room a moment later, and her heart sank.

Nope. Sanity wasn't at issue here. Surprise! Surprise!

Nick was sipping his scotch, and she could see that he was trying to come up with something suitable to say that wouldn't offend her father. She hung back, wondering how he would handle it. The man, she'd discovered, was tact personified, and he didn't disappoint.

"Aunt Bertrice has terrible taste in clothes, Sam." Nick made a face to back up his words. "Not to mention, she's a very small woman and none of her clothes would fit me. And even if they did, it's not really something I'm into. As Mia will attest, I'm not much of a clotheshorse."

"Well, it's not for everyone. And I don't do it as much as I used to. Promised the wife, you know. But every now and then I like to put on the Ritz, especially during the holidays, and on special occasions. Women have such pretty things to wear. Men only get suits. The drabness offends me. We got shortchanged."

"Have you ever thought about having some velvet suits made? Back in colonial times men wore velvet and brocade garments; some were even trimmed with fur and jewels. Expensive fabrics were a sign of wealth and gentility. And, of course, every man who was considered a 'gentleman' wore a wig, though I wouldn't recommend that now." No sense in giving Sam any more eccentric ideas; he had enough as it was.

Sipping his beer thoughtfully, Sam pondered the suggestion. "You don't say? Maybe I should give that some thought. I think it's the dreariness of the menswear that gets me the most. If I could dress it up a—"

"I hope my father isn't bending your ear too much, Nick." Mia took a seat on the sofa next to Nick, flashing him a warm smile brimming over with gratitude. When he returned it, heat climbed her cheeks and her heart gave a definite thump.

"You're not, are you, Dad?" she blurted, hoping to dispel whatever malady she was feeling. She didn't like it, not one bit. Maybe she was coming down with something, like the plague. Yes, the plague would be good. That would explain why she felt all hot and sweaty, and why her heart was racing, like she'd just run a marathon.

"I'm thinking of having some velvet suits made up—men's suits, in different colors. What do you think of the idea, Mia? I think I could carry it off, don't you? Though I worry that velvet might make my ass look big." He lifted his right buttock off the chair and looked, and Nick chuckled under his breath.

"I like the idea," Mia replied. "It's very revolutionary sounding."

"Yeah, that's what Nick says, and he probably knows, him being an author and all."

"I'm not an expert on the subject, Sam, but you can probably find books at the library on colonial dress and customs."

Sam changed the subject so quickly Mia nearly developed whiplash.

"When were you two planning to tell me about what went down at the mall parking garage the other day? I shouldn't have to hear this kind of shit from strangers."

Mia opened her mouth to respond, but Nick cut her off.

"It was nothing," he tried to reassure the older man. "Just a couple of stupid kids out to rob us. Mall security took care of it. It was over in a matter of minutes."

"And neither one of you was injured?"

Mia and Nick exchanged glances, before Mia said, "No, Dad. I fired my gun, and the recoil knocked me on my butt. I hit my head, a little bump, but that was all."

"Well, as hard as your head is it's not a surprise that you weren't hurt. But maybe to be on the safe side I should take you to the shooting range for some additional practice. Sounds to me like that gun you bought is too big for you. You need something with a little less kick."

"But I like my Glock," Mia protested.

"Glock, schmock. What's wrong with a police revolver? Anyway, what do you think? I can see I've been neglecting my fatherly duties. And if you're going to own a gun with the intention of shooting it, then you should know how to use it properly. I don't want you blowing your foot off, or worse, someone else's."

Just like one of those dogs you see in the back of car windows, Nick's head was bobbing up and down in fanatical agreement. But Mia was too happy to be bothered by Nick's lack of faith. Her father had never offered to aid her in any of her "stupid career choices," as he put it, thinking, no doubt, that it would discourage her from continuing with them.

It hadn't. It wouldn't.

"That would be great, Dad. I'd love it." And she would. Though she was somewhat proficient with a firearm, she could always use a few pointers. And having her father show interest in what she was doing was . . . well, wonderful.

Pleased that his daughter was going to be sensible and had actually agreed with him for a change, Sam smiled. "You come, too, Nick. A man should know how to shoot a gun, to defend himself and his family."

"Nick's learning self-defense, Dad. I'm teaching him a few karate moves."

"For chrissake, Mia! Don't hurt the man. He might sue us." Sam slapped his thigh and gave a loud guffaw, which made his earrings tinkle. Mia burst out laughing.

The only one not amused was Nick, who sat back against the sofa cushions and gritted his teeth until they ached. Playing Casper Milquetoast was definitely getting old. Hell, he had a black belt in karate, not that he could brag about it to anyone.

"Hopefully I'll be able to incorporate some of what I've learned in my writing," he said, as calmly as he could, though he wanted nothing more than to kiss . . . er . . . wipe that silly smirk off Mia's face. "Life experiences, and all that."

"Don't take offense, son. We were just playing with you."

"Oh, Nick's not mad, Dad. He always looks grumpy. You should see him after he eats one of my meals. He's positively fierce."

"You're no Martha Stewart, that's for sure," Nick retorted, and this time Sam laughed, but not at him, which made him feel a teensy bit better.

Mia made a face. "Well, thank God for that! The woman is . . . is . . ."

"Phenomenal?" Nick suggested with an arch of his brow.

"A freak. Besides, I bet she has no life outside of her work."

"The same could be said for you, dear."

Rosalie entered the room to let everyone know that dinner was on the table. "I keep telling Mia that she needs to settle down and get married, Nick. A woman is incomplete without a man in her life, but these young women of today don't understand that. All they want is independence. Her sister is married, her friends are married; Mia should be married, too."

Noting Nick's amused expression, the laughter in his eyes, Mia yanked the chair out from the dining room table, not waiting for him to seat her, and fell into it. "I told you, Mom, I have no plans to get married. It's a highly overrated institution, in my opinion. And I'm sure Nick feels the same way, don't you?"

"Is that true, Nick?" Rosalie asked, hope fading slightly from her eyes as she dished out a twenty-pound piece of lasagna and plopped it on Nick's plate.

"I'm not sure where Mia got the impression that I'm against marriage, Mrs. DeNero. You and Sam are such sterling examples of marital bliss. It's not often that I find two people so much in love. It's rather inspiring, to say the least."

Jesus! Where had that syrupy speech come from? If he wasn't careful, he could turn into his nerd-from-hell alter ego.

Mia stuck her finger down her throat and made gagging sounds, before her mother hushed her. Rosalie then smiled, glanced down the table at her husband to find his chin dripping with tomato sauce, and her pleased expression melted as quickly as the mozzarella layering the top of the lasagna.

Mia flashed Nick a "you traitor" look, but he only smiled enigmatically and delved into his dinner.

Paybacks were tough, he thought with a smile.

Staring at her reflection in the oblong mirror that hung on the back of the bedroom door, Mia wrinkled her nose in disgust.

The black-beaded crepe jacket wasn't really her style. It was too fancy, too chic, too Angela, and not at all Mia.

And it was Angela who had convinced her to buy it, who said she needed to dress up a bit for the Graziano-Gallagher engagement party. Though her sister was probably going to wear one of those comfy, stretchy maternity outfits, which was, as far as Mia could tell, the only benefit of being pregnant.

Well, at least I get to wear pants.

The size of her purse precluded carrying concealed in the usual manner, but she wouldn't go unarmed, or be caught unaware. Not after what had happened at the mall. This time she was taking no chances; this time she would protect Nick Caruso or die trying.

Bending over, she felt for the small, manageable gun that was strapped to her ankle. It gave her a Bonnie Parker gun-moll kind of feeling, with a little bit of Wonder Woman thrown in for good measure.

Mia DeNero, defender of the universe.

With hands on narrow hips and legs spread wide, she took the traditional Wonder Woman pose and grinned at the fanciful notion. She was in the midst of the most delightful fantasy when the annoying pounding started on the door.

"Hurry up, Mia! We're going to be late."

Mia snapped out of it. "Hold your horses!" she shouted through the closed door. "I'll be out in a sec."

Nick was so damn persnickety about being punctual. Go figure. She'd decided long ago that thirty minutes either way wasn't going to kill anyone.

"Being late to a social function is rude. I don't like being rude, or late."

Mia took one last look in the mirror, decided that this was the best she could do with what she had, and heaved a sigh. She really didn't look at all like Wonder Woman, who was in reality that gorgeous Lynda Carter, with the big black hair and brilliant blue eyes.

Pulling open the door, she found Nick pacing a hole in her area rug. He was dressed in a black suit, white shirt, and black tie—the grim reaper come to life.

And she was worried about how she looked! Ha!

"What are you, an undertaker in charge of a funeral? Is that the best tie you can come up with? It's horrid."

Nick patted the offending garment, then said, "Yes. Now, let's go. We're late. I—"

"Yeah, yeah, I know. You don't like being late." Her frown deepened. "Wait one minute—" Mia dashed back into the bedroom, leaving Nick speechless and very annoyed.

A moment later, she returned, dangling a bright red tie between her fingers. "I bought this for my dad. I was going to give it to him for Christmas, but I think you need it more than he does."

Nick's eyes rounded in disbelief. "It has snowmen on it!"

Mia squeezed the end of it, and the tie began playing "Frosty, the Snowman." Looking even more aghast, Nick shook his head. *Fuck, no! I am not wearing a tie that has snowmen on it,* he wanted to say, but said instead, "I refuse to wear a tie that plays music. My God! I would be the laughingstock of the party."

"That's what you said about the leather pants, and you survived. Why are you so hung up on what other people think? A man who is secure in his masculinity can wear anything, even pink. My dad is the perfect example."

"Your dad is a cross-dresser. And not exactly someone I want to emulate. Don't get me wrong; I like Sam. I just don't want to dress like him."

She held out the tie, wearing a mutinous expression that Nick had come to dread. "Wear it, or I won't go."

Mia had him, and Nick knew it. He needed to be at that party tonight, to talk to Alfredo Graziano again and meet his friends. The old man's associates were somehow connected to the investigation. He had to find out how deeply they were involved, and he could learn a lot by asking the right questions and gauging their responses.

Grabbing the tie out of her hand, Nick discarded his own and began to put it on, saying, while he fashioned the Windsor knot, "This is blackmail, Mia. And I don't like being blackmailed, especially by someone I'm paying to help me."

"Lighten up, will you, Nick? You need to get into the holiday spirit. You would have scared everyone in that other tie, looking as somber as a fire and brimstone preacher." She squeezed the tip of the tie again, making the music play. "I just love this song, don't you," Mia said, and began singing along.

Nick counted to ten, twenty, and then finally thirty. "There. Are you satisfied?" he said when he was finished.

Mia's smile was full of satisfaction as she surveyed her handiwork. "Not quite. But it's a good start."

A short time later, Nick entered Mama Sophia's and scanned the restaurant as unobtrusively as possible, finding Alfredo and his fiancée engaged in conversation with

Angela and John. The foursome was laughing uproariously, obviously having a good time.

"Let's go greet the affianced couple," he suggested to Mia, who was smiling and waving at a group of four men he hadn't met as yet, though he recognized Eddie Falcone from the FBI surveillance photos.

"Those guys seated over there are Lou's poker buddies," she explained. "They're all very nice men. I hope you didn't get the wrong impression, from what Lou said the other day about the strip poker party. He was only yanking your chain."

And why should she care if he did?

Nick clasped her hand. "We'll go this way. I don't want them laughing at my tie."

"You look very nice, Nick, much better than you did before. No one is going to laugh at you."

"That is still up for debate."

"Mia!" Angela stepped forward to kiss her sister's cheek when she approached. "That pantsuit is perfect on you. I knew it would be. You look lovely."

Mia cast a sidelong glance at Nick and sighed at how handsome he looked. She was disappointed that he hadn't told her she looked nice. In truth, she'd dressed carefully to please him, wanted him to think she was desirable. She knew she was entering dangerous waters; she hoped only that she wouldn't drown.

"Thanks." She smiled up at her brother-in-law, whose handsomeness always made her breath catch. Fortunately he was kind and had the personality to match his good looks. "How's things at Stefano, Franco, and Franco, John? Is my sister driving you nuts yet?"

Gazing adoringly into his wife's eyes, the tall man squeezed Angela's waist, or what was left of it. "Angela's a great addition to the practice. Tony's half in love with her already."

The pregnant woman laughed. "Stop teasing, John! You know the only woman in Tony's life is Marie."

"Everyone loves Angela," Mia said, almost to herself, but Nick heard the yearning in her voice that she couldn't quite disguise, and wished he could say something to reassure her. He doubted Mia would want Angela to know that she felt inferior to her. She was insecure about herself in so many different areas: her looks, abilities, and intelligence. Someone had really done a number on her self-confidence, and he didn't think for a moment that it was Mia's father.

Fortunately Angela was busy talking to Annie and Joe Russo, who had just arrived, and hadn't picked up on her sister's anguish.

"Did I tell you how beautiful you look tonight? I like your outfit."

Mia blushed, and smiled happily. "Thank you. Angela helped me pick it out. As you've probably noticed, I'm not all that good with clothes."

He stared into her eyes and found himself being pulled under. Shaking himself, he said, "Let's go pay our respects to the don, shall we?" Nick winked at Mia, who was clearly flustered.

"Ah, good . . . good idea. You haven't met Lenore yet. She's a lovely woman. I'll introduce you."

As promised, Mia made the introductions, and Nick found Lenore Gallagher to be gracious, soft-spoken, and very attractive.

Shaking Lenore's hand, he noted the large diamond solitaire engagement ring gracing her finger. It looked to be at least three carats, maybe more. Nick figured the ring had probably cost between ten and fifteen thousand. No small piece of change.

Where had Alfredo gotten the money to purchase it?

After the appropriate good wishes, compliments, and questions about the engagement and Nick's book were exchanged, Alfredo and Lenore drifted off to the other side of the room to join two men who appeared to be about Alfredo's age.

Nick recognized the smaller one from an old mug shot the FBI had on file. The other guy, Vincent Palumbo, was Graziano's partner in the car dealership, but he didn't have much on him. The man had no priors.

Paul Buttoni, small-time crook, was connected to the Larry Calzone organization. And judging by the way the two men were hugging each other, he appeared to be a close acquaintance of Alfredo's—an interesting development, and not good for the old man's credibility, to be certain.

Inviting known members of the mob to a social function usually indicated that a personal or business relationship existed.

"Do you know those men, Mia? The ones Alfredo is talking to," he asked, hoping she'd heard some gossip about them. Word on the street traveled pretty quickly in Little Italy.

Glancing across the room, she studied them for a moment. "I'm not sure about the shorter one, but the other guy is Alfredo's business partner, Vincent Palumbo. Alfredo always refers to him as Vinnie. They grew up together, I think."

She looked up at Nick, curiosity sparking her eyes. "Why?"

He shrugged, hoping he appeared far more nonchalant than he felt. "No reason. Just wondering. They seem to be interesting characters. I might be able to use them for a future book."

"You're not here to work tonight, Nick, so quit writing in your head. We're here to have fun. I'm expecting you to dance with me."

He paled at her proposal. "Dance? I don't like to dance." He hadn't done so in years, and didn't plan to start now. Holding Mia in his arms was a tempting idea, too tempting, and definitely too dangerous to even contemplate, let alone carry out.

"Well, I do. And since I have to baby-sit you, the least you can do is be accommodating."

His face reddening, Nick filled with outrage. "Baby-sit? I'm paying you three thousand dollars a month to—"

She grinned up at him. "Gotcha. Come on." She grabbed his hand. "I'm hungry. Let's go see what there is to eat."

"That's the first sensible thing you've said all evening."

"I told you I could be accommodating."

"So you did. But what you didn't say is that you can also be manipulative and stubborn, not to mention bossy."

Mia caressed his cheek. "Now, don't be a sore loser over that tie, Nick. It was for your own good."

The band began playing "It Had to Be You" and Mia stopped in her tracks and tugged on Nick's arm. "Please dance with me this very instant. I love this song. It's so . . ." She was going to say romantic, but thought better of it. "Lovely. Pretty please."

"How can I resist such a plea? You'd think me impolite if I refused. But don't say I didn't warn you."

As Mia snuggled closer to Nick's chest, she listened to the words of the song and wondered if they could possibly be true. Nick certainly wasn't like the other men she'd known. At first she'd thought that a bad thing, but she'd come to realize that she enjoyed his quiet, thoughtful ways, even his stubbornness about trying new things. In some ways, he was as insecure as she was, and she found that rather endearing.

"You surprise me, Mia. I didn't think you'd like dancing. Wrestling, now that seems more your speed."

Nick's teasing grin made her smile. "Quiet or I'll flip you on your back."

His right brow arched. "And have your way with me?"

The idea was certainly enticing. "Maybe. But I find that I'm ravenous . . . for food, so you're safe for the moment."

"Pity," he replied.

Mia's heartbeat and imagination soared into overdrive, and she thought it best not to comment.

When Mia excused herself to use the ladies' room, Nick took the opportunity to move off to a more isolated area of the restaurant, so he could use his cell phone to call Burt. His friend picked up on the third ring.

"Whoever this is better have a damn good reason for interrupting me while I'm watching *The Phantom Menace*. Skywalker's about to enter the pod race."

"Jesus, Burt! It's me, Nick. Shut that damn VCR off and listen. I need you to do something for me."

"It's a DVD player, not a VCR. I just bought it. And I'm busy. Go away, Nick."

"I've only got a minute. Mia will be back at any moment. She's in the john."

"Where the hell are you, boyo?"

"At Alfredo Graziano's engagement party."

A shrill whistle ensued, then a resigned, "Okay, shoot."

"There are two men here, good friends of Graziano's. I haven't been able to find out much on Palumbo. See what you can turn up.

"Are you writing this down, Burt?" The man was notorious for not remembering a thing he was told when he was engrossed in a movie.

"Yeah, yeah, every damn word."

"He's Graziano's business partner in the car dealership. Apparently they grew up together. E-mail me whatever information you turn up."

"Will do. Anything else?"

"Yeah, but it's not something I feel comfortable talking about over the phone. We'll have to try and meet soon." He needed to talk to someone about his growing feelings for Mia. Holding her against his heart tonight as they danced only confirmed what he'd suspected all along, that she'd become very important to him.

"That's gonna be tough, Nick, seeing as how you've got yourself a twenty-four/seven bodyguard. What's it about? You didn't do anything stupid, I hope."

"It's nothing I've done, Burt. It's just—"

"Nick, there you are. I've been looking all over for you. It's not safe for you to be wandering off by yourself. You were supposed to wait for me outside the rest rooms, remember?"

Nick spoke quickly into the phone. "I've got to go, Aunt Bertrice. I'll call you soon."

"You sound henpecked already, boyo."

With Burt's laughter ringing in his ears as he clicked off, Nick smiled apologetically at Mia. "Sorry. I wanted to call my aunt, and the area outside the rest rooms was crowded and noisy. I couldn't hear a thing."

"That's odd. There wasn't anyone there when I came out." Mia eyed him suspiciously. "Just don't do it again. How do you expect me to guard you when I don't even know where you are?"

She slipped her arm through his and smiled. "Come on, Nick. After worrying me like that, the least you can do is dance with me again."

Nick shook his head. "I don't think that's a good idea." In fact, it was a very bad idea. A man could only take so much torment, and Mia was incredibly desirable.

"I'm not taking no for an answer. There are few girly things in this world that I like to do; dancing is one of them."

"You really are a very bossy woman, Mia DeNero. Has anyone ever told you that?"

She grinned, dragging him toward the dance floor. "A few." *Dozen.*

NINE

A man alone is easy prey.
Pale Rider

"You dance very well, Nick. I can't believe you were so worried about stepping out on the dance floor."

"I feel self-conscious. If I don't do something well, I don't like doing it."

So how are you at sex? Mia was dying to ask, and then cursed herself inwardly for her wayward thought.

Not smart, Mia. Stupid! Stupid! Horny, Mia!

But it was heavenly being held in Nick's strong arms, to smell the clean lime scent of his aftershave, and feel his breath tickling her cheek. She could get used to this with very little effort, and that scared the hell out of her. He was still her client, which made him forbidden fruit. But taking a big bite out of that apple seemed awfully appealing. Too appealing.

"Practice makes perfect, Nick. And you really should try being more assertive. If you don't attempt new things, you'll never get better at them."

"Yeah, but there are some things I'd rather practice than others." Nick studied her lips.

Mia pulled back, staring up at him. "That sounds rather suggestive, coming from you."

He didn't lose a step. "I was talking about my computer. I'm not as proficient on some of the programs as I'd like to be."

"Oh."

"What did you think I meant?"

"Nothing. Nothing at all."

Nick pulled Mia closer. "Perhaps if I feel the way your body moves when you dance, I can pick up a few pointers and learn to move better." He pressed into her, and Mia felt his heat, and her own, and swallowed with a great deal of difficulty. *Mount Vesuvius was going to—*

"Uh, I think you're moving pretty good there, Nick. We don't want my father coming over and smacking us on the head for dancing too close, now do we?"

He threw back his head and laughed, and she added, "I'm not kidding. That happened to me at the Holy Trinity seventh grade welcome dance. It was humiliating. I'm still scarred from it."

"Okay, I'll bite. What happened?"

"The chaperone caught me and Timmy Molinari dancing too close together; he bopped us on the head with a newspaper and told us to separate."

Nick grinned, wishing he'd known the adolescent Mia. He bet she was something as a teenager. "And did you?"

"Of course. Then, as if that wasn't bad enough, the next morning I went to my social studies class to find that the chaperone was none other than my new teacher, Mr. Englebright. I had a complex for the entire year. And then the creep gave me a C, and I knew it was because he didn't like me. He thought I was too forward."

"And are you?"

She grinned. "Only if the situation warrants. And—"

"There you are, Nick." Sophia Russo came bounding toward them on the dance floor, wreathed in smiles, and Mia groaned inwardly. The woman had interrupted what promised to be a very titillating conversation. Then she groaned louder when she saw who had accompanied the older woman—only the Venus de Milo herself.

Standing next to Sophia was the most earthy, gorgeous, womanly woman Mia had ever laid eyes on. She was almost six feet tall, dark hair, olive skin, fabulous figure, and large boobs—your basic nightmare.

Mia, who always felt ugly and boyish next to these overblown types, pasted on a sickly smile, noting that Nick hadn't been able to take his eyes off the attractive woman, and decided then and there that whomever this gorgeous creature was, her hatred was entirely justified.

"This is my goddaughter, Gabriella Perillo," Sophia explained to Nick, ignoring Mia, as was her usual practice. "Gabriella is visiting from Italy. Remember, I told you about Joe? Well, this is his daughter. She is *bella*, no?"

Avoiding the loaded question, though, in fact, he thought Gabriella Perillo was very attractive, Nick smiled and stuck out his hand. "Very nice to meet you, Miss Perillo. I hope you enjoy your stay here in Baltimore. Be sure to visit the National Aquarium. It's very informative." He had no idea if that was true, since he'd never been there, but he assumed it was.

"I know that I'm going to find it quite enjoyable here, now that I've met you, Nick. Sophia has told me so many good things about you. I am anxious to get to know you better. And you must call me Gabriella, or Gabi. We are friends now, no?"

Well, Miss Italy didn't waste any time, did she? The she-cat is practically purring.

"I'm Mia DeNero," Mia interjected, deciding she'd better introduce herself, because Nick had obviously forgotten all about her. And it was a pretty good bet that Sophia wasn't going to do it.

Gabriella's smile was like the sun warming the earth. Her teeth were even good. "I am a bit surprised that this party isn't so good," she said with a heavy Italian accent, though she spoke English extremely well. "I thought everything in America would be . . . how do you say? . . . first class. But the food is so-so and the music, no good. In Italy we have live music for such important occasions."

"My dinner was quite excellent," Mia said, noting that Sophia was somewhat surprised and pleased by her comment. "Perhaps you just chose the wrong items. And personally, I think DJs are much better than live bands. You get lots more variety with tapes and CDs."

"Perhaps." Though she smiled prettily, Mia sensed a nastiness about the woman. "In Palermo I go to many restaurants. We have very good food there. This is not as good. I am sorry for speaking plainly; it is my way. Americans should not try to cook like Italians. It is but a poor imitation."

"Well, to each his own, I guess. I happen to love Mama Sophia's food," Nick said, wondering why Sophia hadn't defended her daughter's establishment. Sophia was very protective of her own. It was okay for her to criticize them from morning till night, but she rarely allowed anyone else to do so.

"You must be tired from the plane ride, Gabriella. Perhaps that is why the food has not agreed with you." The older woman was going out of her way to placate her goddaughter.

"It's true, Mary's food is not as good as what I prepare," she went on. "But still, it is very good. Her restaurant is well respected in Little Italy and has received excellent reviews in many prominent newspapers.

"And Uncle Alfredo wanted his favorite Italian songs played tonight, so he chose to have the disc jockey instead of *The Paisans*."

Tossing back her mane of thick black hair, Gabriella looked kindly at her godmother and kissed her cheek. "I'm sure you must be right, Sophia." She then turned her attention on Mia, giving her the once-over, and then wrinkling her nose in distaste.

"Your suit is very unstylish, Mia. I do not like it. It is too mannish. Not feminine at all."

Sophia's face reddened.

Mia stiffened, and Nick laid a hand on her arm to keep her from overreacting. From the fury flashing in her eyes, he knew that she very much wanted to belt the outspoken woman. "I think Mia looks lovely," he said.

Mia was too incensed to respond to either comment.

Gabriella shrugged. "It is a matter of opinion, no? A woman should dress like a woman, not a man, if she has the proper equipment, that is. Perhaps that is the problem." She stared at Mia's bosom.

"Why you—" Red-faced, Mia lurched forward, but Nick held her back. "Let me go! I'm going to show her about equipment."

"Let it go," he whispered for her ears alone. "Gabriella Perillo is foreign. Obviously she doesn't understand our ways here." Mia calmed down somewhat, but she couldn't help remembering that Nick had said something similar about her wardrobe not that long ago.

"I'm sure you didn't mean to insult Mia. Isn't that right, Miss Perillo?" Nick felt very uncomfortable in his new role as peacemaker. "Comments can often be misconstrued and taken the wrong way. I'm sure you understand."

"They should be taken as I have offered them. I have been taught to speak plainly. I was just pointing out that in Italy you wouldn't find anyone dressing like this. We are much more sophisticated. Italian designers are far superior to the Americans. Everyone knows this. We have better food, we have better clothes." She smiled a wide-eyed innocent smile. "But, of course, I was not trying to insult Mia."

Mia pinned the woman with a lethal look, not believing a word of her disclaimer. Behind the simpering smile was a wicked, evil, diabolical—suffice it to say, Gabriella Perillo was a bitch. Didn't anyone realize that fact but her?

"I've been wanting you to meet my goddaughter, Nick," Sophia interjected before Mia could respond. "Gabriella's going to be here a few weeks, and I thought it would be nice if you two got together, became friends."

Gabriella looked pleased by the suggestion. Nick's expression seemed to indicate he was all for the idea. Only Mia looked as if she might puke.

"If Nick wants to date Gabriella, I won't try to stop him. But I will insist on going along on the dates. You see, Gabriella, Nick is under my protection, and I cannot let him out of my sight."

"A grown man needs to be protected? This is not how we do things in Italy."

"You're not in Kansas anymore, Toto."

Confused by Mia's comment, Gabriella replied, "In Italy the men, they know how to take care of themselves, and their women."

"Nick has been marked by La Cosa Nostra," Sophia explained to her goddaughter in hushed tones. "He is writing a book, and they have made threats on his life. One must take these kinds of things seriously. *Capisce?*"

"Ah, mafioso. *Si,* I understand now that you have a problem and need protection. But why don't you get a man, if that is so, Nick?"

She turned toward Mia with malice in her eyes. "Or are you perhaps one of those men who have changed themselves into a woman? I have heard of such things."

Sophia crossed herself. Nick blanched. But Mia merely smiled, in that feral way an animal does before going in for the kill.

"I can assure you, Gabriella, that I am very much a woman." Okay, maybe not as much a woman as the Perillo bitch, but still . . . "Some of us don't need to be overt about it. We are secure in our femininity and find no need to flaunt it."

"I still say a woman should behave like a woman and not a man."

Mia stared meaningfully at the woman's low-cut dress and exposed cleavage. "And how do I know that your boobs are real? I bet you have enough silicone in there to float a ship."

Nick coughed, stifling a laugh behind his palm.

Gabriella gasped in outrage. "Aunt Sophia, how can you let this woman talk to me like that? I am a guest in this country, am I not?"

Sophia nodded solemnly. "Yes, you are, Gabriella. But

you have behaved very poorly tonight. I hope Nick will excuse your behavior."

Wondering how in hell he got into the middle of a cat-fight, Nick smiled smoothly. "I'm sure this is all nothing more than a terrible misunderstanding. Why don't you two shake hands and make up. After all, 'tis the season for forgiveness."

Gabriella clasped his hand instead, and Mia's eyes narrowed into dangerous slits. "Come dance with me, Nicky. You do dance, don't you?"

As an FBI agent, Nick had been in some difficult and deadly situations, but at the moment he couldn't recall one as bad as this one. Mia was staring daggers at him, willing him to refuse the invitation, Sophia was looking hopeful, wedding bells ringing loudly in her ears, and, to make matters worse, a crowd was beginning to gather.

For a man trying to keep a relatively low profile, he was doing a piss-poor job.

"I'd love to dance," he finally replied, smiling at Gabriella and ignoring Mia's sharp intake of breath. He'd face her wrath later, out of the public forum. But for now he needed to defuse the situation. And dancing with a beautiful woman like Gabriella wasn't exactly a chore.

Once Nick and Gabriella were out on the dance floor, Sophia turned to Mia. "I apologize for my goddaughter's behavior this evening. I'm not sure what has gotten into Gabriella. She is much more outspoken since the last time I saw her. I think she still suffers from the death of her mother." Who had died when Gabriella was twelve, but Sophia didn't see fit to mention that.

"You don't need to apologize, Mrs. Russo. You can't be blamed for other people's rudeness, only your own."

And hers was usually abundant, but Mia refrained from saying so. It was so rare when Sophia Russo apologized that Mia wanted to bask in it for a while longer.

The older woman smiled, and there was admiration in her eyes. "You have backbone, Mia DeNero. I like that." She crossed to the other side of the room, leaving Mia staring openmouthed after her.

Sophia had no sooner departed than Grandma Flora sidled up. The old woman was dressed all in black, still in mourning for a husband who had died decades earlier. Mary referred to her grandmother as a "professional mourner." Flora liked to make the rounds of the funeral parlors and pay her respects to the dead, whether or not she was acquainted with them.

It was an Italian thing. Death and dying figured prominently into every Italian's life. They dwelled on it, reveled in it, prayed for it to come, and then cursed the Almighty loudly when anyone fell ill.

"I saw whata happened and heard whata Gabriella Perillo said. You musta protect Nick from this woman. She isa no good. A spoiled brat, I tink. Her father gives her whatever she wants. He hasa no sons, no wife, so he lets her run wild. I don't like the Perillos. They have no class. The daughter, she is just likea the father. *Puttana! Bastardo!*" Grandma made a spitting sound that had Mia's eyes widening.

"I'm not sure what you expect me to do, Grandma Flora. If Nick wants to date Gabriella I can't stop him."

"I tink your Nick has better sense than that. He is a smart man, no?"

"Men don't always think with their brains, unfortunately."

The old woman let loose a loud chuckle. "It'sa true.

For many men, when the root isa hard the brain isa soft. But I tink your Nick is different. I like him. He reminds me of my Sal. A good man, my Salvatore. Frank is all like his father."

"I can try to protect Nick Caruso from the mob, Grandma Flora, but that's all I can do." Mia didn't have the tools, the skills, to compete with a woman like Gabriella. And she could see from the ecstasy smeared on Nick's face as he danced with the man-eater that she was working her wiles on him.

She shouldn't care; he was only her client, Mia reminded herself.

But she did.

Grandma clasped Mia's smooth hand in her wrinkled one. "Sometimes a woman, she needs a little help from her friends, no?"

Mia gazed across the room to where her sister, Mary, and Annie stood talking, and wondered if they'd be willing to help. There was no way she would let Gabriella get the best of her. Mia needed to prove, if only to herself, that she could compete in the womanly woman department.

"You know a lot for a wrinkled, short woman, don't you, Grandma?"

Flora pinched the younger woman's cheek, smiling affectionately. "I likea you, Mia. You reminda me of myself, when I wasa young girl back in Sicily. And you are a good daughter to your mama and papa, and a good sister to Angela, who keeps me out of jail. I tink you will makea very good wife."

Mia's brow wrinkled in confusion. "But, I'm not getting married, Grandma Flora."

The old woman smiled enigmatically, but didn't reply.

* * *

Mia was stuffing her face with a second piece of tiramisu when her parents strolled up, and she nearly choked on the tasty dessert. Her father was wearing a bright red velvet suit that would have made Santa Claus envious.

And Santa Claus, Sam was not!

"I hope we're not late." Rosalie kissed her daughter's cheek, then look accusingly at her husband. "Your father was putting some last-minute touches on his ensemble." She rolled her eyes. "You look very nice, by the way, Mia. Black is a good color for you."

"So, what do you think? Does the old man look good, or what? Your mother can't make up her mind if she likes the suits or the dresses better. Just like a woman. You can never please them."

Rosalie patted her husband's cheek. "You look very nice, dear. It's just so . . . so bright, that's all. It'll take some getting used to."

"You look quite festive, Dad. It didn't take Mrs. Bucco long to make the suit for you. She did a nice job."

He smiled, pleased with the compliment. "The ruffled shirt was my idea. I thought it would dress it up a bit. You know how I hate plain. I'm thinking of adding some rhinestone buttons. I miss my earrings. I feel so naked without them."

"Where's Nick?" Rosalie looked about the crowded room, and Mia couldn't keep anger and disappointment from flooding her face.

With a nod of her head, she indicated the dance floor. "He's otherwise engaged with Gabriella Perillo, newly arrived from Italy." Nick had suddenly become a dancing fool. For someone who'd professed only hours earlier that he hated dancing, he was now the reincarnation of Fred Astaire. It was obvious that he found the woman attractive.

Sam whistled. "*Madone!* She's some—"

"Hush, Sam! Can't you see Mia is upset?"

"I'm only looking. And I'm sure that's what Nick's doing, too. Men don't marry women like that. Trust me."

Crossing her arms over her chest, Rosalie pinned her husband with "the look." "Are you saying that Italian import is better looking than I am, than your own daughter?"

"*Madone!* I can't win. I should keep my mouth shut. I'm going to get a beer." Sam took himself off to the bar.

"Did you and Nick have a fight, Mia? Is that why he's dancing with that creature? Why, she looks like a woman of the streets. Very coarse, if you ask me."

Mia smiled. Rosalie was nothing if not loyal. "That's what I thought, too, Mom. But you know how men are. They like that obvious type."

"I wouldn't worry, dear. He'll come to his senses eventually and realize who the better catch is."

"I keep telling you, Mom, that Nick and I aren't—"

"You're not fooling anyone, Mia. You can't keep your feelings hidden. You're very transparent, if you don't mind my saying so. And it's obvious that you care for this man."

"I do care for him. We're friends. But that's all." She refused to give her mother any ammunition. Rosalie would have the church booked and the invitations ordered, if she gave her the least little bit of encouragement. Her mother was dying for Mia to get married and give her grandchildren, and Nick had apparently been chosen as the sperm donor.

"In my day when a woman wanted a man she fought for him."

Mia looked at her mother as if she'd lost her mind. "I liked you better when you thought the end of the world was coming. I'm not saying I'm interested in Nick, but if I was, theoretically, you understand, how does someone like me compete with someone like Gabriella? Her boobs are bigger than my head."

Rosalie threw back her head and laughed. "But think of how they will sag when she's old."

Mia wrapped her arms about her mother and kissed her cheek. "Thanks, Mom. I needed that."

"Of course, dear. That's what I'm here for."

"I can't believe you actually danced six dances with that . . . that woman," Mia told Nick once they were back at the apartment. "I thought you didn't like to dance. Or is it that you just didn't like dancing with me?"

"Gabriella isn't as bad as you think. She was actually quite nice once we got out onto the dance floor."

"Nice!" Mia shook her head. Men were so stupid. Of course, Gabriella was nice. Nick was a man she was interested in pursuing. Was he really that dense?

Nick rubbed the back of his neck, trying to ease the tension headache that was forming. "You told me I should try new things, experiment a little. I was only taking your advice."

"Where's your loyalty? That Perillo woman treated me quite rudely, and I didn't deserve it."

Nick was tired, and he didn't feel like getting into this tonight. He'd experienced enough drama for one evening. Not to mention that he'd had to fight off Gabriella when she'd cornered him in front of the men's room and tried to kiss him. It had been like skirmishing with an Amazon. The woman was almost as tall as he, and strong, too. He just thanked God that Mia hadn't seen them. He would have never heard the end of it.

"I owed Sophia a favor for setting up the interview with her brother. I was merely being polite."

Mia made a face, then ordered, "Get undressed. We're going to practice some wrestling moves."

Eyes wide, Nick glanced at his wristwatch. "You want to practice now? It's one o'clock in the morning, and I'm tired."

"So? We don't have to get up early, and we have nowhere special to go tomorrow. It's Sunday. And if you have energy for dancing, then I'm sure you have energy for self-defense lessons."

Shaking his head, Nick loosened his tie. "I'm too tired. Let's wait until tomorrow."

Unwilling to take no for an answer, Mia disappeared into the bedroom, emerging a moment later wearing her navy sweats. "You're going to ruin that suit. I'm not in the mood to be gentle tonight."

Nick turned from the sofa, where he was placing his blankets and pillow, and grinned. "Oh, is that what this is all about? You want revenge because I danced with Gabi, and—"

"Now, it's Gabi. Sounds like you two have become very good *friends* in a very short time."

He ignored the implication. "And you want to teach me a lesson."

"Don't be ridiculous. I just want to see if you've learned anything from our previous sessions."

And I want to teach you a lesson.

"And if I refuse?"

"I'll just have to pummel you to the ground in your suit. And if it gets ripped, I'm not paying for the repairs."

Nick tossed his jacket over the arm of the sofa and began to unbutton his shirt. "Aren't you going to turn around while I change?"

Mia didn't flinch. "Why? I've seen naked men before." She crossed her arms over her chest, daring him to continue. She waited, expecting him to turn fifty shades of red and run into the bedroom.

But to her astonishment he didn't. Instead, Nick removed his shirt and stood before her bare-chested. Mia's breath quickened, and she could feel her heartbeat galloping off to parts unknown.

Damn, but he had a fine chest! And the other parts weren't too bad, either!

"I assume you're going to leave on your pants."

"Now, why would you assume that? I certainly wouldn't want to ruin them." Unfastening his pants, he eased down the zipper.

At the evocative sound, Mia went into panic mode. "Now, wait a minute, Nick! I don't think we should be wrestling if you're not wearing pants."

He shrugged. "That's up to you, Mia. You're the one intent on wrestling tonight. But if you're afraid that I'll have some kind of advantage—" He removed his pants and stood before her in a pair of black silk boxers.

Her gaze fixed on the prominent bulge, she heaved a sigh, then looked up to find him smiling, as if he could read her X-rated thoughts. Her face reddened.

"I'm surprised you would have the nerve to take off

your pants in front of a woman. You don't seem the exhibitionist type, that's all."

"I've decided to take your advice and be more adventurous. Isn't that what you're always telling me, that I need to let go, not care what others think? Besides, you told me once that we shouldn't be afraid to expose ourselves in front of each other, that you had very little modesty."

"That's right, I don't." *Two can play at this game,* she thought, pulling off her sweatshirt and sweatpants. "It wouldn't be fair to keep my clothes on, so I'll wrestle you without them."

Her bikini panties and lace bra were black, sexy as hell, and Nick wasn't concentrating on anything but on how hot she looked when she lunged for him and pushed him back on his butt, pinning him to the ground and knocking the air out of him.

When he could breathe again, he said, "Jesus! You took unfair advantage."

"Just like a real attacker would," she said, holding his arms above his head and staring into his eyes. "You don't think an attacker would give you mercy, do you, Nick?"

"Let's try it again," he said with a hoarse voice, feeling himself harden. Mia must have noticed because she smiled knowingly, almost triumphantly, he thought.

"Oh, I think we've had enough lessons for one night, don't you, *Nicky?*" she said, jumping to her feet. "Good night." Laughing, she ran into the bedroom and slammed the door shut, locking it.

"Hey, wait a minute! I need to use the bathroom."

"Too late. I'm already in bed. You'll have to wait until morning."

Cursing a blue streak, and women in general, Nick

marched into the kitchen, wearing a rather significant erection, pulled open the refrigerator door, and reached for the quart bottle of Evian, which he proceeded to pour over his head and down the front of his boxers.

"Damn impossible woman!"

And damn me for wanting her so badly.

TEN

I'm too old for this shit.
Lethal Weapon

Since her run-in with Gabriella, Mia had made and canceled three different luncheon appointments with her sister, Mary, and Annie.

She was determined to best the Perillo woman at her own game, and would work herself into a dither, fully intending to ask her friends for help, only to chicken out at the last minute, inventing some lame reason why she couldn't go.

Only today, thanks to Angela, she had no excuse. When Mia had called her sister this morning to tell her that she wouldn't be keeping their luncheon engagement—her excuse being that she couldn't leave Nick alone—Angela had arranged to send over the one person Mia could hardly refuse as a substitute bodyguard—her father, the ex-cop.

"You're sure you don't mind my dad coming over?" Mia asked Nick. "He won't bother you. I told him you have work to do and that he needs to be quiet. If you turn on the Home Shopping Network, I think he'll be fine."

"As a matter of fact, I don't mind at all. I've invited

Burt over; the three of us can watch a football game, movie, or whatever. So don't worry. I've got it covered."

Mia's eyes widened slightly. "Burt? But I thought you didn't like hanging out with him."

Nick replied smoothly, "He left a message on my cell phone the other day, asking to see me, so I thought I'd invite him over. I've been avoiding him lately, and I feel rather guilty about it."

Nick's reversal of attitude toward Burt seemed very odd to Mia, but she didn't have time to question him further. "I won't be gone long. We're just going to have lunch, maybe do a little shopping. Angela's still buying stuff for the baby. You'd think this baby of hers was the only baby ever to be born. He or she is going to be the best dressed kid in Baltimore, not to mention spoiled rotten. I think my mother and John's are going to fight over who gets to baby-sit."

"Enjoy yourself. I'm sure it'll be good for us to have a little time apart. After all, we've been together constantly since you took me on as a client, and enforced closeness can be difficult at times."

Did she detect relief in Nick's voice? Was he happy— eager—to get rid of her? He sure seemed to be.

Of course, Mia knew someday soon her assignment would be over and she and Nick would have to go their separate ways. But she wasn't ready for that to happen yet.

She wondered if she ever would be.

Mia had broken her own rule. She'd allowed herself to care too much, to grow close to Nick. He'd become part of her life in the short time she'd known him—a very big part. She wasn't sure if it was love, but if not, it was damn close.

She could deny her feelings to others, and would continue to do so, to keep up her professional appearance. But there was no denying the strong ache in her heart, the breathless way she felt whenever they were together.

Nick was becoming necessary.

Mia wanted him, needed him.

And she was scared, afraid of what the future would bring. Or maybe she was afraid of what it wouldn't bring.

A knock sounded at the door, and Mia didn't have time to contemplate further. Inviting her father inside, she explained that no one was to be let into the apartment except Burt Mulrooney, and left for her sister's loft in Fell's Point, hoping that nothing went wrong.

Asking her dad for help always made her feel a little bit uncomfortable. And even though he'd been great about the shooting lessons, praising her improvement in handling a gun and trying not to laugh when Nick failed to hit the target, she wanted to succeed on her own merits, and not because her father was there to help her.

"Well, as I live and breathe! You finally made it over here," Angela said to Mia upon her arrival, taking her coat and hanging it on the brass hall tree.

Angela wore a very flattering red wool maternity dress that accentuated her dark coloring. "You look nice," Mia said.

The pregnant woman smiled gratefully. "Thanks. I feel sort of like the Goodyear blimp, so I appreciate the compliment."

Mia marveled at how large the loft was. There was so much room to spread out that her entire apartment could fit into Angela's living room. "I love this apartment. Someday I'm going to have a place just like it." She heaved a sigh, wondering if that day would ever come, knowing it probably wouldn't. Not on her income, anyway.

Angela studied her sister carefully. "I don't know what's up with you these days, Mia, but I definitely think you need some time away from Nick Caruso. You're becoming a hermit, almost withdrawn, and quite mysterious. Why won't you tell me what's been bothering you? You know you can talk to me. We've always confided in each other." She handed Mia a soft drink, placing a bowl of pretzels before her. "I won't tell Mom, if that's what you're worried about. I promise."

Mia sipped her Coke, then said, "I might as well wait until Mary and Annie arrive. I'd hate to explain everything twice." She glanced at the clock on the mantel. "They should be here any minute, right?"

"Annie called right before you got here and said they'd be right over. She got held up at the store, and then had to pick up Mary." The doorbell rang just then, and Angela grinned. "Like I was saying . . ."

Lunch consisted of cold chicken, pasta salad, and vegetables with dip, and everyone ate greedily, talking of mundane things, like the weather, doctor exams, and the prevailing gossip in the community. While the women munched on Mary's contribution of chocolate cannolis—her specialty—and sipped their coffee, Mia launched into the reason for wanting to meet with them.

"By any chance, did any of you meet Gabriella Perillo at Uncle Alfredo's engagement party the other night? I mean, besides you, Mary. Obviously you've met her before."

"I don't know how my mother stands her. Though come to think of it, the two women are somewhat alike." Mary shook her head. "What goes around comes around, they say."

Annie made a face. "I hated the Italian bimbo on sight. She tried to put the moves on Joe, even after he refused to dance with her. And I saw her hanging all over that author friend of yours, Mia, trying to suck his face off."

Startled by the revelation, Mia didn't respond, but jealous anger began burning a hole in the pit of her stomach, spreading like a cancerous growth.

"Why this interest in Gabriella Perillo, Mia?" Angela wanted to know. "I didn't have the opportunity to meet her, though John was salivating all over himself. She is attractive. And thin." She patted her protruding stomach. "And she doesn't look the least bit cowlike, unlike *moi*."

"Tell me about it," Mary commiserated. "If my skin stretches any more I'll be able to upholster my couch with it. Of course, I've used my pregnancy as an excuse to stuff my face. Speaking of which, anyone want that last cannoli?"

"*Cara,* the doctor will be mad at you," Annie cautioned her friend. "She said you needed to watch your sugar intake, not to mention your fat grams."

Mary rolled her eyes. "Shut up, Annie! You're starting to sound like my mother. I think you've been hanging out with Sophia too long. That's much worse for your health than eating this cannoli, especially your mental health."

Annie flipped her off. "Pregnancy does not become you, *cara,*" and Mary had the grace to blush, knowing it was true. Her mood swings were formidable.

Clearing her throat, Mia tried to regain their attention. "It's because of Gabriella Perillo that I'm asking for your help. You see, she's been coming on to Nick. Not that I have any designs on him, or anything, you understand," she emphasized quickly, and the three women looked at each other knowingly.

"But she insulted me in front of him, intimated that I might actually be a man, then ragged on my flat chest. And she even criticized that nice pantsuit you helped me pick out, Angie."

Angela's mouth fell open. "You're kidding! What's wrong with the pantsuit? It looked wonderful on you. I told you that."

"She said it was mannish, but that's neither here nor there. I need help. I want to compete with Gabriella, to look more womanly and less tomboyish."

"But why, if you don't have designs on Nick?" Annie wanted to know.

Mia sighed, and then smiled a bit sheepishly. "Okay, so I lied. I admit that I do have a small amount of interest in Nick, though I shouldn't, because of the whole client thing. And I have no intention of allowing that woman to get her hooks into him. She's not half good enough for Nick."

The three women exchanged startled glances, then Angela smiled and patted her sister's hand.

"You're a lovely woman in your own right, Mia. You shouldn't let someone like Gabriella Perillo, who obviously has no class, get to you and undermine your self-confidence."

"Angela's right," Annie said. "If you want us to help you, we will, but only if it's for the right reasons. Trying to get even shouldn't be your main motivation for wanting to do a makeover."

"It should be for you," Mary concurred, "because you want to look different or, in my case, get a man's attention. Annie helped me with Dan."

"Annie helped you do a makeover?" This surprised Mia. Mary was a beautiful woman who didn't need artificial enhancement. She was what Rosalie called a "natural beauty."

The pregnant woman laughed. "Annie didn't like my underwear, or style of clothes, so she helped me pick out new ones. If you're trying to attract the attention of Nick Caruso, then I'm all for helping you do that."

"Nick's a client. I feel conflicted. I guess I'm not very professional."

"I think he's cute," Angela said. "I don't blame you for being interested. I'd think there was something wrong with you if you weren't."

"Your author friend is definitely hot, Mia." Annie's grin was downright naughty. "He's got a cute tush, too."

"You guys will help me, then, *if* I decide that I need help, that is?"

"You're getting cold feet already?" Mia's sister looked incredulous. "It took you four tries to get this far, and now you're getting cold feet. I don't believe it."

"Not exactly. I just want to make sure that this is what I want to do. I know I'm not beautiful or sexy like Gabriella, and I don't want to come off looking foolish or desperate. I don't want anyone laughing at me." Especially Nick. She wouldn't be able to stand it if he thought she was a joke.

"You've been afraid of rejection your whole life, Mia," Angela replied softly. "It's the reason you hide behind sweatshirts and baggy jeans and play down your feminine side."

"Because I'll never be as pretty or sexy as any of you. Let's face it, I'm flat-chested, have no curves to speak of, and—"

"Boobs are highly overrated," Mary interrupted with a grin. "And I wasn't that well endowed before I got pregnant, so Annie convinced me to buy a Wonder Bra. And believe me, it worked *wonders*. I have cleavage now. I can stand a pencil up between my breasts, and it will actually stay there."

"But why on earth would you want to do that?" Mia stared at the pregnant woman as if she'd lost her mind.

Mary grinned. "Because I can."

"Damn, we're out of beer." Sam's frown deepened. "Can't believe my daughter invites me over and doesn't stock the fridge. How are we going to watch a football game without beer? That's un-American."

Nick, who had hidden the Bud in one of the cupboards before Sam arrived, smiled smoothly. "Why don't you run down to the corner market and pick us up a couple of six-packs, Sam." Nick pulled a twenty out of his wallet and handed it to Mia's father. "My treat. Burt can baby-sit until you get back."

The older man's eyes filled with uncertainty. "I'm not sure that's a good idea. Mia would be pissed if she found out. I promised my daughter I'd take good care of you, Nick."

"How's she going to find out? I'm not going to tell her. Are you?"

"Hell, no!" Sam turned his attention to Burt. "You think you can protect Nick while I run down to the market? There's a gun in my coat pocket." He reached in, removed the revolver, and set it down on the table. "Just in case there's any trouble."

"We'll be fine. I doubt any Mafia types even know Nick is staying here, and you won't be gone that long," Burt reassured the older man with a confident smile.

Nodding, Sam grabbed his jacket, and then disappeared out the door, shouting, "I'll be right back."

"You're going to get that old guy into trouble if his daughter finds out that he left you alone."

"Couldn't be helped. We can't talk in front of Sam, and I need to know if you've found out anything new about Buttoni or Palumbo that I can use. Besides, I'm not alone. You're here."

"I haven't discovered anything official, mind you, but word on the street is that Palumbo is running a chop shop for the mob. I think it's Larry Calzone's crew."

Nick's brows lifted. "Is Graziano involved?"

"No one knows for sure, but it's doubtful. He's always been a straight shooter. And the business is named for his father. My source doesn't think Al would do anything to smear his old man's name. He revered him, or so I was told."

"We need to find that out for sure. Keep checking. I intend to plant someone inside the business to get some tangible evidence. Adams and Malloy are outside the dealership, monitoring things from the surveillance van. So far nothing of substance has come in."

"The plant might work, but it could be dangerous. Those Mafia types don't mess around with snitches. I heard of one case where some guy talked and they cut off his dick and stuffed it into his mouth, to silence him permanently. I know one thing for sure: I don't want anyone messing with my dick, unless it's a woman. Guess I'm getting too old for this shit."

Nick grinned. "Guarding your pension, old man?" Burt frowned at the truth of his partner's words, and Nick added in a serious tone, "I don't see any other way. Higgins is going to have my ass soon, if I don't produce some tangible results.

"But don't worry, Burt. I don't intend to ask you to do it. Christ! If push came to shove, you couldn't outrun a ten-year-old girl, not with all that extra weight you're carrying."

"Don't be too sure of that, boyo. I ain't anxious to die, but I'm no wimp. I'll do what's needed of me."

Nick wrapped his arm about his friend's shoulder. "I know that, old man. I was only playing with you."

"So what were you so anxious to talk to me about the other night when you phoned? You said you had something to tell me, and I've been dying of curiosity ever since."

"It's got nothing to do with the investigation, not directly anyway."

Burt had been around Nick long enough to know something was wrong. "It's Mia, isn't it? I knew it. She's too damn good-looking for you to ignore. And you two have been playing house for weeks. You haven't screwed her, have you? That would not be good, boyo."

Nick counted to ten, reminding himself that Burt was a friend. "Nice, Burt, very nice. You've got a mouth like a garbage can, you know that? And it's none of your damn business who I sleep with. It's just that I'm attracted to Mia, and I think she feels the same way. There's just something about her . . ."

Mia was getting under his skin. There was no denying

it. He had only to close his eyes to conjure up her sweet smile, picture her feisty and mad as hell when they argued, which was often, recall how she'd felt in his arms when he'd kissed her.

"Sounds to me like you're falling hard, Nick. And you've picked the wrong time and the wrong woman. Don't be stupid and do something rash that you'll regret. I know how important your career is to you, and messing with a civilian is going to get you in big trouble. I tried telling you that from the get-go."

"Don't be ridiculous, Burt. I haven't fallen for anyone. It's just that . . . well, we're living in such close proximity, seeing each other day after day, sometimes in a state of half undress. She's even got me wrestling with her. It's a physical attraction, nothing more. I'm not sure how to handle it, that's all."

"If you want my advice you'll get the hell out of Mia's apartment as quickly as possible. You're playing with fire, and you're gonna get burned."

"You know I can't leave yet, not until we get something more substantial on Graziano." And to be honest, he didn't want to leave. Not until he knew for sure how he felt about Mia. What he felt. And since his career was still intact, he didn't want to blow this current investigation by making the subjects suspicious. If Palumbo and the others knew there was an ongoing FBI investigation into their activities, they'd close down their operation in a heartbeat.

"You've already spoken to Graziano and found out nothing substantial. I don't see the reason for your wanting to stay. At least nothing that has to do with this operation." Nick shot his friend a nasty look for knowing him so well, but the agent ignored him and continued.

"I've been telling you from the beginning that the old guy's not a player. You're wasting your time with him."

"I got a gut feeling about it, Burt. Alfredo is the key to getting these guys. I know it. I just need to figure out how it all fits together, how the money is being laundered."

"Maybe he is, and maybe he isn't. But in the meantime, you could be tossing your career down the toilet. And I know you don't want that. Hell, you've worked too hard to make a success of yourself."

"Nothing's going to happen. What happened in Philadelphia was unfortunate, but everyone makes mistakes. I can't spend the rest of my life worrying about it, or SAC Higgins. I shouldn't have said anything. You always overreact. Jesus! You're worse than my fictitious Aunt Bertrice."

"Obviously you're worried, or you wouldn't have brought the subject up in the first place."

Nick had no response because he knew what Burt said was true. Too damn true. And he didn't know what in hell he was going to do about it, or Mia.

If he could tell her about the operation, it would make things a whole lot easier. He was starting to feel like shit about duping her, but he knew he couldn't compromise his investigation.

Bad enough he had already compromised himself.

Setting her purse down on the hall table, Mia removed her coat, and then stared incredulously at Nick. "I can't believe you actually accepted an invitation to the Russos' for dinner tomorrow night. Are you out of your mind? Did you miss the part about how much I dislike Gabriella I'm-too-wonderful-for-words Perillo?"

Nick affected a stance of nonchalance. "Sophia called

while you were at your sister's. I didn't know how to get out of it, so I said we'd come."

First of all, Mia doubted very much that she had been included in the invitation. And secondly, it was obvious that the real reason Nick didn't want to refuse the invitation was because the gorgeous Gabriella would be there.

The barf factor was tremendous.

"How about no, for starters. I'm busy. I have to work. I hate Italian food. You're a writer. You lie for a living. You could have made something up."

I'm a federal agent and I lie for a living.

"I love Italian food, everyone knows that, including Sophia," Nick replied.

"And Italian women."

"You're Italian," he reminded her with a grin that sent her pulse racing.

"Don't change the subject. You should have checked with me first. It would have been the polite thing to do. Maybe I already have plans for tomorrow evening."

"Well, do you?"

"No. But that doesn't matter. I could have. This is an extremely busy time of year. I'll have you know that I've turned down any number of invitations to—"

"What are you so upset about? It's only dinner, and Alfredo will be there. I'll have another opportunity to talk to him about my book." And maybe ask him a few pointed questions about his childhood friends. Though he'd have to be careful not to arouse the man's suspicions. Alfredo was a shrewd old dog.

"I doubt that's your only reason for going. I'm sure you're anxious to see Amazon woman again."

Nick arched a brow. "Are you jealous? You certainly sound like you are. I'm flattered."

Crossing her arms over her chest, so she didn't smack Nick's smiling mouth, Mia lifted her chin, even as heat rose to color her cheeks pink. "Hardly. You're not my type at all," she lied. "I just can't stand Gabriella. And don't think I haven't heard how you and she were making out at the engagement dinner. Everyone's talking about it. A disgusting public display of affection, like two teenagers, I believe was how it was told to me."

Jesus! Nick's smile melted quickly. "I wasn't making . . . kissing Gabriella. She threw herself at me. I was quite shocked by her behavior, if you must know."

"*Uh, huh.* And I suppose you had to fight her off. Come on, Nick. I've seen you in action, remember?"

"I only kissed you that one time, and I've already apologized for it. I told you it wouldn't happen again."

Why? Because you thought it was so terrible?

And what if I want it to happen again.

"So you've said." Nick might not have kissed her again, but he'd had some whoppers of erections while in her presence. That should count for something, Mia thought.

"Look, if it's going to make you upset, I'll call Sophia back and send our regrets."

"*Ha!* So she can put a curse on me? Do you know what it's like when one of those old Italian women puts a curse on you? I could lose my hair, or worse, develop psoriasis." Mia made a face and scratched her arms, as if the itching had already begun. "Sophia has her mind set on you marrying Gabriella. Don't you know that? Are you so naïve that you don't see what the woman is up to?"

"I know perfectly well what she's up to, and I also

know how to handle myself around women, even ones with psoriasis."

Mia rolled her eyes. "Has it ever occurred to you that Gabriella Perillo might be connected to the Mafia, that maybe she was sent over from Italy—a female hit man, if you will—to take you out? They'd send someone you could learn to trust, perhaps become romantically involved with."

Okay, it was a stretch, but it was the best she had at the moment. And it was possible. Sort of. Maybe.

Nick swallowed his smile. "No, I hadn't considered that."

"Well, it's a good thing you have me, then, isn't it? I'm looking out for you, Nick. Even Grandma Flora said Gabriella was bad news. She told me to watch out for you."

Nick's eyes widened. "Really? Flora said that?"

Mia gave the Scout's-honor sign. "On my honor, those were her very words. And I think Grandma's got a sixth sense about her. She might not see dead people, but she sees something. Some of the stuff she told me made the hairs on the back of my neck stand up on end."

"What kind of stuff . . . er . . . things?"

"I'm not at liberty to say, but it was heavy-duty."

Rubbing his chin in contemplation, Nick replied, "You know, I hadn't considered any of this. Perhaps it would be good to play along, see what Gabriella is really up to."

Panicked that her words had backfired, and that she'd sent Nick into Gabriella's clutches, Mia shook her head emphatically. "No! That's not a good idea."

"Maybe I should pat her down, see if she's carrying a concealed weapon, twin torpedoes possibly."

The vase that sailed by Nick's head missed him by only

a fraction of an inch before it crashed into the wall. The last thing he saw was Mia's retreating backside as she slammed the bedroom door in his face.

ELEVEN

Those are just your emotions
acting without the benefit of intellect.
Passenger 57

"The manicotti is delicious, Mrs. Russo. It has just the right amount of cheese, and the sauce is quite tasty, too. You're an excellent cook."

Smiling warmly at Nick, Sophia indicated with great pleasure the woman seated next to her. "Gabriella prepared tonight's dinner. She is the one you should be complimenting, Nick. Gabriella is a woman of many talents and will make some lucky man a wonderful wife."

Wonderful wife! Shit!

Mia felt like gagging. It seemed Gabriella was not only beautiful she could cook well, too. Well, in her opinion you couldn't trust anyone who didn't eat Stouffer's on a regular basis. And she wasn't going to touch on the woman's perfectly manicured claws . . . er . . . nails. Glancing down at her own, she cringed at the short, broken mess and curled them under, hoping no one, including Nick, had noticed.

"I bet Mia is a good cook, too." Grandma Flora smiled at the young woman next to her, placing her gnarled hand over hers and squeezing gently. "This isa true, no, Nick? You eat her cooking. I tink Mia must cook even better than Gabriella Perillo." Lifting her nose haughtily as she stared down the length of mahogany table at Sophia's goddaughter, Grandma smirked.

"Mia cooks with a great deal of flair," Nick replied as honestly as he could, hoping there wasn't going to be another catfight over who was the best cook. "She's very . . . innovative. We've had many interesting Martha Stewart moments."

Appreciating the eloquent lie that Nick spun so effortlessly, Mia flashed him a grateful smile, which he returned in kind.

"Ah, Martha Stewart. *Bellisimo!* I get her magazine sent to me in Italy. She is a smart woman," Gabriella enthused, sipping her wine, and flashing Mia a spiteful smile.

For the most part, the nasty woman had reined in her viperous tongue this evening, probably because Sophia had threatened to send her packing if she acted rudely toward her guests, namely Mia. "I read somewhere that Martha's husband left her and married her assistant, so I'm not sure how smart that makes her," she stated.

"I bet she neglected her husband ina the bedroom." Looking the image of innocence, Grandma Flora continued sipping her wine, while her daughter-in-law gasped at the outrageous remark, clutching her throat.

"Mama mia, disgratzia!"

Flora ignored Sophia's outburst. "You cannot spend all your time ina the kitchen cooking, ifa you wanta to makea your husband happy. My Sal wasa very happy," she added, filling up her now empty wineglass and taking another sip.

Sophia's face flushed as red as the cranberry candles adorning the table. "Be quiet, old woman! I will not allow that kind of talk at my dinner table." Turning to her husband, she said, "Frank, tell your crazy mother to be quiet." She gazed at the crucifix hanging on the wall and made the sign of the cross, just in case God had been listening. "Flora is ruining my dinner with her sex talk. What will people think?"

The old woman brushed her hand under her chin. *"Vaffunculo!"*

Used to the ongoing hostilities between his wife and mother—World War II had nothing on Flora and Sophia's arguments—Frank said, *"Forgetaboutit!"* ignoring his wife's edict, and earning a hateful glare, as he directed his attention to Nick.

"My wife tells me you're writing a book about the Mafia, Nick. Have you talked to Alfredo? He knows plenty of people who might be able to help you."

Nick glanced over his shoulder at the older man seated on his left. "I'd be delighted to hear more of what Mr. Graziano has to say. I'm sure he has many interesting stories to tell."

Pleased by the respect the younger man had shown him, Alfredo nodded and smiled. *"Si.* I do. But I promised Lenore I wouldn't speak about such things again. It is in the past now."

"Al is done with that part of his life," Lenore Gallagher stated, exchanging smiles with her soon-to-be husband, and Nick wondered if that was true.

He hoped so, for both their sakes. He'd grown fond of the old guy in the short time he'd known him, and wanted to believe that Alfredo wasn't just putting on a good show for the woman he loved.

"Tell Nick about Pauley, Al," Frank urged his brother-in-law, who shot him a disgusted look.

"Al's got a childhood friend who's connected to a local

crime family," Frank explained, disregarding Alfredo's reaction. "Small-time stuff, mostly. Maybe you can get him to introduce you. Pauley's quite a character. He and Al went to school together."

"Pauley's business dealings are separate from our friendship," Al stated. "I don't ask, he don't tell. It's better that way."

"Do you think your friend, Pauley, would allow me to interview him for the book?" Nick asked, praying silently Alfredo would agree, disappointed when he shook his head.

"That would not be possible. I told you before, Nick, talking gets you killed. And I wouldn't insult my friend by asking. We don't discuss his business, or mine."

"Luca Brazzi swims with the fishes," Grandma stated quite matter-of-factly, and Alfredo nodded solemnly.

"That's right. At the bottom of the ocean, with all the other dead things."

"I hear business is booming down at Lucky Louie's, Al." Frank stood and circled the table, filling everyone's wineglass with more Chianti. Everyone's but his mother's, that is. Flora had definitely had enough. Soon, she would start singing "Oh, My Papa" at the top of her lungs, and it would not be a pleasant experience. Flora hit notes only a cat could appreciate.

"Maybe I should come by and see about getting a new car. The Buick's about had it."

"The Buick had it about thirty years ago, Frank," Al told his brother-in-law. "Come down and see what we've got on the lot. I've got inventory we need to unload before the new year. I'll make you an offer you can't refuse."

Everyone thought *The Godfather* comment was wildly funny and laughed, with the exception of the FBI agent.

"Maybe you're in the market for a new used car, too, uh, Nick? I can cut you a good deal, if you're interested," Alfredo said, and Nick could have kissed Frank Russo for providing the opening he needed.

Now, he had a legitimate reason to go snooping around the car lot. And he'd be able to meet Alfredo's partner, Vinnie. "I might just take you up on that, Mr. Graziano."

"But your car is so nice!" Mia blurted, looking at Nick as if he'd lost whatever sense he'd been born with, and wondering what had gotten into the usually sensible man.

Nick wanted to strangle the woman to silence, but said instead, "Yes, but I'm bored with the Volvo. I'm thinking of getting something a bit flashier. Maybe a convertible, or a sports car."

Gabriella clapped her hands. "*Oooh!* I love sports cars. Lamborghini. Ferrari. *Exquisito.*"

She had created a monster, Mia decided. Nick was actually wearing a navy sport coat this evening, with blue jeans. He looked very *GQ*. And now he wanted to buy a sports car, aka, a chickmobile?

When had this transformation taken place? And why hadn't she noticed?

Okay, so she'd wanted him to change. But not so much that other women would notice. Gabriella didn't seem to mind Nick's ugly glasses, either. Of course, blood-sucking vampires weren't all that choosy when it came to their prey. They just sank their teeth in and sucked.

"I know what to look for when buying a car. My dad taught me. I'll be happy to help you pick out a new one,"

Mia offered, noting that Nick didn't seem all that thrilled with the idea.

"Mia isa very smart. She knows lotsa tings."

"Thank you, Grandma Flora," Mia said to the old woman. "My intelligence is often overlooked."

"Gabriella, why don't you take Nick into the front room and show him the Christmas tree, while I get the coffee and dessert." There was a wealth of meaning in the look Sophia bestowed upon her goddaughter, and Mia didn't miss it.

Mistletoe no doubt covered the ceiling, probably the floor, too. And "Here Comes The Bride" was probably blaring from the record player instead of "Here Comes Santa Claus."

Turning to Mia, the older woman asked, "Would you help me in the kitchen, please?"

Apparently Mia's brilliance was lacking at the moment because she hadn't been able to outsmart Sophia, queen of the matchmakers. "Of course," she replied, deciding that the interfering woman might have won the skirmish, but the battle was a long way from over.

Nick pulled the car up to the curb in front of Mama Sophia's and cut the engine, immediately silencing Bing Crosby's rendition of "Silver Bells," which blared from the CD player.

Opening the passenger door, Mia stepped out, glancing up at the night sky. The stars twinkled brilliantly against the black velvet backdrop. And though the December air was bitterly cold, there seemed a bit of magic to it. It made her feel restless, expectant. . . .

Hopeful?

"Let's go for a walk," she suggested when Nick came

around the car to escort her upstairs. "I'm not ready for bed yet, are you?"

"Well, I am kind of tired." He'd had to keep on his toes all evening. First, with Sophia constantly trying to pair him off with Gabriella, and then, with the woman herself, who did everything she could to entice him under the mistletoe. He'd been run ragged, and he felt bone tired. He was getting too old to be playing parlor games with an oversexed, marriage-minded Italian femme fatale.

"Pretty please! It's not that far a walk to the Inner Harbor. We can look at the water, maybe toss a coin in and make a wish."

Nick studied Mia for a moment. Her dark eyes were bright with anticipation, her cheeks chapped and rosy from the cold. She was adorable. And trouble with a capital T. "And what would you wish for?" he asked, bemused by this sudden change in her demeanor.

Unusually quiet tonight, Mia had hardly spoken to him on the ride home. He thought perhaps she hadn't been feeling well after the heavy meal they'd eaten, and he couldn't blame her, if that was the case.

What he thought was going to be a simple dinner when he'd accepted the invitation had turned into an eight-course dining marathon. He was now in need of an Alka Seltzer cocktail.

"If I tell, it won't come true." Mia reached for his hand and tugged. "Come on. The exercise will do us good. I'm sure we consumed at least thirty thousand calories at dinner." She wasn't counting the leaden fruitcake Sophia had served for dessert, which had probably weighed fifty pounds and could have passed for a ship's anchor. Sure felt that way, anyway, when it hit the bottom of her stomach.

Who in their right mind liked fruitcake? Yuck!

Mia had picked out all the disgusting bits of yellow, green, and red candied fruit before taking a bite. And if it hadn't been for the whipped topping she'd lobbed on in copious amounts, she doubted she would have been able to choke it down.

"All right," Nick agreed, curious as to what Mia was up to. "But I can't stay out too long. I need to get back and get some work done on the computer."

She arched a disbelieving brow. "You're going to write tonight? But it's so late." A car pulled up to the traffic light just then, and a boisterous group of laughing teen-agers honked and made faces at them, catching Mia off guard. Startled, she would have fallen if Nick hadn't reached out to steady her.

"Morons!" Mia muttered under her breath, liking the feel of Nick's hands on her waist. But as soon as the thought formed, he removed them, shoving his hands back into his pants pockets and taking a step back.

"Who said anything about writing? I want to check the stock quotes, see how much money I made or lost to-day. I won't be able to sleep until I do."

Shaking her head, Mia laughed. "Guess it's worse when you actually have money invested."

Nick's breath caught in his throat. "You should laugh more often, Mia. You have such a pretty smile."

Prettier than Gabriella's? she wanted to ask. "Thanks. My teeth aren't perfect, but I get by." *Now why did you have to go and spoil it, Mia? The man just paid you a compliment, and all you could do was mention your crooked teeth. Sheesh! Talk about morons.*

The Inner Harbor was relatively deserted when they seated themselves on a concrete bench not far from the water. "It's so peaceful here," Mia said with a sigh. "I love sitting here. I find it very relaxing to stare out at the water and do nothing but think."

Nick frowned. "I hope you haven't been coming here alone at night. That wouldn't be safe, or very smart."

"Let me assure you that I'm very smart, not to mention armed. And I haven't come down here for a while, so you needn't lecture me."

"Just because you have a gun doesn't mean you're safe. A man who is strong and determined can overpower you, take away your gun, and then rape or kill you, or both."

"My, my, but aren't we being pessimistic this evening? Such a pleasant topic you've chosen, Nick. Are you trying to spoil my good mood? I made a concerted effort not to let Gabriella get to me tonight." Although when the woman and Nick had disappeared into the living room, it was all Mia could do not to rush in and attack her. She was positive Gabriella was defiling Nick with smothering kisses.

"Gabriella will be leaving soon, so there's no need to let her upset you."

Mia's face brightened instantly, and she had the uncontrollable urge to clap. To prevent that from happening, she shoved her hands between her knees and tried not to grin. "Really? When?"

"Gabriella told me this evening that her father wants her home for Christmas. And since that's right around the corner, I assume it will be soon. She's invited me to visit her in Sicily."

Mia tried not to let her jealous anger show, but she

was furious. Gabriella had trespassed big-time. "See? What did I tell you? She's with the Mafia. Gabriella's trying to lure you to your death, like they did with Michael Corleone when he went to Sicily."

"I assume you're talking about *The Godfather*?"

She rolled her eyes. "Of course, I'm talking about *The Godfather*. Don't you remember when Michael went to Sicily, fell in love and got married, and the Mafia tried to blow him up, but killed his wife instead? He eventually got even, of course."

"And you think if I go this could happen to me?"

"I'm sure of it."

Mia looked so earnest it was all Nick could do not to take her in his arms and kiss her senseless. But he knew that wouldn't be smart. And Nick needed to play it smart from here on out. There was too much at stake.

His heart?

Jesus! Where had that come from?

"Thanks for the warning. I'll keep it in mind."

Mia attempted a smile, but her teeth started chattering like a monkey's, ruining the enticing effect she'd been hoping for.

"You're freezing. Where are your gloves?" Nick took hold of her icy hands and rubbed them between his own. "Let's go home. It's too cold to be sitting out here. I'll make hot chocolate for us."

Warmed by his concern, and touch, she allowed him to help her to her feet. For what seemed like an eternity, they stood gazing into each other's eyes. It was definitely one of those Kodak moments, and Mia felt this was the opportunity she'd been waiting for all evening.

All her life, if she were truthful.

Leaning toward him, Mia willed Nick to draw her into

his arms and kiss her. The invitation couldn't have been more blatant. Neon signs flashed in her eyes saying, *I want you! I want you.*

But Nick didn't come to the party.

Instead, he drew back and dropped her hand. "We'd better hurry home, or we'll catch our death."

But Mia already felt dead. Her heart was frozen.

She'd been rejected.

Nick hadn't wanted to kiss her.

She wasn't surprised. He'd spent the evening with Gabriella, had probably kissed her under the mistletoe, and would probably kiss her again.

So why, then, would he want to kiss Mia?

He wouldn't. He didn't.

She didn't measure up to the Amazon.

It was time for the makeover, as hideous as that prospect was.

"I don't think it's a good idea that you keep coming around here, Pauley. We gotta keep a low profile, so Alfredo won't get the wrong idea." Glaring at his cohort— the biggest idiot on the entire east coast—Vinnie went back to eating his meatball sub. If there was one thing he hated, it was having his lunch disturbed. A man should be allowed to eat in peace and not get indigestion.

"I didn't think it was smart to phone, Vin, and I needed to talk to you right away."

Vincent wiped sauce from his chin with a napkin. "What's so important it couldn't wait?" He knew Pauley well enough to realize that every mundane matter was important to him. The man was worse than a woman when it came to worrying about insignificant crap.

"Al called last night, asking if I'd be interested in talking to some guy who's writing a book on the Mafia."

Pauley had finally gotten Vinnie's attention. "You're shitting me, right?"

The shorter man shook his head, indicating he wasn't. "If this author should start snooping around, we could have big trouble. I thought I should tell you, so we could figure out what to do."

"So what's the problem? Don't talk to him."

"Are you nuts? Of course I'm not gonna talk to him. Al already told the guy I wouldn't, but he thought he'd ask me anyway. Says he likes this Nick Caruso. The guy's on the level, the real deal, or so he says."

"I never heard of any Nick Caruso. What kind of books does he write? Mysteries? I like mysteries. And those legal thrillers. Those are good, too."

Pauley shrugged. "How the hell should I know? What difference does it make anyway? All I know is, if this guy starts sniffing around, he could get wind of what's going on here, and that's going to make Calzone very nervous."

Calzone wouldn't be the only nervous one, but Vincent didn't like showing his hand when it came to poker, or business. "So take care of it. Why bother me with details? You're the one who's always saying you're the muscle of this arrangement."

"What?"

Pauley's face had whitened. The spineless piece of shit was scared, disgusting Vinnie. He spelled it out. "Get . . . rid . . . of . . . him. We don't need any more problems. Dealing with Alfredo is problem enough. I don't need no author making trouble and screwing up our deal."

"Rid of him? You want Caruso whacked? But he ain't

done nothing yet. You can't whack a man who ain't done nothing. That ain't right."

"What? You want to wait until he turns up something, is that what you're telling me? How smart is that?"

Pauley shuffled his feet, and Vinnie's patience grew shorter. "What the hell's the matter now?"

"I never killed anyone before, Vinnie. I'm not sure I can do it."

"Jesus Christ, Pauley! How the hell did you get in tight with Calzone? You're a fucking amateur."

"I was in the right place at the right time. And I was dating Larry's sister. Carla recommended me."

"So hire it done, if you don't want to do it yourself. I'm sure you know plenty of low-lifes who can use a few extra bucks. How hard could it be to kill a fucking author?"

"Sammy the Bull's an author. You think I want to go up against someone like him? The guy's a murderer."

"And a rat. Never forget who your friends are, Pauley."

Pauley stiffened. "You neither, Vinnie. I'm the one who brought you in on this deal. Don't forget that. One word from me and Calzone will halt the gravy train."

Wrapping his arm around his friend, Vinnie tried to cover his mistake. "No need to threaten me, Pauley. I didn't mean anything by it. I was making a generalization."

"All right, then. I'll see what I can do about Caruso. How hard can it be to kill an author? He sits on his ass all day, right?"

Pauley grinned, and so did Vinnie, pleased that his business partner was such a pushover and had believed his lies.

Buttoni had always been full of stupid sentiment. He'd

never learned that business came before pleasure, and certainly before friendship.

And that money came before anything else.

TWELVE

We're women.
We don't say what we want,
but we reserve the right to be pissed off
if we don't get it.
Sliding Doors

"You expect me to wear *that*? It's indecent. Even I'm not that daring."

Mia felt every tomboy bone in her body rebel at the sight of the skimpy black dress that Annie was holding up for her inspection. It was slinky, barebacked, low-cut, and pretty much nonexistent.

"We just got this in. It's Versace, and it's you, Mia. Trust me," the co-owner of Goldman's Department Store told her reticent customer. Annie's father, Sid, owned the other half of the retail establishment, but it was Annie who was responsible for revamping the outdated clothing store, much the way she was attempting to revamp Mia.

Eyes twinkling, Mary smiled widely. "Oh, this brings back such good memories. I'm so glad Annie is torturing someone else this time, instead of me."

Annie flashed her friend an exasperated look. "*Oy vey!* It worked, didn't it? You're married to Dan. And there was a time when you didn't think you would be."

The two women made silly faces at each other, and then burst out laughing. "You're right, Annie," Mary

188

said, caressing her tummy. "And I'll always be grateful to you."

"Well, I'm so glad I can provide entertainment for you both." Mia grabbed the dress from Annie's outstretched hand and marched toward the dressing room, saying over her shoulder, "I'll try the damn thing on, but I can tell you right now, I'm not going to wear it."

"Now, Mia, be fair." Angela, who was standing right outside her sister's dressing room, tried to reason with her. "The red leather dress you bought is just as revealing as this one. I don't see much difference between the two."

Mia stuck her head out of the curtain enclosure. "Yeah, but I didn't buy the red dress. Nick did. Big difference."

"Which should give you a pretty good idea of what the man likes," Annie pointed out, a bit too reasonably for Mia's comfort. The woman was ten times worldlier than Mia could ever hope to be, and about twenty times sexier.

"You've got a dynamite body. Use it," Annie said, adding when Mia pointed to her boobs and made a face of disgust, "Okay, so you're not Dolly Parton. But a good push-up bra can work wonders for your cleavage. Or better yet, go topless, and I doubt very much Nick will care if you have any cleavage."

Glancing in the mirror again, Mia shook her head. "I'd be mortified to go out in public with this on. I feel naked. You can see every lump I own . . . and don't own." Damn! Why did she have to be so flat-chested? Gabriella had breasts even a cow would be flattered to claim. Next to the woman's watermelon-sized appendages, Mia's looked like walnuts.

"You don't have any cellulite lumps, which is why you can wear this clingy type of dress," Angela pointed out to Mia, who was presently modeling the garment for the three women. She took the chair Annie pushed toward her and seated herself, flashing the thoughtful woman a grateful smile. "And once we get all the accessories for it, like high heels, jewelry—"

"High heels! I refuse to wear those spiky heels that shout 'I'm yours for the taking! Come and get me.' How demeaning." Mia glanced down at her comfy sneakers and sighed. What was wrong with comfort and practicality?

"You'll need to rethink your makeup and hair," Annie said, ignoring the young woman's outburst. She was used to resistance. Mary had had a similar reaction when Annie had insisted her friend wear thong underpants.

"But I don't wear makeup. And what's wrong with my hair? It's curly. There's not a whole lot I can do with it."

"You give Little Orphan Annie a bad name. How long since you've been to the beauty parlor?" Annie studied Mia's hair with a critical eye and grimaced. "Mr. Roy is a miracle worker. I know he'd be delighted to try his hand at redoing your hairstyle. Maybe you should consider adding a dash of color. Nothing too drastic, just some highlights. Color always makes such a dramatic statement."

"You should know, Annie," Mary quipped, referring to the time when her friend had been in the habit of dying her hair to match her moods.

"But I like my hair!" Mia protested. "It's wash and wear. And I don't do beauty parlors. They're too girly for my taste. Usually I just trim my own hair."

The three women looked aghast at each other, trying

to hide the horror they were feeling, before Angela said, "Look, Mia, you can bet your boots that Gabriella Perillo isn't whacking on her own hair. And if you want to get Nick's attention—"

"But the Amazon's leaving! I don't need to go to all this trouble now. I appreciate you guys wanting to help, but if Nick doesn't like me for who I am, then maybe he's not worth pursuing."

Mia, you are such a liar!

"God helps those who help themselves," Mary pointed out, looking like she knew exactly what she was talking about. "And you told us that Gabriella invited Nick to Sicily. He might go, if she makes him the right offer. And you know she will. Unfortunately men don't always think with their brains. An attractive, available woman is a big temptation."

Thinking back to the other night at the Inner Harbor when Nick had neglected to kiss her, Mia knew her friend spoke the truth, and heaved a dispirited sigh. "I suppose you're right. Men are so shallow. Maybe I shouldn't even bother. After all, it's not very ethical to get involved with a client."

Annie rolled her baby blues. "Spare me. I married a former priest. I don't believe in rules when it comes to matters of the heart."

Mia smiled softly at her flamboyant friend. "You really are head-over-heels in love with Joe, aren't you? And it couldn't have been easy bucking Sophia. I admire you, Annie."

"It's still not easy, but it's worth it. When you find the man of your heart, then you've got to go for it, no matter what obstacles stand in your way, including opinionated mothers-in-law."

"Annie's right." Angela reached out to take her sister's hand. "I want you to be happy, Mia, to find someone good and kind, as I have with John. If you don't take a chance, you'll never know what true happiness is."

Mia stared at each of the three women in turn, then shook her head when their meaning became alarmingly clear. "Now wait just a minute! Don't go getting any ideas about wedding bells and orange blossoms. I'm not looking for anything permanent. I just want to have an uncomplicated affair, something we'll both enjoy, and—"

Liar! Liar! Liar! At least be honest with yourself, Mia, if you can't tell your closest friends the truth.

Mary started laughing, and then Annie joined in.

Hands on hips, chin thrust in the air, Mia demanded to know, "What's so damn funny? And why are you laughing at me?"

"We said the same thing once." Mary wiped her eyes with the edge of her sleeve. "I swore up and down that I didn't want to get married, especially after achieving my independence with the restaurant."

"Me, too," Annie said. "Joe was the last man on earth I ever thought I'd end up marrying."

"I guess you can count me in on that, too." Angela smiled widely. "Funny how fate steps in and slaps you upside the head when you're not looking, isn't it?"

"So you're saying that I do want to get married and just don't know it?" Mia looked skeptical. "I think I would know if I wanted to get hitched for the rest of my life."

"I think what we're trying to say, and not very well, apparently," Angela replied, "is that it took all of us a while to figure out that our hearts were engaged long before our bodies entered into the equation."

"You mean . . . love?" Mia swallowed, her face a mask of horror again, though for entirely different reasons this time.

"It's not so bad." Annie's blue eyes filled with tenderness. "There are definite benefits to being married. It's nice to wake up each morning to find the man you love lying next to you. It gets your motor running much more effectively than caffeine, I can promise you that."

"I can do that without getting married," Mia pointed out to her grinning friend.

"It's not the same," Mary went on to explain. "When you finally find that one special person it's like two halves coming together to make a whole. You wonder how you ever survived without him for so long."

Mia shook her head. "Well, I'm telling you right now that I'm not going to fall in love with Nick Caruso."

I'm not! I'm not! I'm not!

"I like him a great deal, but we have next to nothing in common. And he's just too conservative and stuffy for my taste. I admit that he's a really good kisser, and that he looks awesome in his underwear. I figure that's more than a lot of women get."

"Should we try to convince her?" Annie asked her companions, who shook their heads in unison.

"It's no use." Mary shrugged. "When it happens, it happens. And there won't be a thing Mia can do about it then."

"You make it sound like a terminal disease or something. I'm grateful I haven't succumbed." She'd almost died of a broken heart the last time.

"Haven't you, Mia?" Angela asked, unable to hide the concern in her voice.

But Mia refused to discuss the matter further. Angela had always been too smart for her own good. "I thought you were going to help me get laid. That's my top priority at the moment. I'd like to have sex again before my parts rust.

"Let's get busy with this damn makeover before I change my mind and decide to forget the whole thing. I don't have all day, you know. I've got to get home to Nick. Dad wasn't all that thrilled about baby-sitting again." Actually, Sam had been excited at the prospect of another poker game with Nick, but she thought it sounded much more dramatic this way.

Heaven forbid! Mia thought. She was turning into Rosalie, the drama queen.

"You won't change your mind."

Mia threw her hands up in exasperation. "Damn it, Annie! Quit looking so smug. Just because you're getting sex on a regular basis is no reason—"

Annie's laughter filled the store, making some of the other customers turn their heads to see what was so funny. "This has nothing to do with sex. You're in love. As soon as you admit that to yourself, life will be a whole lot easier for everyone, and we can get on with making you look gorgeous."

"I'm not in love!" Mia declared.

But it was clear that no one believed her protestations, Mia most of all.

Stomping his feet to get the blood circulating, Nick gazed out at the frozen ice rink full of skaters, seeing none of the activity going on around him, hearing none of the laughter and shouts of joy that filled the frigid air.

His mind was elsewhere. On Mia, if he was truthful. The same place it had been for days.

The object of his thoughts skated by with a group of acquaintances, laughing and waving at him. "Come on and join us, Nick," Mia shouted, her cheeks rosy from the cold. "We're having a great time."

Waving back, Nick smiled perfunctorily, and shook his head to the negative. He hated lying to Mia, hated the pretense he'd developed, hated having her think he was someone he wasn't.

The fictional Nick Caruso was a much better person than FBI agent Nick Caruso. He was kind and considerate to his aunt, polite and caring to people he barely knew, and he didn't come across as the love 'em and leave 'em type of male that most women detested.

None of that had mattered to him before. He'd never been concerned about what other people thought of him. But Mia was different. She trusted him, believed in him. Went out of her way to include him in everything, like this community fund-raiser for the local hospital she had brought him to.

The pediatric wing at Mercy Hospital was to be renovated, which Nick thought was a very worthwhile endeavor, so he hadn't complained overly much when Mia insisted on dragging him along. She'd explained that she would be armed, just in case. And that she had gone over the list of potential contributors and found nothing to be concerned about. He had to give her credit; Mia continued to be thorough and vigilant.

Nick had become part of Mia's life, just as she'd become part of his. Only it wasn't his life he was sharing, but someone else's, someone who didn't exist. He was living a lie, and someday that was going to become painfully apparent to everyone.

But he was duty-bound not to reveal his true identity and motives for being in Little Italy. Nick couldn't afford to blow his cover. He had a job to do, and he intended to do it to the best of his abilities.

He just hadn't counted on getting involved, letting his emotions take a holiday, finding people he was beginning to care about. And he wasn't just thinking about Mia, though, of course, she was the biggest part of it. He'd grown quite fond of the Russos and DeNeros and genuinely liked them, warts and all, and enjoyed being part of their lives.

What would happen when they discovered his real motives for befriending them?

They would feel betrayed, especially Sophia. The older woman would never forgive him for duping her to get close to her brother. And Nick liked the fact that he had earned her respect.

But mostly he worried about what Mia would think. If she would be able to understand why he'd been dishonest with her. Even though Mia lived by her own set of rules, she was honest, had integrity, and didn't play games and lie to people to get what she wanted.

Mia would hate him. She would—

"I thought you said you didn't mind coming to the fund-raiser. You look miserable, sitting there all hunched over."

Nick looked up to find Mia standing at the railing. Her nose was as red as Rudolph's, but she looked adorable in her multicolored knit cap and scarf.

Mia fastened her blade guards, opened the gate, and came through the opening, climbing the few steps to sit on the bench seat next to him. "We can leave if you want to," she offered, though he knew she was having a good time. "But you haven't skated, not even one time. So I'm not sure I should let you off the hook that easily. I told you before we arrived that I checked the place out and deemed it safe, in case you're worried about it. I doubt very much that there are many ice-skating hit men in Little Italy."

"I'm not much for ice skating, I told you that. I'm not very good at it. But I've enjoyed watching you and your friends having a good time."

Mia glanced down at her watch. "It's nearly five. We'll be leaving soon for my parents' house, anyway. Mom will kill me if we're late for dinner. She made me promise to be on time."

Hesitating a moment, Nick tried to choose his words carefully. "Are you sure I should go? I feel funny about eating at your parents' house again." *And taking advantage of your family this way.*

"Are you kidding? Mom and Dad are crazy about you. Besides, Rosalie lives to cook. She'd be very disappointed if she couldn't try out her famous recipe for veal Marsala on you. Not to mention that Dad wouldn't have a reason for dressing up in something pretty and outrageous."

Nick sighed, and Mia added with a bit of uncertainty in her voice, "If you don't want to go, just tell me, Nick. I know my parents aren't the easiest people to be around."

Hurt filled her eyes, and Nick clasped Mia's hand, pleased that she'd taken his advice and worn mittens. "I like your family very much, Mia. Please don't misunderstand. I just don't want to inconvenience anyone, that's all."

"Don't be silly. It's no inconvenience. You're doing everyone a favor, including me. I get to fulfill my familial duty as a good daughter, while being your bodyguard at the same time."

"If you're sure."

"I'm very sure. So quit worrying about it."

Nick glanced across the skating rink to find Sophia and Gabriella glaring at him from the other side. He waved in greeting, but they didn't respond. "What's wrong with those two?" he asked, his brow furrowing in confusion. "They look furious, for some reason."

Mia grinned. "They are. I think Sophia might be putting the evil eye on you. She mentioned something to me earlier about inviting you over for dinner this evening, and I was pleased to inform her that you were my guest tonight. Isn't it fun having women fighting over you? I'm sure it makes your ego huge."

"Fun isn't exactly the word I would use." Nick studied Mia more closely, his right brow arching. "You look different tonight. Are you wearing makeup?"

Mia's cheeks blossomed pink. "Just a touch. I've been experimenting a bit." While at Goldman's, Annie had loaded her up with an assortment of lipsticks, blushers, and eye shadows, and had even thrown in a few lessons on how to apply the stuff. Mia thought it would be best if she eased into the makeover slowly, and wearing a small amount of makeup now and then seemed like a good place to start. After all, she didn't want Nick to go into shock at her sudden transformation from tomboy to femme fatale.

As if.

"You have beautiful skin. You really don't need artificial enhancement."

His compliment warmed her all the way down to her frozen toes. "Thank you. Annie talked me into buying the stuff yesterday, while I was shopping at Goldman's. She's a very persistent salesperson, and I found it hard to say no."

"That's the kind of attitude that gets nice girls into trouble, especially if they're wearing cherry red lipstick."

At Nick's teasing grin, Mia's entire body tingled, and her heart soared to new heights. Maybe Nick did find her attractive. His ardent look certainly said so, and filled her with hope that maybe things would turn out differently this time.

She swallowed with some difficulty, pasted on a teasing smile, and replied, "Who says I'm a nice girl?"

Nick and Mia decided to walk the relatively short distance from the ice skating rink to her parents' house. The frigid air smelled of snow, and they huddled in their parkas, walking briskly against the cold. Night had fallen, but streetlamps and holiday decorations illuminated the way.

When they turned the corner, Mia's face lit; she clapped her hands excitedly, the sound muted by the mittens she wore. "Look! Dad's put up the outdoor lights." She pointed toward the brick house on the left side of the street. "Doesn't it look pretty? I know everyone uses the tiny white lights these days, but I still love the multi-colored twinkle ones."

Smiling at Mia's enthusiasm, Nick could easily imagine her as a child of six on Christmas morning. She probably had a great many happy childhood memories to draw from, and he wondered if she knew how lucky she was. He thought she did.

Tongue planted firmly in cheek, he replied, "I think my eyes are frozen shut, or maybe I've just gone blind from the cold. But I'm sure if I could see I would think the sight spectacular."

She knocked him on the arm. "Oh, Nick, quit being a wuss. It's not that cold. In fact, I'm hoping it will snow. Wouldn't it be great to have a white Christmas this year?"

He huddled deeper into his jacket, shivering at the thought. "Since when did you turn into an Eskimo?"

"I'm a winter person. I love the cold, and snow. I admit that I don't like jogging much during cold weather, but once I get going I find it invigorating." She hadn't gone jogging since Nick's arrival, and she missed her morning routine. Mia had thought about asking Nick to accompany her, but didn't think he'd be able to keep up.

Despite his muscular physique, he didn't seem to be very athletic. Case in point: he didn't know how to ice skate. She wondered if he'd ever played football or base-ball as a child. Perhaps his elderly aunt had frowned on such activities.

"I admire the fact that you work out every day," Nick told Mia, his comment surprising her. "I hear you in your room at night, grunting and moaning, while performing your push-ups and sit-ups."

Her smile was incredibly sexy, and Nick felt heat in his lower extremities, despite the cold. "How do you know exercise is responsible for the moaning you hear? Maybe I'm doing something terribly wicked."

Reaching the front lawn of her parents' modest home, Nick threw back his head and laughed, unwilling to conjure up that provocative image. "Doesn't sound like you're having that good of a time to me, but if you are, perhaps you should let me in on what you're doing."

Giggling, Mia opened her mouth to reply, just as the first shot rang out.

The bullet whizzed by Nick's head, pinging the metal garbage can waiting at the curb for tomorrow morning's pickup. It happened so quickly that Mia didn't have time to scream.

Without thinking, Nick reached for his gun, then realized he didn't have it. "Shit!"

At the same time, Mia ordered, "Hit the ground," throwing herself in front of him as the second bullet struck. They fell to the ground, she on top of him, and all Nick could see when he looked up was bright red blood gushing out of the woman he'd just come to realize he loved.

THIRTEEN

*If anything in this life is certain,
if history has taught us anything,
it's that you can kill anyone.*
The Godfather

Mia's keening wail frightened the hell out of Nick. He looked around to make sure the gunmen had fled, and then, as gently as he could, picked up the injured woman and carried her toward the house, moving quickly but carefully, hollering as he drew near for someone to open the front door.

Sam DeNero's face whitened at the sight of his daughter's prostrate form. "Mia! Jesus Christ!" His eyes glittered dangerously. "What the hell happened to my daughter, Nick?" He hauled Nick and his precious bundle inside, slamming the door shut before anyone in the neighborhood could see what was going on.

"Call 911! Mia's been shot. It was too dark to tell, so I don't know how badly she's been wounded." *Please, God, don't let her die,* Nick prayed, fear making him break out in a cold sweat. The thought of never seeing her impish grin, hearing her raucous laughter again, made him sick to his stomach and light-headed.

"Carry Mia into the back bedroom and put her on the bed," Sam ordered, his tone ringing authority. "Rosalie, bring the first-aid kit," he shouted to his wife, who was still in the kitchen preparing a dinner that no one was likely to eat.

"Aren't you going to call 911?" Nick asked, depositing Mia on her bed and turning on the lamp. He drew a shaky forearm across his forehead to wipe the dampness from his brow, wondering why the older man was hesitating.

Red cabbage roses climbed the walls of Mia's room, but none appeared in her cheeks. She looked pale as death in the lamplight, and Nick was scared shitless that she was going to die.

Jesus Christ! How had this happened?

The entire fiasco was his fault, of course. And somehow he had to make it right; the surveillance operation be damned. The decision made, he reached inside his coat pocket and pulled out his cell phone. "Mia needs to go to the hospital ASAP, Sam. I'm going to—"

"No!" The older man shook his head. "Not yet. We'll call if it's necessary. But if we call 911 now, the police are going to come and investigate, and I doubt either you or my daughter want them snooping into matters that don't concern them. Am I right?"

The knowing look Mia's father flashed made the hairs on the back of Nick's neck stand at attention. He nodded, watching as Sam tenderly removed his daughter's coat and sweater, then covered her up with a sheet as best he could, to protect her modesty. She looked pale, had obviously lost some blood, but the wound didn't look as serious as Nick had first thought.

"She's been hit in the upper arm. It's just a flesh wound," Sam pronounced with no small amount of relief, continuing to probe the wound with practiced fingers.

"There's no bullet lodged here; it just grazed her. It was small caliber, most likely a .22, and won't leave much of a scar."

Nick, who wasn't normally a praying man, thanked the Almighty. "But she's not moved a muscle or made a sound. Are you sure she's going to be okay? She sure as hell doesn't look it."

"Mia's always had a low threshold for pain. She's just passed out. It's for the best. I need to clean out this bullet wound and get it bandaged before she awakens."

Rosalie came rushing into the room, carrying clean towels and a first-aid kit. "Is Mia alive?" she asked. "Will she be all right? My baby, my baby." She rushed to her daughter's bedside, smoothing back Mia's sweat-dampened hair and kissing her forehead. "Mommy's here, baby. Everything's going to be okay."

Sam spared a glance at his wife. "Keep it together, Rosalie. Mia's going to be just fine. She's fainted, that's all. The wound isn't deep. The bullet grazed the fleshy part of her upper arm. Once I clean it up and get it bandaged, she'll be as good as new."

"Are you sure? You wouldn't lie to me, Sam." Rosalie wiped tears from her eyes with the back of her hand, and he squeezed her shoulder reassuringly.

"I promise. Now, I need you to go into our bedroom closet and fetch my black leather bag, the one with the medical supplies. I'm going to give Mia an injection of antibiotics."

Rosalie nodded, then hurried to do his bidding.

Nick didn't ask why Sam had medical supplies on hand, but he surmised that the ex-cop had done this sort of thing before when he worked for the Boston Police

Department, though probably not while wearing a gold lamé dress.

Funny, but Nick hadn't even noticed what Sam was wearing up until now. He'd either been too distracted by Mia's injury, or he was getting used to the man's outrageous ways. He hoped it was the former.

Noting Nick's questioning gaze, Sam explained, "I was a medic in the Army. I know how to do this kind of stuff. And I'm good at it, so don't worry."

"What can I do to help?" Nick asked, feeling guilty he hadn't offered before now. He was usually so in control and never lost his cool. But right now he felt like a newborn colt on wobbly legs. He hadn't been able to remain detached and objective where Mia was concerned.

He loved her, and that was going to prove a major problem.

But for now, Nick needed to get himself together, find out who was trying to kill him, and why. He'd worry about the other later, when he had time to figure out what in hell he was going to do.

Sam looked up for a moment, studied the younger man, and frowned. "You can sit yourself down on that chair, son. You look as if you're about to pass out, and I don't have time right now to scrape you off the floor."

Nick did as instructed, holding his head between his hands. "Mia saved my life. That bullet was meant for me."

"The Mafia?"

Having no idea who had shot at him, Nick nodded to keep up the pretense, though he wondered if Sam knew more than he let on. Cops had a nose for intrigue, even ex-cops. "I'm not sure, but that would be the logical explanation."

Eyes narrowing, Sam fastened the bandage around his daughter's arm. "Would it?"

Rosalie returned a few moments later, handing her husband the items he requested, and Nick was spared from answering.

A few minutes later, Mia's eyes fluttered open, then widened. She seemed surprised to see her father and mother hovering over her. Then it all came back to her in horrifying detail, and she grew alarmed, trying to sit up. "Where's Nick? Is he okay?"

Sam pushed her back down gently. "Don't be stupid, Mia. You'll pass out again."

"I'm fine, thanks to you," Nick replied, moving to stand by the bed and reaching for her hand. "Saving my life is getting to be a bad habit with you, Miss DeNero."

Mia smiled softly and squeezed his hand, though it was a weak effort at best. A lump formed in Nick's throat at the sickening realization that he could have lost Mia tonight.

"What do you mean?" Rosalie crossed herself, looking even paler than she had earlier. "Has this sort of thing happened before?" Her gaze moved from Nick to her daughter. "You said what you were doing wasn't dangerous, Mia."

"Nick's just teasing, Mom. I saved his neck at the ice skating rink today. Isn't that right, Nick?"

"I'm a terrible skater, Mrs. DeNero. I kept falling down, and Mia had to come to my rescue more times than I care to admit." The lie fell smoothly from his lips.

"I'm not sure I believe either one of you, but I'm too upset to press you for answers now. But when my daughter is fully recovered I want a complete explanation about what happened tonight. Do you hear me, young man?"

"Mom, you're overreacting. No doubt this was some kind of drive-by shooting. You know that happens all the time here in Baltimore. A drug deal gone wrong, or a case of mistaken identity. I don't think they were shooting at us."

Mia knew full well that the bullet had been meant for Nick, that the Mafia must have gotten wind of where he was, and that his life was still in danger. They had attempted to kill him and weren't likely to give up any time soon.

"I don't care. You'll both spend the night here," Mia's mother ordered, brooking no refusal as she smoothed back the stray strands of dark blond hair that had come loose from her bun. "Nick can sleep in the spare bedroom. I don't want you going home tonight."

"That's fine, Mrs. DeNero." Nick didn't see any point in arguing with the woman, who was justifiably distraught. "I don't think it's a good idea to move Mia just yet, anyway. Tomorrow will be soon enough."

"I feel fine, but we'll do it your way, Mom. I'm still planning to eat dinner, so don't go getting any ideas about not feeding me. The veal Marsala sure smells good. When do we eat?"

Rosalie looked aghast. "The veal! I hope it's not ruined." She dashed off to the kitchen.

Sam shook his head. "Only your mother would worry about burned veal at a time like this. You call me if you need me for anything, Mia, or if that arm starts to swell. I gave you a shot of antibiotics as a precaution, but we need to keep an eye on things, make sure no infection sets in."

"But what about dinner? I'm starving. Almost getting

killed has increased my appetite. I'm sure Nick's hungry, too."

"I'll call you when it's time for dinner. You can come to the table if you're feeling up to it, or we'll bring you and Nick a tray and you can eat in here."

"Thanks for everything, Dad. And don't worry. I'll be fine. I've got Nick to keep me company."

Sam didn't say what he was thinking, but Nick could read the disappointment in the older man's eyes before he walked out of the room, shutting the door behind him.

"Your father thinks I failed you, and he's right, Mia. I should have been more alert. You'll never know how sorry I am that this happened. I feel totally responsible."

She looked into his eyes and saw sorrow and regret; it confused her. "Why should you take the blame? It's not your job to be alert. I'm the bodyguard. I'm the one who should have been more aware of my surroundings, instead of mooning over Christmas lights, and . . ." And the man seated next to her.

Mia blamed herself for what happened. If she hadn't been distracted, by Nick, by their sexual banter, she might have seen the gunmen before they hit.

Her lack of professionalism had endangered both their lives. She vowed it wouldn't happen again. She knew it had been a mistake to become enamored of Nick.

But how was she supposed to stop feeling?

How could she stop loving Nick?

Annie and the others were right. She had fallen in love with Nick, as stupid and irresponsible as that was.

Mia closed her eyes and heaved a sigh, unwilling to gaze upon the face that haunted her every waking moment, and most of her sleeping ones, too.

Who would have ever thought that tomboy Mia would fall hard for a computer geek? Certainly not Mia.

But she had.

And now she had to find a way to turn off her feelings, to get back her perspective, and be the bodyguard Nick had hired her to be.

She had to concentrate on protecting Nick, not loving him, for that was the surest way to get him killed.

But that seemed about as easy as keeping Nick safe from the Mafia. And she wasn't at all sure that either one was possible.

"What do you mean, you're not coming to my Christmas party? This is my first official party since marrying John. You have to come, Mia."

Mia leaned back against the bed pillows and heaved a sigh, wishing her sister hadn't come over to visit today, and hadn't made the request that she had.

It had been difficult enough these past two days since the shooting to keep her mind occupied with things other than the width of Nick's back, or how good he looked in his jeans, which he was now wearing more often. If she had to attend a party with him . . . well, she just didn't want to put that much temptation before her. Not now that she was certain that she loved him. It would be pure torture.

She touched her injured arm, trying her best to look pathetic, though in truth she felt perfectly fine. "I've been shot, in case you haven't noticed. Give me a break. I don't feel like going to any Christmas party, yours included."

Angela was clearly unimpressed with Mia's theatrics. "I've seen your wound. It's nothing. Dad did a great job of patching you up. I doubt you'll even have a scar. Granted, wearing a sleeveless dress could be a problem because of the bandage, but—"

Was her sister being purposely obtuse? "Hello! I'm not going to any party. And I'm certainly not wearing that hooker dress you guys picked out."

"Why the sudden change of heart? I thought you were interested in snaring Nick to your bed."

"I've decided that it wouldn't be smart to pursue Nick, as I had originally planned. That whole Gabriella competition was a bad idea. And she's leaving for Italy tomorrow, so I needn't bother.

"Not to mention that I almost got him killed by thinking about *matters* that I shouldn't have been thinking about." And that had scared the hell out of her. "I've got to get over this infatuation I have for him. And I will. I just need time and space."

Seating herself on the edge of the bed, Angela reached out and took her sister's hand. "When did you finally realize you were in love with Nick?"

A look of panic crossed Mia's face. "*Ssh!* He might hear you. Keep your voice down."

"He won't. Nick's got his earphones on. I noticed he was wearing them when I went to fetch your Coke earlier."

"He's probably listening to that opera he likes." Mia wrinkled her nose in disgust.

"I don't think so. He seemed to be rocking out."

Mia's eyes widened. *Nick, rocking out? No way.*

"I guess deep down I've known for a while that I loved Nick, but I didn't want to admit it. After all, it wasn't part of my job description.

"Dammit! I've made a mess of everything as usual, Ang. I never do anything right. Dad's right—I'm a loser."

"Falling in love is as right as it gets, Mia, so quit talking like that. I know Nick is pleased by the job you're doing. He told me so."

"He was being kind. Nick feels guilty because I was shot protecting him."

"From what you told me, Nick doesn't hand out compliments that freely. I get the impression he cares a great deal about you, Mia."

As much as she wanted to believe it, Mia couldn't allow herself to hope, to think along those lines, not any longer. And she wouldn't encourage her sister to think that way, either. She shrugged in a noncommittal way. "Whatever. Anyway, I don't think it's a good idea that we attend your party together. It would only complicate matters, and my life is complicated enough at the moment."

"Just in case you change your mind I've brought you a present." Angela retrieved the Macy's shopping bag she had left by the foot of the bed, handing it to Mia. "I hope you like it."

Mia's eyes widened, and she let loose a small squeal of delight when she discovered the most gorgeous emerald green knit dress hidden within the folds of the tissue. It was very classy, with long tight sleeves, scooped neck, and slits running up the sides of the skirt—clingy and sexy, yet conservative.

"I love it! It's so . . . me. Thanks, Ang." She leaned forward and pecked her sister's cheek. "I take back all the horrible things I've said about you over the years."

Angela smiled. "Will you come to my party, then? I'll beg, if I have to."

Mia considered making her sister beg. It would be a new experience, and payback, for when Angela had charged her little sister twenty-five cents a sheet to use her pretty scented stationery when Mia was ten. "Oh, all right. But if things get out of control with Nick, I'm going to blame you."

"What could happen?"

The possibilities had Mia's toes tingling and filled her with an eagerness that was sure to be her undoing.

Nick spoke softly into the receiver, hoping Mia and her sister would remain occupied in the bedroom a few minutes longer so he could finish his conversation with Burt. "Did you learn anything from the informant about the shooting? Talk fast. I've only got a few minutes."

"I hope you appreciate the irony in this, Nick, but it looks like your writing a book on the Mafia has made a few people around town nervous, namely Larry Calzone and his crew, which, as we suspected, includes Paul Buttoni. They're trying to shut you up, so you don't get wind of their illegal doings."

"Jesus! Art imitates life. Even my fabrications get me into trouble."

Burt's voice filled with trepidation. "You need to be extremely careful, Nick. Those assholes are likely to try another hit. It might be best to lay low during the Christmas holidays. Nothing much is likely to happen then, anyway. I'll keep my ears open on this end and see what develops."

"All right. I want to give Mia a chance to recover from the ordeal before I decide what the next step will be."

"The next step should be your getting the hell out of Dodge. You've caused that woman enough trouble. I tried to tell you that something like this was going to happen. If Higgins hears about the shooting, your ass is toast, boyo."

Nick rubbed the back of his neck. "Thanks for re-minding me, Burt. Fortunately not many people know what happened. Mia's father had the presence of mind to keep me from bringing in the authorities."

"Do you think Sam suspects something?"

"I think his cop's antennae are twitching, but I doubt he's figured out anything yet. I'll need to throw him off track, somehow."

"What about Mia? What are you going to do about her?"

Ah, the million-dollar question. The one Nick had no answer for. None that he cared to contemplate, anyway.

FOURTEEN

I would rather have one breath of her hair,
one kiss of her mouth, one touch of her hand
than an eternity without it.
City of Angels

"Your sister is going to kill you when she finds out we left the party early."

Though Nick wasn't the least bit sorry. After taking one look at Mia in her tight, green knit dress that hugged every curve of her luscious body, he wanted to have her all to himself, wanted to make love to her, as foolish and impractical as that idea was. And he wanted to do it tonight, before reason and logic took over and warned him away. He'd thought of little else for days, except how much he loved her.

Taking her eyes off the road for a moment, Mia smiled softly at Nick. "I promised Angela we would attend, but I didn't say how long we would stay. We were there for over an hour, enough time to eat and make merry with everyone. My sister has no right to complain. I did what she asked of me."

"Weren't you having a good time?" he asked, concern creasing his brow. "It seemed like you were. Your arm isn't hurting, is it?" Since the shooting he'd been watching Mia carefully, checking for signs of infection, and making sure she didn't overdo. Of course, she fought him tooth and nail, had even called him a few colorful names, but he'd persisted until she finally gave in and agreed to rest more.

The sound of her laughter surrounded him like a warm and comforting quilt. "It's fine. I'm fine. Quit worrying. You're worse than my mother, and that's saying a lot. And since when did you turn into a party animal? I thought you'd be happy we didn't stay long."

Gazing out the car window at the surrounding area, Nick didn't recognize their location. They'd gotten off the freeway some miles back and were on one of the secondary roads. "If you don't mind my asking, where are we going? It doesn't take this long to get back to the apartment from your sister's place. That much, I know."

"Be patient. I'm taking you somewhere that is sure to infuse you with the spirit of Christmas present. What you're about to see would even make old Ebenezer Scrooge stand up and take notice. It's awesome."

"Hey, I thought I was doing pretty good in the Christmas spirit department. You didn't see me complain when you dragged me out into the center of the Francos' living room and made me dance to 'Jingle Bell Rock,' as humiliating as that was."

"I had the distinct feeling that I was the lesser of the two evils," Mia tossed back with a grin. "Your other choice of dance partner was Sophia. I saw your face pale when she asked you to dance, so I decided to rescue you, just in case she still had the hots for her old flame, Joe Perillo, and was planning to transfer them to you."

The memory made Nick cringe. Being the object of Sophia Russo's affections was too daunting a prospect, even for a seasoned FBI agent. "Don't get me wrong. I'm not sorry we left early. To be honest, I'm anxious to get home and on the computer to check the stocks. I want to see if those tech stocks perform the way you predicted they would. I've been leery about investing in that segment of the stock market again, but your past hunches have been right on target."

"Why leery? Technology is here to stay. I know the NASDAQ had a downturn, but the whole market did. I think things are going to break wide open again, you'll see. I feel it in my gut."

"What does your gut say about what time we'll be home? Those hors d'oeuvres your sister served were good, but I'm getting hungry again."

And not just for food.

He'd never before wanted a woman the way he wanted Mia, with his heart and soul, and not just his body. Loving her was fraught with complications, but he couldn't help himself. Although it broke all the rules about getting involved during an investigation, and totally defied logic, he didn't care. He was crazy about her. And there wasn't a damn thing he could do about it right now, except show her in that age-old way how he felt.

Mia didn't answer. Instead, she turned down 34th Street and waited for Nick's response. She wasn't disappointed.

"Holy sh . . . smoke!" Nick's eyes widened. "I've never seen anything like this." The entire residential neighborhood had been adorned with all kinds of Christmas decorations, not to mention a gazillion lights. Each homeowner had tried to outdo the other with their exterior illumination display. The result was spectacular and beautiful, if a bit gaudy.

"Wow! Santa won't have any trouble finding this place. I didn't know this street existed."

"Me, either, until the other night when I saw it featured on a Maryland Lotto commercial. Isn't it pretty? I'm so in awe. I wonder what their electric bills are like."

"I wouldn't want to know," Nick replied with a shudder as they cruised slowly down the brightly lit street, one car of many who had come to see the colorful display.

"I'm so glad you like it. I couldn't wait to show it to you."

"It's beautiful, Mia, but not as beautiful as you. You put every one of those lights to shame when you smile and your face lights up."

Embarrassed by Nick's uncharacteristic effusiveness, Mia's cheeks reddened, but she couldn't contain the grin spreading slowly across her face. "I was wondering when you were going to notice my new dress. You didn't say a word when I came out of the bedroom tonight."

He'd been so in awe of Mia's beauty when he'd seen her standing there he was afraid his voice would betray just how deeply he loved her. "Your beauty rendered me speechless."

"Oh, Nick. You always say the sweetest things. Your aunt should be proud of the way you turned out. She raised you with such good manners. My mom's always commenting on what a nice person you are." Nick flinched, but Mia didn't notice.

For all his fabricating, Nick didn't feel like a nice person, just a man in love. And though he hated carrying on the charade, he couldn't help himself. If he told Mia the truth, she would hate him. And that was something he couldn't risk.

Reaching out to touch her hair, he confessed, "You make me feel things I've never felt before, Mia. You're very special. I hope you know that."

The tiny hairs on the back of her neck sprang to attention, and she felt her throat constrict. "You shouldn't talk that way when I'm driving, Nick. We're liable to have an accident." She could feel her body heat, and it had nothing to do with the car heater being turned up full blast.

If only Nick felt the same way about her that she felt about him. But Mia knew that wasn't going to happen. If history had taught her anything, it was that she had no luck with men, especially the ones she cared deeply about.

An awkward silence filled the car and she tried to make light of the moment. "You're just grateful because I saved your life. Admit it."

"I am. But that has nothing to do with the way I'm feeling right now. Let's go home."

His voice held promise, and something else she couldn't quite discern. Mia swallowed the grapefruit-sized lump in her throat before asking, "To check on the stock market?"

Nick shook his head, and her heart began tap dancing around in her chest. "I've got something else entirely in mind. Something much better."

Mia wasn't naïve; she knew what that "something" was. It was the same something she'd been fantasizing about for weeks. But now that the time had come to "get laid," as she had so eloquently put it to her sister and friends, she was nervous, and not at all sure this was such a good idea.

Her heart was involved. Taking their relationship to the next level could only spell heartache for her in the end. But she knew if he asked she wouldn't say no.

She loved him, wanted to be with him, always, if she were truthful. But she knew based on past experience that a lifetime of happiness wasn't likely. So she would take what Nick offered, treasure their time together, and face the heartache when it arrived.

Removing her coat, Mia draped it on a nearby chair. Nick was already seated on the sofa, glass of wine in hand. She expected him to be nervous. After all, she was pretty certain that he wasn't that experienced when it came to women. But he sure didn't look nervous. In fact, he seemed a whole lot calmer than she.

"Come sit down, Mia. I thought we'd have a glass of wine, to relax."

Moving to the sofa, Mia sat down beside him, and he handed her a glass of Bordeaux. He must have purchased the wine, because she hadn't any on hand. "Thanks."

"You wore that dress for me tonight, didn't you?"

Her cheeks grew hot at the intensity of his gaze, which was filled with admiration, but there was no sense in denying what was true. "Yes. I wanted to look nice for you."

"It worked. You look incredible, and I want you. Want to take you to bed and make love to you."

"You do? I . . . Uh. I'm not sure what to—"

Taking the glass from her hand, Nick set it down on the coffee table. "Don't try to deny that you feel what's between us, Mia. I know you do. The attraction is too strong to ignore. I've seen the desire in your eyes. You already know you make me hot."

"I do?" He placed her hand on his crotch, and she felt the hard length of him, her eyes widening in surprise as she swallowed. "Oh, right."

Clasping the back of her head, he drew her to him.

"I'm going to kiss you. Stop me now, if this isn't what you want. But I should probably warn you I'll most likely kill myself if you say no."

She couldn't help herself; she smiled. "And here I thought I was the only drama queen."

Their lips melded together, and when Nick thrust his tongue into her mouth, Mia didn't resist. She couldn't have, wouldn't have, if someone had offered her a million dollars at that moment. In fact, she couldn't get enough of Nick's kisses and pressed closer, until she was practically lying on top of him. "Mmmm. You're a good kisser."

"So are you," he replied, his hands moving up and down her back, igniting every one of her nerve endings.

She reached up and removed his glasses. "I think these are steamed up anyway, so let's get rid of them."

Nick didn't think he could get any harder, but he felt like he was about to burst through the zipper of his pants. "Jesus, Mia! You make me crazy. I want you so much. I think I've wanted you from the first moment I saw you, with that banana smeared on your nose. You were so adorable."

"Not my best moment." She caressed his cheek. "Let's go into the bedroom and do this right. I'm too old to make out on the sofa like a horny teenager, and so are you."

He arched a brow. "I was going to suggest the kitchen table."

"That's been done before. It's sacred ground. Mary made me promise not to defile it."

"Mary?" Nick's eyes widened, then he eased into a slow grin. "This apartment has seen its share of action, I'm thinking."

She tugged his hand. "Shall we add our own to it?"

When they entered the bedroom, Mia discovered that she wasn't the least bit nervous anymore. She was also grateful that she'd had the presence of mind to change the sheets and make the bed this morning.

Women's intuition? she wondered.

"I need help with my zipper." Turning her back, Mia filled with anticipation as she waited for Nick to assist her.

He tossed his sports jacket on the chair. "My pleasure," he said, then lowered the zipper, kissing his way down her neck and back, until Mia wanted to scream out in frustration. "You're not wearing a bra."

She smiled at the surprise in his voice and dropped her dress to the floor, then removed her thigh-high stockings, never taking her eyes off him. "That's right. Are you shocked?"

Nick dropped his gaze and stared at the dark patch of curls covering her mound, noting that Mia wasn't wearing any underpants, either, then looked back up at her pert breasts. He lost whatever slim thread he'd been hanging on by. "Jesus!"

Despite her squeals of protest and laughter, he picked Mia up and deposited her in the center of the bed, joining her there.

"Aren't you going to take off your clothes?"

"Yes, but I have something to do first." His lips closed around each of her nipples and he sucked, making Mia gasp aloud in pleasure. Feeling as if she would fly straight to the ceiling, she gripped the sheets to anchor herself.

With a sexy grin, Nick stood, shrugging off his shirt,

then his pants and boxer shorts. Mia's eyes widened at the sight of his erection. And the size!

"I had no idea," she said, unaware she'd spoken her thoughts aloud.

"About what?" He settled in next to Mia, drawing her naked body into his arms.

"Ah, nothing. I can see I'm not the only one full of surprises tonight."

"You talk too much." He kissed her again, deeply and thoroughly, until a deep moan erupted from her throat. Kissing his way down her neck, chest, and abdomen, he paused when he reached the apex of her thighs.

Anticipation had butterfly wings beating wildly in her chest, and Mia sucked in her breath. "Nick," she uttered in a breathless voice that sounded nothing like her own when his mouth settled on her most intimate place and he began tonguing her. "Oh, Jesus!" she cried, feeling her body tighten as he played her like the finest instrument.

When she couldn't stand the delicious torture a moment longer, she wiggled out of his grasp and pushed him to his back, kneeling before him and taking him full in her mouth. Mia had never done this for any other man, but she wanted to do it for Nick, because she loved him.

After a few moments, Nick choked out, "Stop, Mia, or we'll be done before we get started."

Looking up, and noting that his face was bathed in sweat, she smiled wickedly, pleased she'd had the same effect on him. "Paybacks are tough, aren't they?"

With a sexy growl, he covered her body with his own, drawing her legs apart gently and making sure she was ready to receive him. He reached for one of the condoms he'd set on the nightstand and sheathed himself. "I've never wanted any woman the way I want you."

A lump formed in her throat, and she tried hard not to let his words matter. It was just sex talk, she told herself. "Isn't that line pretty standard?"

"Did I tell you that you talk too much?" he said, thrusting his tongue into her mouth, then entering her and replicating the motion with his body.

Mia wrapped her legs about Nick, welcoming him in. She matched him stroke for stroke, kiss for delicious kiss, and their climb to the top was frenetic and quick. With several powerful thrusts, Nick had her climaxing and shouting out his name. A second later he exploded into her.

When she could form a coherent thought, Mia decided two things: Nick had been incredible—the stuff erotic dreams were made of; and she was never going to let him out of her bed, or out of her heart.

"Mia," Nick whispered a few moments later, brushing sweat-dampened curls away from her face. "That was wonderful. You're wonderful."

"I bet you say that to all your bodyguards."

The smile she expected didn't materialize. "I'm being serious, Mia. I— There are things we need to discuss, important things, but I'm not at liberty to reveal them just yet."

At first Mia looked confused, then her face whitened. "Oh my God! You're married, aren't you?" *Please, please, let it be anything but that,* she prayed silently. Twice in one lifetime would be too cruel a joke.

"No!" He shook his head. "I'm not married, or in a relationship with anyone, other than you."

She let loose the breath she'd been holding. "Then what? You look wracked with guilt, Nick. I'm not expecting a marriage proposal because we had sex, if that's what you're worried about. I'm a big girl. I know how the game is played."

"It's not that, Mia. It's just difficult for me to explain. I can't right now. But I want you to know that I care. I care very much."

Mia caressed his cheek, wishing that were true, but knowing it was not. She'd heard that before, from Greg, and it had amounted to a big fat nothing. It was guilt talk, nothing more, so she let him off the hook. "You're worried about your aunt, aren't you? Worried what she might say if she knew what we had done?"

Nick cursed inwardly, and then piled on another lie. "That's part of it. Aunt Bertrice is old-fashioned. Men and women don't do this kind of thing outside of marriage, to her way of thinking."

At his words, Mia filled with resolve to do away with Nick's aunt Bertrice. "Does that mean you don't want to make love again?"

Wrapping his arms about her, Nick drew Mia to his chest and cuddled her. "Hell, no! But I'm starving. Do you think we could make some sandwiches, then pick up later where we left off?"

"It's a blow to my ego that you're so easily lured from my bed by the prospect of eating. If I tried really hard, I could make you forget all about your hunger." She licked the sworl of his ear, then blew into it, smiling when she heard his quick intake of breath.

"You're not playing fair, Miss DeNero."

"I'm very competitive, in case you haven't noticed, Mr. Caruso, and I like to win."

You've won my heart, Nick wanted to tell her, but knew he couldn't.

Not yet.

But soon.

Soon this investigation would be over and he'd be able to tell Mia exactly how he felt about her.

He'd been lonely a long time. Mia had filled up all the empty spaces in his heart, in his life, and made him yearn for things he once thought were impossible, like marriage, family, and happily ever after.

"Once this book is finished I'll—"

She pressed her fingers to his lips. "Don't make promises, Nick. I'm content to live one day at a time. I don't expect anything. It's better that way."

"For now," he agreed, then he kissed her again and they both forgot about pasts, futures, and all that had happened in between.

FIFTEEN

And don't forget to fasten your condom.
Father of the Bride

"Oh, look!" Mia pointed toward the double-hung window that faced the back alley, then rushed toward it. Dark clouds covered the gunmetal sky, making it seem like midnight, instead of eleven o'clock in the morning. "It's snowing, just as the weatherman predicted. The guy finally got something right.

"Good thing we already bought the Christmas tree. Now we can spend the day decorating it." They'd spent the last two days in bed, making love, not bothering to answer the phone, barely bothering to eat, so Mia decided they were making progress.

Not that she was complaining, mind you. The sex had been fabulous. But Christmas was only a few days away, and she'd always put up a tree during the holidays. Life went on, even for those in love.

The small Douglas fir they'd purchased from the local vendor down the street was five feet tall and perfectly formed; it smelled divine. She intended to decorate it in a patriotic theme this year, all red, white, and blue lights and bulbs, with maybe some cranberry garland thrown in, for good measure.

Nick smiled regretfully as carols played softly in the background, hating to disappoint Mia. She had a thing about Christmas, and he knew she'd been looking forward to decorating the tree and the apartment with him.

But he'd spent the last two days neglecting his duties, and he needed to check in with Burt to see if there were any new developments surrounding the investigation. He wanted to wind up the money-laundering inquiry and get on with his life, so he could tell Mia he loved and wanted to marry her.

Though he loved his job, the only regret he had is that his work had kept him from forming any significant relationships, although that could also be blamed on his unwillingness to open himself up to hurt and abandonment. He'd played it safe, but now realized he no longer wanted to.

Mia had changed all that. He wanted a life with her, a family, though he wasn't sure how he would overcome her fear of having children. But, of course, he was jumping the gun.

"That'll be a good job for you to do today, sweetheart. I need to work, or I'm never going to finish this book. And then my publisher will kill me, saving the Mafia the trouble."

"You're always working, Nick. When are you going to let me read your work in progress? I promise I won't be too critical. I have a very good eye for things." He'd been working practically nonstop for weeks. Surely he had something substantial to show for it, so why wouldn't he let her read it?

"I'm sure you do, but I don't have any pages printed out. It's all on disk."

"Isn't that an odd way to work? If it were me, I'd

rather have a printed copy, so I could make changes if I needed to. Why don't you print out a copy, and—"

Nick shook his head. "Why don't you let me finish what I have to do so we can enjoy ourselves later. I promise I'll make it up to you." The look he cast her was purely erotic, and Mia felt her toes, and various other parts, tingle.

"The least you can do is type naked. Then I could get some pleasure out of watching you work."

"You keep looking at me like that and I'm going to ravish you beneath the Christmas tree." He wiggled his brows nefariously.

With a mischievous grin, Mia lifted her sweatshirt to reveal her naked breasts. "Promises, promises."

Nick bolted out of his chair, his ardor quite evident, and Mia squealed when he turned toward her. Just then, a knock sounded on the door.

"Damn!" He bit back a curse. "Wonder who that could be? Whoever it is has pretty rotten timing, that's for sure. What am I supposed to do with this?" He indicated the prominent bulge in his pants and frowned, almost painfully.

"Keep that thought while I answer the door and get rid of whoever it is. A good erection is a terrible thing to waste."

But when Mia opened the door, she found her parents standing on the other side, and knew that she and Nick wouldn't be having mind-numbing sex under the boughs of the Christmas tree any time soon. Which was really a shame because she'd planned to do a rousing Madeline Kahn–type rendition, à la *Young Frankenstein*, of "O Christmas Tree" during climax.

Sam and Rosalie's arms were laden with gaily wrapped

packages, and Rosalie had a red Macy's shopping bag draped around her wrist.

"Hope we're not interrupting," Mia's mother said. "We got worried when you didn't answer your phone, so your father suggested we come over and make sure everything was all right. I bought some ornaments for your tree. Macy's had them on sale yesterday for fifty percent off."

Kissing her mom's cheek, Mia wished she'd had the presence of mind to check in with Rosalie to keep her from worrying. But she really hadn't been thinking about anything or anyone besides Nick, who looked as disappointed as she felt.

Pasting on a smile, she welcomed her parents inside, shaking the snow off their coats and hanging them on the hall tree. "We were just about to decorate the tree," she explained.

"It's a nice one," Sam said, perusing the evergreen from top to bottom. "Though I don't know why you want to bother with fresh every year. The fake ones are just as nice. And you don't have all those damn needles everywhere."

Mia made a face. "Next year I'm going to go into the countryside and cut one down at a tree farm." But then she remembered that Nick wouldn't be here next year to share in the fun, and her smile disappeared.

Suddenly the prospect of celebrating the holidays, celebrating anything without Nick, was too hideous to even consider. She didn't want a life without Nick in it.

Dammit! She'd been hoping he would confess his love for her, so she could do the same. Once that happened, she might actually put forth the idea of them getting married to gauge his reaction. She knew it was a bit unorthodox for the woman to bring up the subject, especially a woman who'd found the word *marriage* abhorrent. But things had changed. She wanted to be with Nick, always, and he might never get around to asking Mia to spend her life with him.

After her first experience with falling in love, she didn't think she would ever want marriage. She'd been young and naïve back then, more in lust than in love with an older man. Now she knew for certain that it was Nick who was her soul mate. She still didn't want to have kids—big chicken that she was—but having Nick for a husband had suddenly become very appealing.

Why didn't he tell her he loved her? They'd been intimate, grown very close, revealing details about their pasts—she'd even told him about pouring glue in Angela's hair. Though the one thing she hadn't confided in him was about Greg Farris. The time had never seemed right.

So why didn't Nick say the words she longed to hear?

Because he doesn't feel the same way you do, Mia.

"What's wrong, dear? You look preoccupied about something." Rosalie seated herself at the kitchen table, while Sam stayed in the living room to keep Nick company. "You and Nick aren't having a fight, are you? Maybe we should go."

"No, Mom, it's nothing like that."

"Do you have your period? I always got out of sorts during my monthly. It's the hormones, you know."

Sighing, Mia seated herself next to her mother. "It's not that, Mom."

"Well, it's something. And unless I miss my guess it has to do with that man you've been guarding. You're in love with Nick, aren't you?"

Mia glanced into the other room, relieved to see Nick and her father occupied in front of the television set with the volume blaring. "Does it show?"

"I'm your mother. I'm trained to know these things. So what are you going to do about it?"

"I think we've had this talk once before, Mom."

Rosalie nodded. "About the Perillo woman. And the advice is the same: you go after what you want, and you let nothing stand in your way until you get it."

"I was hoping Nick would confess his love for me, but he hasn't. I need to be sure about his feelings. I feel so frustrated I've actually thought about proposing, just to see what his reaction would be."

Rosalie's eyes widened at the admission. "I don't want to be nosy and butt into your personal"—translation: sex—"life, dear, but if you and that handsome man aren't having relations, I'll be quite surprised. How can you make love with a man and not know if he loves you back? It's in his touch, his kiss, every word he whispers."

"Jesus, Ma! You've been watching too much *Oprah*."

Rosalie smiled. "I've been around a long time, Mia. I know you and your sister don't believe this, but I know something about love."

Mia rolled her eyes. "If you start singing 'If that guy gets into your blood, go out and get him,' I'm leaving."

"Oh, there's a song like that?"

"Don't play innocent with me, Rosalie DeNero. I know you watch *Ally McBeal*."

"Not so much, anymore. I don't like it now that Billy's dead."

"So you think I should just go for it with Nick?"

"You almost gave your life for the man. What else do you have to lose, except the man himself?"

"I hate it when you're right."

Rosalie smiled softly and patted her daughter's hand. "I know, dear. So does your father."

"Nick is holding back. He told me he cares, but that there are things standing in his way."

Worry filled Rosalie's eyes. "His elderly aunt?"

Mia shrugged. "I don't know. He wouldn't elaborate." And she'd been wondering about his enigmatic statement ever since.

There was a lot about Nick that made her wonder. Sometimes he sounded like a nerd, other times cool and macho. He certainly was commanding in bed. He made love like a man with vast experience, not like someone who didn't date much, as he'd claimed. He was always working on his book, but she'd never seen any results of those efforts.

Mia sighed. Obviously, she was starting to get paranoid.

"Your father thinks Nick is hiding something. I know Sam is suspicious about most things—it's the cop in him—but sometimes his instincts are right on target."

Her father thought that? Though Mia made a mental note to ask him about it later, she felt the need to defend Nick. "What could Nick be hiding? He sits in front of his computer all day, working on his book, or checking stock quotes.

"The only person I've seen him talking to since he arrived, and with whom I'm not very well acquainted, is his friend, Burt Mulrooney. And he certainly seems harmless enough. In fact, I like Burt. He's a movie nut, just like me."

"What does his friend do for a living?"

"I'm not sure. I think he might be a journalist, or used to be, at any rate."

"You and Nick haven't known each other that long, Mia. Perhaps you should take things more slowly and disregard what I told you before. I don't want to see you get hurt again."

Perhaps, but things were already careening out of control at a breakneck pace, like a runaway train that couldn't stop, and Mia didn't know how to put on the brakes.

The Christmas tree was lit, its colorful lights twinkling, the Pillsbury cinnamon rolls were baking in the oven, smelling like manna from heaven, and Mia was seated on the floor at the foot of the tree, waiting impatiently for Nick to open his present.

"I hope you like it. I promise it's not another pair of leather pants, though I was tempted. You do look hot in leather."

"Too bad you didn't buy them. I was thinking about going for the Val Kilmer look," he teased, tearing off the wrapping paper. Nick opened the box and discovered a handsome brown leather-bound set of the works of William Shakespeare, and his eyes widened in appreciation and gratitude. It was a thoughtful gift, and one he would treasure always.

"I tried to find something for your home library. I'm sure you have a huge one." Her cheeks filled with color. "Library, I mean. Stop looking at me like that. It's not nice to have dirty thoughts on Christmas morning. This is a religious holiday, after all."

Nick laughed. "I love the books, sweetheart. Thank you. I've always wanted a set of Shakespeare. How did you know? It's the perfect gift."

She smiled happily. "I just figured that authors read a

lot, and that every library should contain Shakespeare. I think someone made a rule about that eons ago."

Reaching under the tree, Nick handed Mia a red foil-wrapped box. "My gift is a bit more selfish, but I hope you like it anyway."

"Selfish? How so?" Intrigued, Mia ripped at the paper, her eyes widening when she pulled back the tissue to find the teddies and thong underpants that Nick had supposedly purchased for his aunt on their shopping expedition. "You tricked me, Nick Caruso, making me think this lingerie was for your aunt. I should have known better, but you lied so convincingly."

Nick blushed as the truth of her words hit home. "I can't wait to see you in them. And out of them. Especially out of them." He wiggled his eyebrows suggestively. "Now would be a good time, in fact."

"You're as randy as a goat. But I guess I'll have to put up with you since it's snowed nearly a foot overnight, and we won't be going anywhere any time soon."

"I don't mind if you don't. I'd much rather stay inside where it's warm. I can't get my fill of you, Mia. I . . . I . . ."

Say it! Say it, Mia willed. But he didn't declare his love. With a frustrated sigh, she replied, "Well, if we're feeling really adventurous, I suppose we can go outside later and build a snowman."

"And pretend that he is Parson Brown?"

" 'He'll say are you married we'll say no man . . .' "

Embarrassment stained Mia's cheeks once again as she sang the rest of the lyrics to herself. "I thought we'd build a lady snowman, a snowwoman, just to give our side equal recognition."

"I think I'd rather stay in bed and snuggle under the

covers with you. It sounds far more appealing, and I won't run the risk of getting frostbite."

The prospect of making love with Nick had Mia getting excited all over again. How was it that just a simple look, a phrase, could get her all hot and bothered? No man had ever had this effect on her before. She supposed the fact that she loved him had something to do with all those raging pheromones that were multiplying at an alarming rate.

"I refuse to let my culinary talents go to waste, just to satisfy your carnal urges. Let's eat breakfast first."

"Opening a container of refrigerated rolls can hardly be called culinary talent. What would dear Martha think if she knew?"

"If Martha Stewart had spent as much time in bed as I have lately, she wouldn't give a damn about making all those stupid homemade confections. She wouldn't have the time, or the inclination, and neither did I. So be happy you're getting rolls and shut up."

Nick threw back his head and laughed, and the deep, rich sound sent tingles down Mia's spine. "You know, you look damn good in that apron. Very domesticated."

She tossed him an annoyed look. "Like a cat?"

"Cats don't wear T-shirts, or have as nice legs as you do. Plus, you're a lot less furry. I'm thinking you should take off that T-shirt and put on just the apron. We could play restaurant. I'll be the customer and tell you in graphic detail what I'd like to eat."

Mia threw the dishtowel at Nick and hit him square in the face. "You're shameless! What a disgusting thing to say on Christmas morning."

She bent over the oven to take out the rolls and a moment later felt Nick pressed up behind her. "Did I explain the advantages of having just an apron on?" he whispered in her ear, raising gooseflesh on her arms. "The bib goes in the front, and—"

Turning, Mia shoved a warm roll into Nick's mouth to keep him from continuing. "Time for breakfast." She smiled, wondering if things would always be this fun and romantic between them. But then she remembered that Nick would be leaving once his book was finished, and her heart twisted painfully.

Seating herself at the table, she picked up her coffee cup, hoping she looked far more nonchalant than she felt when she asked, "Are you almost done with your book?"

Nick reached for the pitcher of orange juice and filled both glasses. "Almost, but not quite. Why?"

"I was just thinking that you'll be leaving once it's finished and you've turned it in to your publisher. I mean, you won't have any further need for protection."

"But I'll always have need for you, Mia. I told you, I care about you, a lot."

"Then let's get married!" she blurted, and Nick spewed orange juice all over the kitchen floor.

He looked at Mia to see if she was serious. "Married! You want to get married?"

Mia shrugged, suddenly feeling stupid for mentioning such a thing. Obviously, Nick didn't feel the same way, just as she'd feared. He'd turned as white as the snow falling outside the window. She tried to cover her mistake and forced a smile. "Gotcha! I was only joking."

Nick smiled, too, but only halfheartedly, unsure if she was telling him the truth. "Mia, I told you before that there were things I couldn't—"

"I was joking, okay? Just drop it and eat your breakfast rolls before they get cold. I'll make some scrambled eggs to go with them." She stood and crossed to the stove, praying Nick wouldn't follow her. She'd made a mess of things, that was for damn sure.

But, of course, that was nothing new. Mia was the champion when it came to screwing up her life, and every good thing that happened to her. Why couldn't she just be happy with the way things were and leave it at that? Why did she feel compelled to propose marriage and ruin things?

Stupid, stupid, Mia!

"Are you okay?"

Turning to face him, she pasted on a smile filled with happiness she didn't feel. "I'm great. How many eggs do you want?"

"Two, I guess. So, you were only kidding?" Relief welled up inside Nick, as well as disappointment. Marriage meant commitment, and right now, he wasn't in a position to offer Mia that. But someday soon he would.

Mia lied through her teeth. "I told you a long time ago, Nick, that I have no interest in settling down, getting married, or having kids. That's just not who I am."

"Then, who are you?"

"I'm the woman who saved your life and wants to go outside and make a snowwoman, hopefully in her own likeness, and who insists that you accompany her. That's who I am." *I'm also the woman who's dying inside.*

"You're beautiful, courageous, and incredibly sexy, so I won't be a spoilsport and thwart your plans. I figure when we get back inside we can jump in the shower and heat things up again."

"Aren't you forgetting one small thing?"

He shook his head. "I stocked up on condoms."

"Dinner at my parents'. They'll be expecting us at

noon." Mia plopped the scrambled eggs down on Nick's plate and watched his self-confident grin deflate. She couldn't help but feel the tiniest bit of satisfaction. Looked like they'd both be doing a bit of crying tonight.

SIXTEEN

*The greatest trick the devil ever pulled
was convincing the world he didn't exist.*
The Usual Suspects

"They're running a chop shop. I haven't been able to find out more than that. My source tells me Calzone is definitely behind the operation. Vincent Palumbo's the brain and Pauley's the messenger, just like we figured. I guess it's time to take action."

Burt sounded tired, and Nick hoped he was taking care of himself. Without Nick watching over his shoulder, his friend was no doubt eating and drinking too much and not taking his vitamins. "How does Graziano fit in?" he asked, peeking into the bedroom to find Mia still asleep, and then shutting the door behind him as quietly as he could, so as not to awaken her.

"He's the patsy. My best guess is that Graziano's been set up to take the fall. Poor bastard probably doesn't suspect a thing. These guys are his best friends. Some friends."

"Are you confident that your source is telling the truth?" Nick didn't put a lot of faith in jailhouse snitches. Most were only out to save their own asses. "Snitches have been known to lie."

239

"Calzone screwed him out of some money a few months back, revolving around a stolen computer scam he'd been running. The guy wants revenge. He also wants to lessen his prison term. He got caught, Calzone didn't, and he's pissed."

"To get the goods on Calzone and the others, we need someone on the inside. We're not getting enough information to make a case stick."

"Yeah, that was my feeling, too. Guess I could volunteer. I don't know a hell of a lot about cars, but . . ."

Nick heard the hesitation in Mulrooney's voice, the dread, and couldn't bring himself to ask it of him. Burt was nearing retirement age and getting too old to bust the bad guys. "Thanks, but I'm not sure you'd be right for this job, Burt. We need someone they wouldn't suspect, and your profile at O'Grady's is pretty high. Someone might recognize you and put two and two together."

"Well, shit! As much as I hate to admit it, I'm relieved. My ex-wife has agreed to see me. Muriel's a widow now, and we're going to have dinner next week."

Nick arched a brow, surprised by the revelation. "You think you two will get back together?"

"Doubtful," Burt said, and he could almost see him shrug. "But we might become friends, and that would be good enough for me. Ain't no fun growing old alone, I can tell you that much, boyo."

Nick had already formed that conclusion. He'd been alone all of his life, and now he didn't have to be; he had Mia. "I'm happy for you, Burt. I hope things work out for you and Muriel. I always thought you made a nice couple."

"Thanks. Now, getting back to our problem. What

about trying to get Graziano to cooperate? Surely he'll be pissed off when he discovers what his friends have been up to. I know if it were me, I'd be tempted to blow off their balls."

"I've thought about that. But what if loyalty to his childhood friends overrides Alfredo's anger and he tells them what we're up to? That would ruin months of hard work." Nick took a moment, then said, "Let me think about this further before making a final decision. I don't want to fuck it up now."

"Well, whatever it is you decide, you need to act fast," the older agent said, concern peppering his words. "Time's running out, Nick. Higgins has been asking a lot of questions about the way you've been handling the investigation. He might be getting ready to pull you off the case." Burt continued on quickly to forestall Nick's argument. "He hasn't said as much, but when SAC Higgins gets antsy that's usually his M.O."

Nick knew Burt was right and cursed beneath his breath, damning Higgins for his impatience and unwillingness to allow him to use his own judgment, just because he'd made one mistake.

This investigation had been his from the get-go, and he had no intention of letting Higgins foul it up. "That's not going to happen. I finish what I start, you know that."

"Then finish it. Your mind's been on other things lately. You need to refocus."

Unable to comprehend what he was hearing, Nick replied in an accusatory tone, "You're the one who told me to take it easy over the holidays. Remember?"

"Yeah, but since when do you ever listen to me? Besides, by now whoever shot at you has to be thinking they scared you off. They're bound to let down their guard a bit."

"Nick, who are you talking to?"

Mia's voice floated through the bedroom door, and Nick covered the phone's mouthpiece with his hand. "I gotta go, Burt. I'll call when I can."

Clicking off, he stuck his phone in his pants pocket, opened the door, and pasted on an innocent smile. "Hey, sleepyhead. I was wondering when you were going to wake up. How are you feeling?" Mia had complained of a headache last night, and she didn't look much better this morning.

Mia snuggled deeper under the covers. "You keep me up all night. I need my sleep. What's for breakfast? I'm starving."

Well, at least she hadn't lost her appetite. Mia could eat most men under the table. "There's no milk, eggs, or bread. I'm going to the market and pick up a few items we need. Then I'll fix you my special pancakes. The one thing we have is plenty of maple syrup."

Mia grew instantly alarmed at Nick's plan, and shook her head. "No, absolutely not, Nick! I don't want you going out alone. It's too dangerous. Just give me a second to get dressed, and I'll come with you."

"You told me last night that you weren't feeling well and might be coming down with a cold. I don't want you outside in this nasty weather. You'll only make yourself worse."

"But I'm your bodyguard." She sneezed. "And I take my job very seriously." She sneezed again, wiping her nose on the bed sheet and making Nick cringe. "I can't let you go alone."

"Bless you. Now, quit worrying. I'll be fine. It'll only take a few minutes to walk down to the corner market. I won't be long, I promise." He leaned over the bed and kissed her forehead. "Be good while I'm gone, and miss me."

"You know I will. Please be careful. I'll be worried the entire time you're gone." *If anything happened to Nick . . .* The thought was too hideous to even consider. She wouldn't think such a thing; it was bad luck. He'll be all right. He had to be. She wasn't finished with Nick Caruso yet. She never would be.

After the door closed behind him, Mia heaved a sigh and dragged herself out of bed. Feeling the beginnings of another headache coming on, she hoped she wasn't coming down with the flu and headed for the bathroom and some Tylenol.

Tugging on her new robe—a Christmas gift from her parents, which she'd promised her mother she would wear—Mia spied her computer in the corner of the room and decided that Nick's absence had provided the perfect time to check her E-mail, which she hadn't done in days.

She was expecting a note from her old college buddy, Stef Ann, who still lived in Boston. Mia and Stef had had some pretty good times at Boston College—too good, if she was truthful—and her grades had suffered because of it. Stef wanted Mia to come for a visit, but Mia hadn't been able to afford it, and now that she could, she just plain didn't want to go off and leave Nick.

Independence didn't seem quite as important to her anymore. She was enjoying being part of a couple, a half to a whole relationship. Mary had been right in that prediction, as had Annie, because Mia loved waking up next to Nick every morning and feeling his body pressed against hers.

He made her feel safe and secure, which was odd, since she was the one who'd been hired to protect him.

Turning on the computer, Mia waited for it to boot up. And waited. And waited. But, of course, her computer had a mind of its own and wouldn't cooperate. "Damn stupid thing! You never work when I need you to." She banged on it. Her theory being: when all else fails, beat it to death. Only that didn't work, either.

The computer was dead. All that was left was a proper burial.

Damn! How was she going to check her stocks this morning? She'd bet Nick ten bucks that Gateway had risen overnight—another one of her gut feelings—and she had no intention of losing that bet.

Entering the living room, she stared longingly at Nick's computer and wondered if she dared use it. The temptation was strong. He had booted it up and left it on—a rarity in itself. Nick never left the room without shutting down his computer—and it looked to be working just fine.

Glancing at the front door, she mentally calculated how much time she would have until he got back. She didn't want him to catch her borrowing his precious computer. The man was anal about other people using his stuff. Obviously, his aunt Bertrice hadn't taught him to share as a child.

Creeping closer until she was standing right in front of it, Mia looked down at the laptop and bit her lip, pondering. Should she, or shouldn't she? Nick would never know. She would just spend a few minutes on the Internet, get her mail, check the stocks, then put everything back exactly as she had found it.

Finally deciding that she *should*, Mia sat down at Nick's makeshift desk. Since his arrival she'd avoided his workspace, mostly at Nick's insistence. He'd demanded absolutely privacy regarding his work in progress, and she'd grudgingly stuck by her word not to trespass.

Mia's forehead wrinkled in confusion at the absence of notes, papers, and all the usual clutter surrounding a workstation. Nick was certainly the tidiest author she had ever come across, not that she'd met any before him.

There were a few research books on organized crime and the like, but they looked brand-new, like they'd never been opened. She picked one up off the top of the pile, noting that the spine hadn't been broken, and thought it odd that anyone could read a book or take notes from it without breaking the spine. Of course, most people weren't as persnickety as Nick, who probably still had the plastic coverings on his lampshades at home.

Staring at the computer screen, Mia noticed several unlabeled yellow folders and was immediately filled with curiosity as to what they contained.

Nick's book, perhaps?

She knew it would be an invasion of his privacy if she peeked in them, and she had promised, but somehow that wasn't reason enough to deter her.

Just click on AOL and forget about the other, Mia, she told herself. *Don't go back on your word.*

But I just want to take a peek, to see what Nick's writing is like, then I promise to quit.

You're asking for trouble, her conscience rudely informed her. *Stop now, before it's too late!*

But, of course, Mia rarely listened to her conscience, and clicked open the first folder.

Nick entered Ming's Mini-Mart to find the place deserted, due to the inclement weather, which wasn't fit for man or beast, only besotted FBI agents.

Ming's was the first Asian-American–owned market to debut in Little Italy, so Nick figured the hardworking guy would be open for business, bad weather or not.

Walking about the store, green plastic basket in hand, he gathered the foodstuffs he needed, noting that the shelves were almost empty of merchandise.

Snowstorms had a way of instilling fear into the hearts of Baltimoreans, who had probably rushed out to their neighborhood grocery stores at the weatherman's first prediction of snow.

Nick managed to find a quart of milk—the last one in the refrigerated case—bread, and the other essential items he had come for. Locating the drug section, he picked up cold medication and extra tissues for Mia, then headed to the checkout counter, where he spied a heart-shaped, red satin box of chocolates.

It was a bit early for Valentine's Day, but he decided he would buy them anyway, to perk up Mia's spirits. Women went nuts over chocolate, and he knew his lovely bodyguard had a sweet tooth.

Handing a twenty-dollar bill to the red-haired, pimply faced boy behind the counter, he waited for his change, not noticing the two men who had entered the store and were walking up behind him.

"Hey, Nick! Is that you?"

He turned to find Alfredo Graziano, his weathered

face wreathed in smiles. "Nick's an author," Alfredo explained to the shorter man standing next to him—Pauley Buttoni, suspect number two in the investigation.

As dapper as Alfredo looked in his black cashmere overcoat, Buttoni looked just the opposite, wearing a tattered blue parka that had seen better days. You'd think with all the money he'd been skimming off the car dealership that he could afford better threads, Nick thought.

Nick cursed his bad luck. He didn't want to engage Buttoni in conversation, didn't want to make the man any more suspicious of him than he was already, but he had no choice. Alfredo was grinning and urging him forward. He just prayed Buttoni wasn't armed.

Gut instinct told him that Buttoni, or one of his paid henchmen, was responsible for the failed hit on Nick's alter ego, and the one who would pay for injuring Mia.

"Hello, Mr. Graziano," he said, smiling at the older man. "Nice to see you again."

"Pauley, this is Nick Caruso. He's the one I told you was writing a book on the Mafia."

Pauley nodded at Nick in a perfunctory way. "So what kinds of things are you finding out?" he wanted to know, trying not to appear too interested, but failing. Nick decided the man looked nervous.

"Not as much as I'd like. Just the information I've gleaned off the Internet and gathered from the library."

The mobster looked relieved. "Probably better for your health. I hear those mafioso types don't like their business messed with."

"I've already explained that to Nick. He understands the way things work. Right, Nick?"

"I certainly do. I understand perfectly."

"So where's Mia?" the older man asked, glancing about the store. "I thought you two were joined at the hip."

"She's got a cold, so I volunteered to come down to the market. The storm left us short of provisions."

"Tell her that we've been very busy at Lucky Louie's, and if she decides to change professions and needs a part-time job, I can put her on. The pay's not great, but it's safer than doing what she's doing. I made her the offer a while back, but she never got back to me on it."

"What's this broad doing that's so risky, Al?" Pauley asked, biting into a candy bar he had yet to pay for.

"Mia is Nick's bodyguard. He hired her to protect him, while he's working on his book."

Pauley threw back his head and laughed. "No shit! You got a woman bodyguard? Don't say much for your masculinity, if you don't mind my saying so, Caruso."

Rather than be insulted, Nick was delighted at the man's conclusion and tried to further it by assuming a mild-mannered posture. If Buttoni thought he wasn't a threat, he'd leave him and Mia alone. "I'm not very good with fisticuffs or weapons. I can't abide violence."

"Fisticuffs?" Pauley's brows wrinkled, making him look like a ferret. "What the shit does that mean?"

"Nick means that he doesn't like to fight. And I don't blame him one bit," Alfredo explained.

Pauley knocked his friend on the arm. "You've become a pussy since you got engaged to that Gallagher woman, Al. She must be good in the sack, huh?" He raised his brows up and down, like they were sharing a good joke.

But Alfredo didn't think it was one bit funny and stiffened, his eyes darkening dangerously. "Don't talk like that about my fiancée, Pauley. I don't like it. Show some respect. Lenore is a fine woman. And she's going to be my wife. *Capisce?*"

"Sure. Sure, Al. Don't get your shorts twisted. I didn't mean nothing by it. I like your old lady just fine, you know that."

Nick listened intently to the exchange and felt like smiling. For the first time since the investigation began, he felt certain Alfredo wasn't involved, and that the older man would probably do anything to protect the woman he loved from the harsh realities of life, especially with regard to organized crime.

"I'd better be getting back to Mia. She needs this cold medicine," Nick said, eager to think this latest development through and formulate a plan.

"Give Mia my love." Alfredo held out his hand to shake Nick's. "And don't forget to tell her about the job offer."

"I won't forget." In fact, Mia might be just the ticket to getting what he needed, he thought, hurrying out of the store and sucking in his breath when the cold wind hit him smack in the face.

He headed for home, and Mia.

"You bastard! You lying, conniving, cheating, underhanded, smooth-talking, imposter-of-a-bastard!"

Mia continued to read the pages within the file, unable to believe what her eyes were telling her: Alfredo Graziano, that sweet man, whom she adored—Mary's uncle, no less!—was a suspect in a money-laundering scheme, and was being investigated by none other than FBI Agent Nick Caruso.

FBI Agent. FBI Agent. FBI Agent.

The words echoed around in her head, until she could no longer stand it. Her heart hurt so much she thought it would burst from her chest.

"Bastard!" Mia reached for the tissue in her pocket and blew her nose, then wiped her eyes.

How could she have been so stupid? To think she'd gone to bed with an imposter, a liar, a man who claimed to have cared for her.

A man she loved.

History repeats itself, Mia. And she couldn't decide which instance was worse.

"Ha! You never learn, do you, Mia?"

Stupid, stupid, Mia!

It was all so crystal clear now why a man like Nick would walk into the office of an inexperienced body-guard such as herself, and hire Mia right on the spot, without checking references—not that she had any—without knowing she could actually do the job. Well, at least she had proven herself in that respect; she'd saved the bloody bastard's worthless life.

Her inexperience and stupidity are what drew him to use her. She was the perfect person to dupe—so trusting, so naïve, so *STUPID*! And what made matters worse was that she'd had her suspicions, knew something wasn't quite right. But she'd let her love for Nick blind her.

This was what Nick had alluded to all those weeks ago, the big mystery as to why he couldn't commit. As if he ever intended to. The bastard!

Mia heard Nick's key turn in the lock. Rising to her feet, she braced herself for what was to come, slamming down the lid to the computer, and her feelings for him as well.

Fool me once, she told herself. *Well, not anymore. Mia DeNero is no longer anyone's fool.*

Wearing a huge grin when he saw Mia, and holding a bag filled with groceries, Nick hung his jacket on the hall tree and moved toward her. "Hi, sweetheart! How are you feeling?"

"I feel like shit, if you want to know the truth, Nick. And do you know why?"

The animosity in her voice confused him, but he passed it off to her not feeling well. "Because you have a headache? Your eyes are watering. I bought some tissues." He reached into the bag and handed her the box, which she promptly threw back at him, almost hitting his head.

"Hey! What's wrong?"

"My eyes aren't watering, you bastard. I've been crying. And do you know why, Nick? Do you have any idea why I've been crying?"

Nick shook his head, but an uneasy feeling was beginning to form in the pit of his stomach. "Because you were worried about me?"

She laughed, but there was no humor in it. "Oh, that's rich. Why should I be worried about you, Nick? I'm betting you know how to take real good care of yourself."

Glancing toward his computer, Nick saw that it was shut and almost breathed a sigh of relief, until he remembered that he had forgotten to turn it off after calling Burt. He searched Mia's face, noting the pain in her eyes, and knew the gig was up.

"Mia, I can explain."

"Save it. I just want you to get out. Pack up your stuff and get out of my apartment. The sooner the better."

The charade no longer necessary, he removed his glasses and tossed them aside. "I can't do that."

Her eyes widened. "What do you mean you can't do that? Of course you can, Agent Caruso. I'll help you." She rushed into the kitchen, grabbed some grocery bags, and began clearing off his desk, dumping everything that wasn't nailed down into them.

Nick moved forward and clasped her wrist. "Stop, Mia! If you know who I am, and why I had to lie, then you know that I can't leave just yet. We're very close to breaking open this case."

"How could you think Uncle Alfredo was involved in something so nefarious? The man is a *mensch*. He always has a kind word for everyone, goes out of his way to be helpful. I adore him."

"Alfredo's penchant for bragging about his connections to the Mafia raised suspicions down at the Bureau when they got wind of a money-laundering operation going on here in Little Italy. The leads led us to Lucky Louie's, which, as you know, is partly owned by Alfredo. So naturally he became a prime suspect."

She dug in her heels, her expression mutinous. "I won't help you destroy him."

"I have no intention of doing that. I don't believe Alfredo's involved. I did at first, but now I know differently. Let's sit down and talk about this. I'll try to explain everything, okay?"

"Oh yeah. I'd love to hear all about how you just had to make love to me to further your investigation, Agent Caruso. I'm sure that'll be interesting. And then maybe you can confess why it is you told me that you cared. You must have been laughing down your sleeve at my stupidity."

"I do care, dammit! Mia, please believe—"

"Shut up, Nick! Just shut the hell up. I don't believe anything you say. But I'll listen to your story about why you felt it was necessary to hire me. I've always been fond of fiction. And you are . . . *were* . . . a writer, after all."

SEVENTEEN

Shame on me for kissing you
with my eyes closed too tight.
That Thing You Do

Arms crossed over her chest in defiant posture, Mia sat on the couch, still as a corpse, her expression unreadable, and waited for Nick to spin his tale of deceit. She had no intention of forgiving him for what he'd done, but she was curious to know why.

Why he'd broken her heart the way he did.

Jesus! Two times in one lifetime. She was a magnet for creeps.

After listening to his feeble explanation, she would kick him out of her home, and her life. Mia never wanted to see Nick Caruso again, as painful as that prospect was.

"Are you just going to sit there and sweat?" She'd never seen a man look so nervous—except maybe when her father caught Jack Ratz with his pants down—which made her feel a teensy bit better. Maybe Nick had a conscience. And maybe pigs really did fly. "Or are you going to explain why you used me? I'm eager to hear what you have to say." *Here comes lie number sixteen hundred and fifty-three,* she thought, steeling herself for what was to come.

Wiping sweating palms on his jeans, Nick took a deep

254

breath and began to explain. "I needed access to Alfredo Graziano, to set up surveillance. Your connection to the family through your sister and friends, as well as your apartment's proximity to Mama Sophia's, were my reasons for choosing you."

Mia tried to keep her voice even, determined not to give him the satisfaction of knowing how he had wounded her. "So I was convenient, is that it?"

His voice held regret. "In a manner of speaking, yes."

A watermelon-sized lump rose in her throat, and Mia balled her hands into fists, so she wouldn't lash out with more than her tongue. She didn't like being anyone's convenience, especially after what she and Nick had . . .

"Everything you told me about yourself—your background, your aunt, your books—they were all lies, weren't they? I don't really know you at all, do I, Nick?" And that hurt. That hurt very much.

"It wasn't all a lie. I was raised an orphan, just as I said, but I don't have an Aunt Bertrice. I wish I had. I've been alone all my life."

She harrumphed. "No surprise there, not the way you treat people. Have you always been a callous bastard, or is that an acquired trait?"

Nick winced, his eyes filling with sadness, and for a moment Mia almost felt sorry for him. *Almost.* Until she remembered what a consummate actor he was. "I never meant to hurt you, Mia. I wanted to explain, but I couldn't. You know how I feel about you. I—"

She held up her hand. "Don't you dare confess feelings for me now. Do you hear me, Nick? I am through listening to your lies and half-truths. I've been down this road before. Just stick to the facts of this so-called investigation of yours and leave anything personal out of it."

"Mia, please!" He rubbed the back of his neck, trying to ease the tension the situation had created. "I can't do that. You've got to understand. I had a job to do. I never meant for our relationship to go so far. It just happened. *We* happened. And I won't apologize for—"

"Screwing me? Using me under false pretenses? You lied to everyone, Nick, used all of us shamelessly. Didn't you stop to think what you were doing to my family? They cared about you, believed you, as I did, and you betrayed their trust, and mine."

"I'm sorry. Truly."

"Don't expect me to forgive you, because I won't. You and I are done. Finished. Kaput. End of story. Not that we had much of a story to begin with, nothing real, at any rate. It was all just a piece of fiction, without the happy ending."

"I love you, Mia."

Pain knifed through Mia, twisting in her gut like a jagged-edged blade, and she lashed out, slapping Nick's face as hard as she could, the sound reverberating off the walls, and the chambers of her heart. With the exception of bodyguard training, she had never struck another human being before, especially someone she cared about. But Nick had hurt her deeply, cruelly. "Don't you dare say that, not now."

She bit her lower lip, trying to get her emotions in check. "I hate you, Nick. Do you understand? I hate you for what you did to me." *If only that were true,* Mia thought with great sadness, unable to turn her feelings off quite so easily.

But in time she would learn. She would learn not to trust, to wear her heart on her sleeve, to accept people at

face value. In time Nick Caruso would become an unpleasant memory, like the other unpleasant memory she
had stored in her heart.

Angela had tried to warn her not to be so gullible, but
she hadn't listened, and now she had learned a painful
lesson, the way she'd learned all of her lessons: hard.

Nick rubbed his burning cheek, and Mia felt remorse.
It was on the tip of her tongue to apologize, but she refused to listen to her conscience. He deserved every bit of
her wrath, and more.

"I'm starting to get the picture."

"My father suspected there was something fishy about
you. As much as he liked and respected you, Sam still
had doubts. Wait until I tell him, tell everyone about
your real motives for coming to Little Italy. Won't they
be surprised? I can't wait to hear what Sophia Russo
has to say. I wouldn't want to be in your shoes when she
finds out. The woman gives new meaning to the word
vengeance."

"You can't tell anyone, Mia. Doing so would corrupt
the investigation, and I can't allow that. What we're doing is too important, and it must be done in secrecy."

Her eyes widened in disbelief, then she smiled spite-
fully. "What are you going to do, Nick? Have me
arrested?"

"If I have to, but I'm hoping it won't come to that."

"Bastard! Go ahead. Arrest me." She held her hands
out in front of her. "And when I get in front of your supe-
riors I'm going to tell them how you violated not only my
trust, but my person as well. I doubt it's in the FBI
manual to fuck the hired help."

Nick reeled as if he'd been slapped again. "First of all,
I didn't fuck you. I made love to you, Mia. There's a big

difference. And secondly, instead of being vindictive and trying to ruin my career, why don't you use the training you've received and put it to good use?"

"What are you talking about?"

"I want you to become involved in this operation. You're capable, have proven yourself, and you're smart. I can use your help, if you're willing."

Mia's heart rate quickened. There it was, tossed out like forbidden fruit—the chance to prove herself, the opportunity to do something important and worthwhile with her life, and make everyone—her father—proud.

Her curiosity was piqued. And damn that curiosity, which was what had created this whole mess to begin with. Sometimes ignorance really was bliss. "Involved in what way?"

"Normally I wouldn't ask—I really don't want to put you at risk. And there will be a certain amount of risk; you should know that going in. I want you to go undercover as an employee of Lucky Louie's Auto World. I need someone on the inside that I can trust, someone with computer experience, and I'm positive they won't suspect a woman."

Her mouth dropped open, then she said, "Weren't you listening, Nick? I told you I won't do anything to hurt Uncle Alfredo, not even for the FBI, and especially not for you."

"You'll be doing it with his blessing. I ran into Alfredo while I was at the market. He said to tell you that there's a job opening at the car dealership. He wants to hire you, if you're interested. Said he made you the offer once before."

"He did." Her brow wrinkled in confusion. "Then he knows who you really are?"

"No, of course not. His offer was just coincidental. But he will. We're going over to his house to talk to him, as soon as we're done here. There are things he needs to know about his business partner and boyhood friends. I think once he hears what they've been up to, who they're working with, he'll be only too willing to help us."

"You're awfully quick to be throwing around *we* and *us*. Why should I believe anything you say? How do I know you are who you say you are? You showed me a fake ID once before."

"No, I didn't. Niccolò Caruso is my real name. I just neglected to show you my FBI credentials when we first met, for obvious reasons." He reached into his back pocket and pulled out a black wallet, handing it to her.

Mia studied the official badge, the photo of the man she had come to love, and heaved a sigh, tossing it back at him. "What will people think if I suddenly show up at Lucky Louie's? I'm supposed to be working for Nick Caruso, the author, remember?"

"You'll tell them that my book is done, and that I no longer have need of your services."

Mia winced. "Well, that much is true, isn't it?"

"No, Mia, it's not. Once this investigation is over—"

"We're over and done, Nick. I could never trust you again. Not after the way you used me. If I decide to help you, and that's a big *if*, depending on whether or not Uncle Alfredo decides to go along with this scheme of yours, after this investigation is over I never want to see you again. Do you understand?" It was the only way she could protect herself from being hurt any further.

"Perfectly."

"You said there might be risk. Who's going to watch my back, if you're not going to be there?"

"I'll have Burt Mulrooney keep an eye on you, and I'll be . . . around. I won't leave you vulnerable."

Too late for that, Caruso.

"Burt's involved in this, too? Who else, Grandma Flora?"

"Burt's an FBI agent. He's been in on this operation from the beginning. He's my partner."

"I should have guessed. I doubt you have any real friends."

"I guess I deserved that."

"Isn't it going to seem odd to everyone if you remain in my apartment, since I'm no longer protecting you?"

"I've already thought about that. You'll have to pretend that we're lovers, Mia."

Mia's look was incredulous. "What? You expect me to carry on this charade, lie to my family and friends? Pretend that I have feelings for you when I don't?"

Now who's lying, Mia?

"Only until this investigation is completed. It's necessary, Mia. I wouldn't ask it of you otherwise."

She took a few moments to make her decision, weighing his reasoning and finding it sound. Finally, she heaved a sigh and nodded, asking, "What makes you so sure Alfredo Graziano will go along with spying on his friends? You don't give the man much credit for loyalty."

"That's where you're wrong, Mia. I give him all the credit in the world. Alfredo Graziano is an honorable man, who's in love with a wonderful woman, whom he intends to marry. Once he learns what's been going on right under his nose, he will want to protect his reputation, rectify the wrong by doing what's right."

"Well, well, Agent Caruso. You finally told the truth about something. How refreshing."

*   *   *

Standing on the front porch of Alfredo Graziano's 1950s-era brick house—the kind the family of *Father Knows Best* might have lived in—Mia snuggled deeper into her down jacket, feeling genuine concern over what they were about to do.

"Try not to be too blunt," she told Nick. "Uncle Alfredo is old. You might give him a heart attack, if you blurt everything out all at once."

"I realize you're worried about him, Mia, but give me some credit for knowing how to do my job. Some people actually think I'm quite good at it. I promise that I'll be as tactful as I can."

She snorted. "Like you know how to be tactful." *Or truthful.*

Nick was spared from responding when Lenore Gallagher opened the door. She was dressed in navy wool slacks and a red sweater, looking slim, youthful, and very together.

"What a nice surprise! What brings you to our neighborhood? Come in, come in. It's freezing outside."

"Is Mr. Graziano here, Mrs. Gallagher?" Nick asked, trying to sound officious, but warming to the woman's welcoming smile. "I have some business to discuss with him."

"About the book?" Without waiting for an answer, she ushered them into the front parlor, which was decorated, quite to Nick and Mia's surprise, in a very modern, garish black and red motif that screamed '70s.

"Don't mind the decor," Lenore said with an engaging grin. "I'm planning to change it after we're married. I think this is Al's failed attempt at a swinging bachelor's pad."

Mia couldn't help but smile at the mental image Lenore's words formed.

Alfredo hurried into the room just then, smiling when he saw who had come to visit. "I was just getting ready for work," he explained, straightening his tie. For all the years he'd worked at Lucky Louie's he'd always worn a jacket and tie to work. "Not that we'll have much business today, with this nasty weather. But still, I like to keep an eye on things."

"Lucky Louie's is the reason I'm here, Mr. Graziano," Nick informed the older man, dreading the conversation they were about to have. He knew that what he was about to confide was going to hurt the old guy, and he wished that he could spare him. Contrary to what Mia believed—with good reason, he supposed—he got no pleasure from lying and duping nice people. It was the part of his job that he hated.

"Sit, sit. Lenore will bring coffee. And call me Al. I don't stand on formality. So, Nick, are you planning to buy that new car we discussed? Is that why you're here? I can give you one hell of a good deal, if you are."

Setting the tray of coffee cups that she'd just retrieved from the kitchen down on the chrome and glass coffee table, Lenore seated herself on the black Naugahyde sofa next to her fiancé and patted his hand. "I think Mr. Caruso and Miss DeNero are here for another reason, Al."

"Ah, the book." He threw up his hands. "Sometimes I forget things. I'm not as young as I used to be, you know."

"It's not the book, Uncle Alfredo," Mia blurted, and Nick shot her a warning look.

"Mia's right, Mr. Graz . . . Al. I'm not really an author." Nick reached into his back pocket and withdrew his identification, passing it to the older couple. "I work for the Federal Bureau of Investigation."

Lenore's eyes widened. "The FBI? But why did you pretend to be an author?"

"I didn't know, either, Mrs. Gallagher . . . Uncle Alfredo, so please don't think I was part of this," Mia said. "I just found out this morning." She shot Nick a dirty look.

"I don't understand, Nick," the older man said, his gaze darting between the two young people. "What about the book you were writing on the Mafia?"

Nick explained as best he could the situation at Lucky Louie's and the involvement of Vincent Palumbo, Pauley Buttoni, and Larry Calzone in a money-laundering scheme.

"From what we've been able to ascertain, Lucky Louie's is being used as an after-hours chop shop. Stolen cars are cut up for parts, and then the used parts are put on customer cars that come into the dealership for repair, maximizing the profits for Palumbo, and subsequently Calzone. The remaining parts are sold on the black market. Two sets of books were used to launder the money."

"Are you sure about this?"

Nick nodded. "Some of the stolen cars are being reworked and repainted, then sold as new or used. The vehicle identification numbers are faked, so the paperwork can't be traced back."

Alfredo's face whitened. "I've been selling stolen cars?"

"Way to be tactful, Agent Caruso," Mia whispered.

"I swear I didn't know such a thing was going on behind my back," Alfredo said, making the sign of the cross. "Vinnie and Pauley are my best friends. We grew up together. How could they do this to me?" He sat back hard against the cushions, looking old and defeated.

Concern filled Mia's eyes, and she reached out, taking the old man's hand. "I'm so sorry, Uncle Alfredo. Greed makes people do terrible things. And sometimes those closest to you lie for their own purposes, thinking that the end justifies the means, but it never does." She turned her attention on Nick and glared; he had the grace to look away.

"What can we do to help?" Lenore asked, patting her fiancé's knee, in an affectionate show of support.

"Yes, yes!" Alfredo agreed, nodding enthusiastically. "I will do whatever it is you tell me needs to be done, Nick. As far as I'm concerned, I have no more friends named Vincent Palumbo and Pauley Buttoni. They are dead to me." His expression said he wished they were.

"For the time being, you're going to have to act as if nothing has changed. We don't want to raise their suspicions. We need hard evidence to convict both men."

"You want me to pretend that nothing is wrong? I must lie and be friendly to them?" The old man heaved a sigh. "It will be hard, but I will do it."

"And you won't be able to tell another living soul about this. You and Lenore must promise to keep what I've told you to yourselves. Outside of Mia, and now you, no other civilians are privy to this information. I want to keep it that way. Mia's life may depend on it."

Lenore gasped, Mia's eyes widened, a shiver of apprehension traveling down her spine, before Alfredo asked, "What do you mean? What does Mia have to do with this?"

"I want you to hire her to work for you, just as you offered this morning in front of Buttoni. She's good with computers. I want her to start snooping around the dealership and hopefully find the evidence we need to get a conviction."

"But if they find out what she's doing they'll kill her." Alfredo shook his head. "No, it's too dangerous. I can't allow her to risk her life. Bad enough when she was your bodyguard, but this . . . this is madness. Look at her, Nick. She's a small, helpless woman."

Mia winced at the label that had always branded her. "I want to do it, Uncle Alfredo. Otherwise what they've done could smear your business. That wouldn't be fair to you or Mrs. Gallagher. And it isn't fair to all the honest people those crooks are ripping off."

"But, Mia," Lenore declared, "you are putting yourself in great danger. It isn't worth it. Alfredo knows he's an honorable man, and so does everyone else who lives in Little Italy. We will survive this."

"I have my own reasons for doing this, Mrs. Gallagher, aside from helping Alfredo. It's important to me. And I feel confident that I can handle whatever's thrown at me, despite my diminutive size." Mia spoke with more bravado than she felt. The truth was, she was scared shitless.

Lenore pinned Nick with a disappointed look. "Where will you be in all this, Mr. Caruso, if you don't mind my asking?"

"I'll be living at Mia's, as before, only now we'll be using a romantic relationship as the basis for my staying there. Mia will be wearing a wire the entire time she's at work, so I'll be monitoring her every move. And I'll have another agent posing as a customer to keep an eye on her, as well. Plus, we've got Alfredo to assist Mia, if need be."

"There are times when Vinnie leaves the dealership,"

Alfredo told Nick. "Mia can search then. But if this has been going on as long as you say it has, then I think Vincent has hidden his tracks very well."

"I'll show Mia what to look for. I suspect Palumbo is gloating over the fact that he's put one over on you. His guard will be down."

Alfredo's lips slashed thin. "That stupid bastard! Why didn't I see what was going on?"

"Don't upset yourself, Al. It isn't good for you," Lenore cautioned. "With Mr. Caruso's help, and Mia's, we're going to pay back Vincent Palumbo in kind. What's done is done. Now we have to fix things."

Wrapping his arm around his fiancée's shoulders, Alfredo kissed Lenore's cheek. "Now I know why I love you so much, *mi amore*."

Mia was touched by the couple's display of affection and glanced at Nick, who was staring at her with the oddest look on his face. A lump formed in her throat.

Okay, so maybe he did care a little. But that didn't make up for the lies he told, the way he had used her.

Just keep reminding yourself of that, Mia. Just keep reminding yourself.

EIGHTEEN

You'd better take care of me, Lord,
because if you don't,
you're going to have *me* on your hands.
Fear and Loathing in Las Vegas

Mia's first day on the job at Lucky Louie's Auto World had been nothing short of disastrous.

Vincent Palumbo was furious that his partner had hired someone to work at the dealership without his consent, and had coldly informed Alfredo that Mia's salary would be coming out of his half of the business. To which Alfredo had replied, "Fine with me, Vinnie. As president and founder of this company I deserve an executive assistant. Mia works for me."

Vinnie had flipped him off, and then spent the remainder of the day giving Mia nasty looks, not to mention the cold shoulder. Which didn't bother Mia at all, because being around Vincent Palumbo, whom she had dubbed "The Fat Bastard," gave her the creeps.

Day two hadn't been much better. Vincent had blown off Mia's title of executive assistant and had assigned her the mundane task of sorting through the various auto parts and restocking the shelves. But she had gotten the carburetors mixed up with the fuel pumps, and Vincent had cursed a blue streak upon discovering her error, using some expletives she had never heard before.

Vincent cursed a great deal when Mia was around.

She knew the bastard was looking for a reason to fire her, so she had apologized profusely, but only after bursting into tears and begging his forgiveness, all in the space of five minutes.

Her performance had been nothing short of brilliant. Vincent had been on the brink of rendering his own apology, but then thought better of it, throwing his hands up in defeat instead and walking away. Nick, who'd been listening in on the exchange, told her later that she deserved an Oscar.

The situation between Mia and Nick at home was even more stressful. Nick was sleeping on the couch again, but that didn't lessen the pain and yearning Mia experienced every night upon going to bed alone, with memories of Nick's kisses and caresses fresh on her mind.

They kept their conversations to the business at hand, speaking only when necessary, to relay pertinent information about the day's activities, or to ask the other to pass the butter at dinnertime, which was also a strained and torturous affair.

As Mia made ready to leave for the car dealership on the third morning, Nick followed her to the door, handing her a tube of lipstick that was in reality a miniature camera.

"Use this if you find any material you think might be useful to the investigation. It'll be easier than making copies on the Xerox machine. Check Palumbo's calendar for notes regarding deliveries, or his desk pad to see if he's made any reference to deliveries or the receiving of merchandise from someone other than their legitimate suppliers. And you might also take a look in his trash container."

Mia made a face at the last suggestion.

"And if you get a chance, try to locate his telephone bills. No doubt he and Calzone have been in touch, probably after hours, and that information can be used as evidence." He'd tried to get a wiretap, but the judge didn't deem there to be sufficient evidence to warrant it.

Wrapping her fingers tightly around the camera, Mia smiled, thrilled to be part of the investigation. It was the most exciting thing she had ever done, with the possible exception of making love with Nick. But she wasn't going to count that.

"This is getting to be real James Bond–like, isn't it?"

Nick didn't share her obvious enthusiasm. "Yes, and just as dangerous. If Palumbo finds out what you're up to . . . well, I don't have to tell you what will happen."

She searched his face, finding concern, which didn't make her feel any better about her chances for completing the mission unscathed, and something more personal that she refused to consider. "You're trying to scare me."

"You're damn right, I am. This isn't a game, Mia. You shouldn't be enjoying it as much as you are."

"I'd be enjoying it more if I had found something useful, but so far I've turned up nothing."

"It's only been two days, and Palumbo is naturally going to be suspicious of newcomers. But that'll change in time. So look again, and use a critical eye this time. Things that look like nothing can oftentimes turn out to be something. Criminals are known to hide things in plain sight."

Mia listened intently and nodded, impressed with Nick's

knowledge and abilities. He was dedicated to his job, and for that she couldn't fault him.

"Like I told Alfredo, criminals think they're too smart to get caught, and that everyone else is stupid. As many mistakes as you've made these past two days, Vincent probably thinks you're just a dumb female without a lick of sense."

She stiffened. "I wasn't that bad!"

"I'm not criticizing. In fact, we want him to think you're inept. That'll make what you have to do that much easier. He'll grow more confident, start to get careless, and go off and leave you alone. And that's when we'll get him. You've got to get access to his computer somehow. I'm positive that's where the files are being kept."

"I've tried, but he watches me like a hawk. He told me never to touch it. I pretended that I didn't know how to use one."

"You may have an opportunity today. Alfredo told us that Palumbo's meeting someone for lunch, away from the dealership. We think it might be Calzone. But your time will be limited, so use extreme caution and don't take any unnecessary chances.

"The sooner we get the evidence we need, the sooner I can get you the hell out of there. I'm nervous about your involvement in this. I have been from the beginning." But Higgins had been breathing down his neck, and he hadn't seen any other way.

"I'll do my best." Mia stuck the camera in her purse and adjusted her shoulder strap.

"I know you will, Mia, and I . . . we at the Bureau appreciate everything you're doing. By the way, don't act surprised if you see Burt there today. He's planning to come by and look at some cars, play the interested customer."

"Thanks for the warning. I'll feel better knowing he's around."

"He's been around, Mia. Just look across the street and you'll see a parked van marked PARROT PLUMBING. Burt and I have been inside the van during the day, monitoring your movements and listening to your every word. You talk to yourself a lot, did you know that?"

Her eyes widened. "You're on stakeout, just like in the movies! But why didn't you tell me? I would have felt safer knowing you were there. And what do you mean I talk to myself? I do not."

He smiled at her indignation. "We wanted you to get used to your surroundings first, make sure you wouldn't give yourself, or us, away. I promised I would keep an eye on you. I'm not going to let anyone hurt you, Mia."

"Too late for that, Agent Caruso," she said in a pain-filled voice so low he could barely hear her, and then with head held high, she walked out the door.

Nick slammed his hand against the wall, then wished he hadn't, because it hurt like hell. He shook it to get some of the sting out. "Fuck!" He hated himself for what he'd put Mia through, was still putting her through. He'd messed everything up, and now he was paying the price.

The only woman he had ever loved hated him, and with good reason. He'd lied, used her, and done everything she'd accused him of. He couldn't defend his actions, except to blame it on his job. And he couldn't even do that because he hadn't been acting as a federal agent when he'd gone to Mia's bed and made love to her. That he had done for himself, because he loved her.

Nick knew he deserved every rotten thing she had said to him. It was no more than he'd said to himself a hundred times over.

So how could he fix what was broken?

He still loved Mia with all his heart and soul. He didn't want to lose her.

But the truth was, he was afraid he already had.

Holding her nose as she stuck her hand into Vincent Palumbo's black plastic trash can, Mia almost gagged when she felt a meatball squish between her fingers. "*Eeuwe!* Gross!" She grabbed some tissues off Palumbo's desk and wiped her hands.

As Nick had predicted, Vincent had gone to lunch, and hopefully wouldn't be back for a couple of hours. Alfredo was outside on the lot with Burt, looking over some of the most recent arrivals to the dealership, while Mia continued her search, in the hope of finding something that could be considered incriminating evidence.

After a few more minutes of searching the trash, she found several pieces of wadded-up paper and opened them. They appeared to be dates, possibly of incoming car shipments, along with some numbers that could prove to be serial numbers. She didn't know, but Nick probably would, so she shoved them into the front pocket of her slacks.

Mia then perused Palumbo's desk calendar, but there were no notations of any importance there. Then she recalled what Nick had said about hiding in plain sight, and looked again, thumbing through the pages, to find a weekly notation made on the same evening of every week that said "The Zone, 10 P.M." She had never heard of The Zone, but figured it could be a sports bar or meeting place. Or it could hold some significance to Larry Calzone, so she took out her lipstick camera and took a shot of each page.

That left one major task to do—and the most important. Vinnie's computer loomed large, and she seated herself in front of it.

It took only a moment to boot it up. Clutching the mouse like a lifeline, Mia prayed silently that God was watching out for her and would keep her safe. She didn't want to think about what would happen if Vinnie came back early and found out what she'd been up to. A mental image of that squished meatball formed in her mind, and she cringed.

Using the computer's find function, she searched for files that made reference to the buying and selling of cars and auto parts. After a few minutes, she finally hit pay dirt.

"Yes!" she mouthed silently, her fingers flying over the keyboard as file after file appeared, with all sorts of vehicle numbers and descriptions of cars, some marked with an LL, for Lucky Louie's—she figured these were the legitimate entries—and some marked with a C—for Calzone?—just as Nick had suspected.

Retrieving the computer disk Nick had given her from her pants pocket, she set about to copy the files, staring over her shoulder every few minutes, expecting to find Vincent Palumbo standing there, relieved as hell when she didn't.

It didn't take long to copy what she needed, and Mia had just finished shoving the filled disk back into her pocket when the door opened and Vincent strolled in.

His face turned beet red when he saw her seated in

front of his computer; hers turned deathly white—a poor choice of words, she decided. He looked as if he was about to spit nails; Mia merely felt like throwing up.

"What the fuck are you doing in my office? I told you to stay away from my computer."

She thought quickly, trying to come up with a plausible excuse. *When all else fails, play dumb.* "Al said it would be okay if I practiced my typing, Mr. Palumbo. I didn't hurt anything. I couldn't figure out how to do much on the computer, anyway, what keys to push to make things work. I'm really sorry. I hope I didn't mess up anything."

He glanced at the blank screen, and the anger left his face. He obviously assumed she was too stupid to know what she was doing, and Mia breathed a sigh of relief. "Get out! And next time you want to use the computer, you ask my permission, not Al's. It's an expensive piece of equipment. I don't want it broken."

"I won't do it again, Mr. Palumbo."

His eyes narrowed as he studied her, and Mia could see that he was trying to make up his mind as to whether or not she was telling the truth. "I was told you had a bodyguard business. Why are you working here, if that's the case?" he wanted to know.

Mia brazened it out. "I had only the one client. No one else would hire me. I guess because I'm a woman. When the case ended I had to find a way to earn money to pay my rent. Alfredo's job offer was like an answer to my prayer. He's a wonderful man."

Vincent snorted in disgust. "Yeah, yeah. Get out! There's plenty for you to do in the parts department. I think another shipment came in this morning. See that it gets catalogued and put away. And don't screw it up this time, or you'll be looking for another job, you hear me?"

Shutting the door behind her, Mia ran down the hallway, as if the devil himself were on her heels. She was taking in huge gulps of air, trying to calm herself, when Al and Burt walked into the front office and saw her.

"What happened, Mia?" Alfredo asked, a concerned look on his face. "You look pale. You're not sick, are you?"

Shaking her head, she mouthed, "Not here."

Having witnessed Vincent's return, he understood. "Come, I think you could use a bit of fresh air. I want to show you the beautiful Cadillac that Mr. Burton just purchased. This is Mr. Burton, one of our newer customers. He's just moved here from San Antonio."

Mia and Burt exchanged smiles. "Pleased to meet you, little lady," Burt said in a fake Texas twang that sounded pretty realistic. He even had on a white cowboy hat.

Rolling her eyes, Mia followed her co-conspirators out the door. "Where's this car that's so wonderful? I've got something to give you, and I don't want to do it out here in the open. Palumbo almost caught me. I've never been so scared in my life." Getting shot had been a piece of cake compared to facing an angry Vincent Palumbo.

Alfredo took Mia by the arm and led her across the car lot. "I'm sorry I couldn't warn you about Vincent's return. He came back sooner than I expected. I had my head under the hood when he arrived, and there wasn't time to give you any warning."

"That's okay. I just played dumb and he bought it. It was kind of insulting, come to think of it. Anyway, I copied his files. I've got a disk in my pocket that might prove useful." She prayed it would, because she didn't want to come back here tomorrow. Bravery went only so far, and she'd used hers up for this week.

Being an undercover operative was a lot tougher than it looked.

Burt indicated with a nod of his head the red Caddy two rows over. "Go sit behind the wheel, like you're admiring the car. Stick the disk, and whatever else you've got, in the glove box. I'll retrieve it and take it from there."

"All this cloak-and-dagger stuff is making my stomach hurt. I think I have heartburn."

"Have you eaten lunch?" Alfredo asked.

"No. I was too busy playing Mata Hari."

"After we're done here, you and I will go to lunch. Let Vincent think what he will. He's already accused me of having an affair with you. Called me an old fool."

Burt masked a laugh by coughing.

Mia's mouth fell open, and then she smiled. "I'm flattered Palumbo would think that a handsome gentleman such as yourself would be interested in me, Alfredo."

The old man chucked her chin. "You are a good girl, Mia. But a terrible liar."

Didn't she know? She'd been lying to herself for days.

"I don't see why we have to keep up this pretense. I don't like lying to my parents. And having dinner at their house, pretending we're an item, is a big fat lie. Besides, I thought you told me the disk would probably cinch the investigation, and that I wouldn't have to go back to Louie's."

Behind the wheel of his Volvo, Nick looked over at Mia, wishing like hell things could be different between them. Had it only been a couple of weeks ago since they'd gone to her parents' house for Christmas dinner? They'd had such a wonderful time, joking, singing, and laughing, as if they hadn't a care in the world.

It seemed like an eternity ago. And sometimes it seemed as if it had never happened, that it had all been a wonderful dream.

"I sent the disk and notepaper to Quantico to be analyzed. Once we determine that there's enough evidence to warrant arrests, we can end the charade. I may have you call in sick tomorrow, just in case something goes down. But until we know for sure, we have to pretend to be a loving couple, just as we agreed."

"Even I'm not that good an actress."

"I'll do my share to help convince them."

"And what happens when this is all over and they wonder why we broke up?"

"It doesn't have to end that way, Mia."

"Yes. It does."

"Only because you want it to."

"You're the one who lied, Nick. Not me."

"Mia, dear, you hardly ate a thing for dinner. I thought you liked my lasagna."

"It was great, Mom. Thanks for going to so much trouble for us. I'm just not that hungry. I had a late lunch with Uncle Alfredo."

"Well, at least you had a good appetite, Nick. I like a man with a good appetite."

Nick, who was seated on the sofa next to Mia, wrapped his arm around her shoulder, felt her stiffen, and drew her closer to his side. "I think Mia's just tired, Mrs. De-Nero. She's not used to working regular hours."

"How's your job at the car lot going, dear? Your father and I were quite surprised when we heard you had accepted Alfredo's offer to work there."

"Mia's finally come to her senses and is going to give up her bodyguard business. Isn't that right, Mia?" her father pressed, unable to hide the pleased smile on his face. "It's not a good profession for a woman, especially a woman of your size and inexperience. I tried to tell you that."

Some things never change, Mia thought, heaving a sigh. "I don't know, Dad. I haven't made a decision about it yet." Which was true. Mia had been debating whether or not she would continue her business, wondering if she still had the heart for it.

"Mia's been an excellent bodyguard, Sam. Anyone would be lucky to have her. I intend to provide her with references now that I'm finished with the book and no longer in need of her professional services."

"She would make a better wife, I think," Rosalie said, not daring to look at her daughter, knowing she would find outrage on her face.

"I keep telling her that, Mrs. DeNero, but Mia's not anxious to marry and settle down just yet. I've been trying to convince her."

"Men aren't the only ones who like to sow their wild oats."

Rosalie gasped, then looked quickly at Nick to see if her daughter's comment had offended him. "Shame on you, Mia! And in front of Nick, too."

"I know she's only joking, Mrs. DeNero. Mia and I have already formed an understanding, of sorts." Ignoring Mia's sharp intake of breath, Nick smiled warmly at her mother, who clapped her hands in response.

"How wonderful! When do you think you'll get married? I can't wait to start making the arrangements."

"Your mother's been making the arrangements since the day you were born," Sam told his daughter with a wink.

"Don't book the church yet, Mom. It won't be any time soon. I can promise you that." Mia elbowed Nick in the ribs, then softened her tone when she said, "Please don't push. You'll frighten Nick away."

"That's not going to happen, sweetheart." Nick leaned over and brushed his lips over Mia's. At first she responded, then remembering that she hated him, drew back, a startled expression on her face.

"No need to be embarrassed in front of me and your mother," Sam said, noting his daughter's odd reaction. "We've done our share of making out. Still do, huh, Rosalie?"

His wife blushed. "Really, Sam! Kissing and telling is not considered gentlemanly behavior."

"Just be glad I didn't tell them what went on in the back of that '69 Chevy Impala."

That brought a grin to Mia's face. "Oooh! Is that where Angela was conceived?" Her anger dissipated momentarily.

"Never you mind, young lady," Rosalie told her daughter. "Some day when you have children you won't want them knowing every little detail about your courtship with Nick."

Mia scoffed, then replied, "That's for damn sure!" and Nick choked on his beer.

NINETEEN

Me? I'm scared of everything. I'm scared of what I saw, I'm scared of what I did, of who I am, and most of all I'm scared of walking out of this room and never feeling the rest of my life the way I feel when I'm with you.

Dirty Dancing

Mia tiptoed around the car dealership the next morning, as if she were walking on eggshells. She'd been hoping and praying that she wouldn't have to return to Lucky Louie's today, but the results they'd been expecting from Quantico hadn't come in yet, and Nick didn't want to raise Palumbo's suspicions. So she was forced to endure the fat bastard for one more day.

"What's wrong with you, girl?" Vincent blurted as he came up to Mia, who was standing behind the parts counter, lost in her own thoughts. "You look nervous. You got something to be nervous about?"

"No, sir!" Mia glanced about, looking for some sign of Alfredo, but knew he was still outside with a customer. She was alone with Vincent, and even knowing Nick and Burt were across the street in the van didn't alleviate her nervousness. "You startled me, that's all." Her voice sounded higher pitched than normal. She hoped he hadn't noticed.

"You done cataloguing those parts yet?"

"Yes, I just finished."

"Good. Then come into my office. I want to talk to you in private." He licked his lips, and she almost gagged, not liking the way he'd been staring at her chest—what there was of it.

"About what, if you don't mind my asking?"

"That's for me to know, and you to find out. And don't keep me waiting."

Mentally making the sign of the cross, Mia followed Palumbo into his office, and watched in horror as he locked the door behind her. "Why did you do that?"

His smile was sinister. "That should be obvious. I don't want to be disturbed."

"If this is about yesterday and my using your computer, Mr. Palumbo, I already told you that I'm sorry."

"Let's just see how truly sorry you are, Mia. You're an attractive woman. I never realized that until yesterday when I had a chance to really take a good look at you."

"Jesus, Burt! I've got to go in there. Mia sounds terrified. And that bastard might hurt her. What if he moves on her? I'll kill the bastard if he touches her."

"Calm down, Nick, and give Mia some credit. She knows how to take care of herself. If you go busting in there now, you'll ruin everything."

"Where the fuck is Alfredo? He's supposed to be keeping an eye on her."

"He's on the lot. Look, I know you care about Mia, but—"

"I love her! She's the most important thing in the world to me. I couldn't live with myself if anything happened to her. I should have never asked Mia to help us."

"What's done is done. Now take a deep breath and try

to relax. You asked Mia to help because you know she's good at what she does. She can handle Palumbo, I'm telling you. Don't underestimate her."

Mia stared down at the meaty hand grasping her arm and nearly puked. Then she got angry. "Take your hand off me, Mr. Palumbo. I'm not interested in anything you have to offer, and I'm insulted that you would think I would be."

"Why? You've been fooling around with Alfredo. I got lots more money than he does, not to mention that I'm better in the sack. Why shouldn't he share? After all, we're partners. And you owe me for snooping around here yesterday. I didn't buy that feeble story of yours for one minute. Who put you up to it? Alfredo? I didn't think he was that smart."

Mia fought to keep her face perfectly impassive, and her tone even. If he thought for a moment that she'd been spying on him, he would kill her. She had no doubt about that. "No one put me up to anything. I told you the truth. And for your information, I am not fooling around with anyone, including Alfredo. Now leave me alone or I will scream down this building."

Vincent laughed and pulled her close to his chest, until she could smell his fetid breath and the overpowering scent of his bay rum cologne. "I like a woman with spunk. I had you pegged for a scared rabbit, but I can see that you got more guts than I gave you credit for. You and me, we could work well together."

Mia opened her mouth to scream, but Palumbo covered it with his lips and kissed her. She struggled to escape his embrace, wiggling like a worm on a hook, but he was stronger and kept her in place. She thought about using karate on him, but opted not to, fearing it might raise his suspicions even further and hamper the investigation. But she had no intention of allowing him to rape her, either, which seemed to be his intent. She yanked her head back. "Let me go!"

At that moment, Alfredo's voice roared through the closed door. "Goddammit, Vincent! Where's Mia? I told you she was my assistant and I need her. Is she in there?"

Palumbo released her suddenly, and Mia stumbled, drawing her hand across her mouth to erase his touch, needing desperately to throw up.

Vincent smiled. "Next time I won't take no for an answer."

She hurried to the door and threw it open, not about to confess that there wouldn't be a next time.

She quit!

Two days later arrests were made in the money-laundering operation, including those of Larry Calzone and his crew, Vincent Palumbo, and Pauley Buttoni, who'd started crying the minute the handcuffs were slapped on and had promised his full cooperation.

The information Mia had produced from her search of Palumbo's computer had been enough for a judge to issue multiple search warrants.

The FBI had scoured Lucky Louie's Auto World with a fine-tooth comb, as well as the various businesses that Larry Calzone operated, and had found enough evidence to put all of the participants involved away for a long, long time.

As a bonus, agents had also found a cache of illegal

weapons in the basement of Calzone's mansion. ATF had been called in and had already issued their subpoenas.

Proud of her involvement in the operation, Mia finally understood Nick's need for subterfuge during his surveillance of Alfredo, Vincent Palumbo, and their car dealership.

But that didn't mean she had forgiven him.

She wasn't sure she ever would.

He'd hurt her far worse than Greg ever had. Mia had loved Nick with the heart and soul of a woman, not a child. He'd taken her heart and crushed it, taken her trust and mocked it, and he'd taken her love and defiled it.

She had no forgiveness for Nick Caruso. Maybe it was wounded pride, or ego. Or maybe it was her Italian heritage that rarely forgave an insult. She didn't know. She knew only that she was finished with men, and Nick, most of all.

"I'm almost done packing, Mia, then I'll be on my way." Nick stood in front of the sofa over an open suitcase, dressed casually in jeans and a green sweater, folding his shirts and slacks carefully, as if they were treasured possessions, and tucking them inside.

Leaning against the bedroom door, Mia dangled by her finger the wooden hanger that held the pair of black leather pants he had purchased a lifetime ago, and wondered why she always had such rotten luck with men.

No, not just rotten luck. No luck!

"Don't forget these. I don't think they'll fit me."

Looking up, Nick smiled softly when he saw the pants, and her heart did a somersault. "How could I? I'll save them for my next Halloween party. I may decide to go as

Val Kilmer portraying Jim Morrison. And when I wear them, I'll think of you." His eyes filled with sadness.

Heart attack alert! Heart attack alert!

Mia fought back tears, trying to keep her features perfectly impassive, though she was dying inside. *Did one actually die of a broken heart?* She thought it was possible. "I've checked my closet. I didn't find anything else that belongs to you. But if I should come across something, I'll send it to the work address you gave me."

"I'm sorry about the way things turned out, Mia. I know you don't believe that, but I am. If I could change what happened, I would. But I will never be sorry for loving you. In my heart I know that wasn't a mistake."

"I understand you had a job to do. Let's just leave it at that." Any further discussion would be too painful, and her emotions were already raw and ragged. She was a hair's breadth away from throwing herself into Nick's arms and begging him to stay. And that would be a huge mistake. Not to mention humiliating.

A knock sounded just then, and Mia rushed to the door, grateful to have something to do that would dispel the awkward moment between them. "Are you expecting someone?" she called out over her shoulder.

Nick shook his head and resumed packing.

Alfredo and Lenore waited on the landing, looking happy and content with the world. Mia invited them in. "I'm surprised to see you. I thought you'd be up to your ears in wedding preparations by now. It's this coming Saturday, isn't it?"

Lenore kissed her cheek. "Yes, it is. That's why we dropped by. We were hoping to catch up with Nick. We heard he was leaving today. I, for one, will be sad to see him go. He was such a nice addition to our Little Italy family." The bride-to-be looked as if she had more to say on the topic of Nick's departure, but mercifully she refrained, much to Mia's relief.

With a nod of her head, Mia indicated the living room. "Nick's packing. Go on in. He's almost done. I'm sure he'll be happy to see you."

Wreathed in smiles, Alfredo shook Nick's hand, and then hugged him to his barrel chest. "I owe you a debt I can never repay, Nick. You have saved my reputation, and that of my business. A man is nothing without his reputation. I think John Gotti told me that." The older man winked at the FBI agent, who threw back his head and laughed.

Nick was going to miss all of the colorful characters that he'd come to know and had grown so fond of. But most of all, he was going to miss Mia—beautiful, headstrong, impossible Mia. He was mad about her, crazy in love, and she was just plain old mad.

"I'm glad it worked out so well, but you're thanking the wrong person, Al. Mia's the one who risked her neck to get the evidence we needed. Without her help, we may never have gotten the goods on your partner, and the others."

Mia's cheeks blossomed at the compliment. She'd received a lot of compliments since the newspaper broke the story last evening. Her father had called late last night to tell her how proud he was, before reading her the riot act about not confiding in him.

Sophia Russo had called early this morning, claiming that Nick had turned out to be a big disappointment. Mia hadn't disputed her opinion, though unlike Mia, the woman had decided to forgive him, for helping her brother clear his name.

"Oh, I haven't forgotten little Mia. Her reward is parked downstairs in front of the apartment building." Alfredo handed the startled woman a set of keys. "It's the red Cadillac—the one Burt looked at. I hope you like it."

Mia's eyes widened. "Of course I like it. But I hardly know what to say, Uncle Alfredo." She kissed his cheek, wondering what she would do with such a huge car, wishing she'd had it as a teenager. She could have gotten into some serious trouble at the drive-in. On second thought . . .

"Thank you. But giving me a car is totally unnecessary. I was happy to help in any way I could. I told you that."

"I figured that if you don't need another car, or if it's too big for you, you can give it to your parents. The Caddy was Vincent's favorite vehicle. I wanted it off the lot and this seemed like a good opportunity to get rid of it."

She smiled in understanding. "Maybe I will give it to my dad. I think he would love it. It's certainly flashy enough for Sam. And red's his favorite color."

"The other reason we're here," Lenore said, squeezing her fiancé's hand, "is to invite both of you to our wedding. It's going to be a small affair. The reception will be held at Mama Sophia's. Please say you'll come."

Nick grinned. "I'd love to see you two tie the knot. Thanks for the invitation." And he'd be able to see Mia again, if only for a few hours.

Mia said nothing, for she'd hoped after today she

wouldn't have to lay eyes on Nick Caruso again. The whole situation was painful enough without having it go on forever. And seeing him again at a wedding, no less, was going to be cruel and unusual punishment.

"Mia? I hope you don't already have plans. I'll be crushed if you can't come." Lenore twisted her engagement ring nervously, waiting for the younger woman to answer.

Happy for the couple, Mia smiled. "Of course, I'll come. I'm looking forward to it. I was just trying to decide what to wear."

"You always did look good in red leather," Nick quipped, but Mia said nothing.

There was nothing more to say.

"Whatsa matter? Why aren't you dancing with that handsome Nick? I tink you and him would make lotsa beautiful *bambinos*. You shoulda get married and start a family."

In truth, Mia had taken the chicken's way out and avoided Nick the entire evening. She told herself it was better for both of them this way, especially for her sanity.

Smiling down at Grandma Flora, she listened patiently as the old woman went on and on about what a wonderful couple she and Nick made, when all she really wanted to do was run upstairs and hide under her bed.

Mia had heard similar accounts from other well-meaning, misinformed people all evening, including her own traitorous parents, who had forgiven Nick everything, and couldn't quite understand why Mia was so upset with such a "nice man," as her mother put it. Her father had accused her of being unreasonable, saying that Nick had only been doing his job, and that Mia should cut him some slack.

How had she ended up being the villain in this fiasco?

She was the wronged party, not Nick, who had come out of this whole miserable affair smelling like a rose. She was the one who had been victimized, not him.

So, why then was everyone taking Nick's side?

"It doesa no good to go againsta fate, Mia," the old woman was saying. "Your destiny lies with thisa man. I havea seen it."

"Thank you, Grandma Flora, but I think you need a new crystal ball. I have sworn off men, including Nick. I am not going to get involved with another man for as long as I live. They are nothing but trouble. And I've decided to remain single." *And celibate.*

Sex was highly overrated anyway. Okay, maybe not with Nick, but she'd just make do.

Nodding in understanding, the old woman patted Mia's cheek. "You havea been hurt. You willa get over it. Ita takes time. Soon—"

Mia shook her head emphatically, watching Nick out of the corner of her eye as he danced with Lenore. He looked achingly handsome in his dark suit and red tie. Without the hideous glasses, he was definitely Chippendale material.

She'd seen the adoring looks the female guests had been giving him all evening. It wouldn't take Nick long to replace her. Handsome, charming, and considerate— strike considerate! There was nothing considerate about lying through your teeth—men like Nick always landed on their feet.

The bastard would go on as if nothing had happened,

while she would sit home alone, night after night, with only a half gallon of fudge ripple for company, consoling herself.

And no doubt gain weight in the process!

Everyone knew unhappiness pounds were the hardest to lose.

"No, Grandma, I won't. I don't want to get over it. Don't you see? Nick lied to me, used me to get to Alfredo. What he did was wrong and unforgivable."

Tugging Mia's hand, Flora led her to a nearby dining table, where they sat. "I am too old to standa for long periods ofa time. Now, I explain tings and you listen. *Capisce?* Men havea been using women for centuries. Itsa the way of tings. God took the rib from Adam and made Eve to be hisa companion, and to givea him babies. This is how itsa been since time began."

Who wrote that version of the Bible? A man?

"Yeah, and look what happened. Eve finally got fed up with that whole male macho thing and got Adam kicked out of the Garden of Eden. And why? Because he was too weak to resist a stupid apple, that's why.

"Hello! Then those two sons of hers couldn't get along, and one ended up killing the other. Some family. Not exactly a great example of domestic bliss, if you ask me, and certainly not one that I care to follow. Though a good enough reason for never getting married."

The old woman absorbed everything Mia had to say. Compassion and understanding burned bright in eyes that had seen much over a lifetime. "You are young, Mia, which isa why you see tings thisa way. When you are old, likea me, and havea been married with many children, then you willa see the great gift God hasa given you."

MAD ABOUT MIA   291

"All He gave me was a broken heart, Grandma. And He didn't even do that; Nick did." Mia shook her head. "No. I'm swearing off men. From here on out, I'm going it alone. As a matter of fact, I think it's time that I say my good-byes to the bride and groom and be on my way."

"Itsa no good to run away from problems, *cara* Mia. They will stilla be there the next day, and the next."

"My problem is out there on the dance floor, laughing and dancing and acting like nothing is wrong with the world. After tonight I won't have to see Nick again. No more problem." She made a swishing motion with her hands. "All gone."

But if Mia thought that ignoring Nick, refusing to answer his phone calls or the letters he sent pleading to see her, would solve her problem, she was wrong.

There wasn't enough fudge ripple ice cream in the whole world to make the hurt go away.

And believe it or not, Mia had tried.

Staring down at the scale, she couldn't believe her eyes. She'd actually gained two pounds in the last two weeks. And Mia never gained weight!

Six empty half-gallon containers of various flavored ice creams spilled out of the bathroom trash can and onto the floor, so it was no surprise where the additional weight had come from. And there was also the onion dip and potato chips, peanuts, pretzels, and those damn chocolate candies she had found in her lingerie drawer, which had obviously been put there by Nick.

Damn him, anyway!

But wasn't it sweet?

Well, she never said he wasn't sweet.

Just a damned liar!

Mia used the bottom of her T-shirt to wipe her eyes, which were running again. Damn! She'd been leaking like a sieve for weeks, unable to control her crying jags.

She looked wretched, hadn't gotten dressed in days, and hadn't even bothered to wash her hair, which looked like a Brillo pad at the moment. And she sure as hell hadn't cleaned her apartment, which looked and smelled rather disastrous, too.

Nick would never have tolerated such behavior. He was such a neatnik. At least the Nick whom she thought was Nick was a neatnik. She had no idea if FBI Agent Nick Caruso was obsessively tidy, though she suspected so. No one was that good an actor!

Just because she could, Mia took the trash can and dumped it on her bed, then climbed up and started smashing the containers into the mattress. "Take that, Nick Caruso!" she shouted, waving her hands above her head like a crazy woman. She stomped the cartons under her bare feet, wishing they were Nick's head that she was pummeling.

Or maybe his heart.

It would have been nice to smash Nick's heart the way he had smashed hers.

"Can anyone join this game, or is it a private party?"

At the sound of her sister's voice, Mia stopped bouncing and turned around, her mouth hanging open when she spotted Angela framed in the doorway. She'd been so busy screaming and carrying on, she hadn't heard the front door open.

"How did you get in here?"

Angela dangled a key. "You gave this to me when you

moved in, remember? At Mom's insistence, I came by to check to see if your body had decomposed yet. She's convinced you're dead. When you didn't answer the door I started wondering if she might be right."

Mia plopped down on her butt. "As you can see, I'm still alive." Only parts of her had died.

Angela glanced at the mess her sister had made and shook her head, arms akimbo. "All this because of a man? I thought you were made of stronger stuff than that, Mia."

Mia made a face. "Oh, bite me! Like you didn't carry on over John when you thought he had deceived you."

"All right. I'll concede that you have a good motive for being upset. But was it necessary to lock yourself away for weeks and not call Mom and Dad? They are frantic with worry."

Mia felt a twinge of guilt. "They always worry, and I couldn't bear to face them. Mom's crazy about Nick; Dad, too. They blame me for not being more understanding and forgiving."

"They love you, Mia, and they're very worried about you. When push comes to shove, you're the one who matters most to them, you know that."

Mia scooted off the bed. "Do you want some coffee? Oh, wait." She smiled apologetically. "I probably don't have any. I haven't been to the grocery store for a couple of weeks."

"I suspected as much, so I stopped by Fiorelli's Bakery on the way here and picked some up, along with a few dozen doughnuts. I figured by now you must be getting low on comfort food."

"I've gained two pounds."

Angela's brow rose while her eyes lowered to Mia's abdomen. "Are you sure you're not pregnant?"

"Quite sure. I had my period last week." Which was the reason she'd devoured the two pounds of chocolates Nick had bought. She'd given serious thought to dumping them, but then reason prevailed. Tossing out perfectly good chocolate was a sacrilege, or, at the very least, un-American.

"Why don't you go take a shower?" Angela suggested. "You stink. I'll clean up the mess in here, and then go fix you a proper breakfast. I also brought eggs, milk, and cereal, just in case you were tired of eating junk food."

Mia sniffed her right armpit. "Not a bad idea. I'm starting to get a bit ripe. I'll be back in a flash."

By the time Mia rejoined her sister in the kitchen, she felt refreshed and a wee bit rejuvenated. Bacon sizzled in the Teflon-coated skillet, and a tall glass of milk sat at each place setting. The bacon smelled divine, and Mia's stomach grumbled, making her realize how famished she was for real food.

"Thanks for doing this, sis. I guess I am pretty hungry."

Angela placed the bacon strips on a plate and set it on the table, along with a bowl of scrambled eggs. "So what are your plans now?"

Biting into the crisp bacon, Mia shrugged. "I don't have any. Guess I'll just coast along like I always do until something comes along."

Angela eyed her sister for a few minutes, then said in a firm but loving voice, "I think you've coasted long enough, Mia. You have a business to run. Have you forgotten that?"

"It's not much of a business. And why do you care?

You were the one who didn't want me to become a body-guard. I should have listened to you, Angela. If I had, I would never had met Nick, and—"

"Fallen in love with a pretty great guy?"

"I hate Nick Caruso! I really thought things would be different this time, that it would work out between us, but loving a man never works out for me, Angie. You know my track record. I always pick the wrong ones. I've no intention of traveling down that dead-end road again."

Having been in Mia's shoes a time or two, Angela heaved a sigh. "Hate and love are strong emotions, Mia. You can feel both at the same time. It's the way our hearts and minds work. Did you ever tell Nick about Greg?"

Mia shook her head. "No. I doubt it would have made any difference. Nick had a job to do, and he did it, and damn the consequences."

"I don't think you're thinking too clearly right now, Mia."

"Don't you ever get tired of being rational and com-posed, Angela? Don't you ever feel like throwing your hands up in the air and screaming at the top of your lungs, or running away?"

"Of course I've felt like that, many times. But I'm too damn stubborn to give up, and so are you. You've got a lot to offer the world. You've proven, over and over again, that you can do whatever you put your mind to. I think that's pretty wonderful."

Heartened by her sister's words, Mia said, "I was a pretty good bodyguard. I did save Nick's life."

"Dad says you're a crack shot."

"He did? Dad said that?"

Angela nodded. "He did. And when he spoke of you and what you'd done to help Nick . . . well, I can tell you that the man was bursting with pride. And envy."

Mia's brows wrinkled in confusion. "Envy? Dad's never been envious of anyone."

"I think he misses being on the police force and busting the bad guys. And I don't think it would take much to convince him to join you, if you're looking for a partner in your bodyguard business."

"A partner? I've never thought about that." She shrugged. "But even if I thought it was a good idea, I don't have any clients. So what's the use?"

Angela smiled knowingly. "Mia, word is out about what you did to help Nick and the FBI. You've been featured on radio stations and in newspapers, not to mention TV, for the last two weeks. Haven't you seen or heard any of it?"

"No! I've been . . ."

"Wallowing? This place does resemble a pigsty. If Mrs. Foragi should come by, you'd probably get your ass kicked out."

"She's out of town, left this morning. Mrs. Foragi and the undertaker are doing their thing in the Bahamas for a few days. She left a note under my door, asking me to take in her mail and newspaper."

"Well, I suggest that you get this place cleaned up, then stop by Mom and Dad's. They've saved all the newspaper clippings for you, as well as some videotapes of the news broadcasts."

"So what you're telling me is that I'm sort of famous?"

"I believe Dan Wilson of NBC4 referred to you as the FBI's secret weapon."

Mia grinned. "Dan said that? How sweet. Remind me not to rag on his haircut again."

"Think about what I suggested, with regard to Dad, Mia. I think you'd be doing him a big favor by inviting him to join your company."

"Hmmm. Dad as a Guardian Angel. Well, I guess he's always been that to us." She thought a moment, then reached out across the table and clasped her sister's hand.

"Thank you, Angela. Thank you for giving me some space, and convincing Mom and Dad to leave me alone for a while."

"How did you know?"

"Are you kidding? Mom would have called the police by now. I'm sure you were the one to hold her back."

"Well, she is rather high-strung."

"No shit? Really?"

Both women laughed, then Mia said, "You're the best big sister a crazy woman like me could ever have. I hope you know that."

"Stop, or you'll make me cry. You know I cry about everything these days. The other day John told me my breasts were the size of watermelons and I burst into tears. And I think he meant it as a compliment."

Mia grinned. "You and John do make a case for marital bliss. But now that I've sworn off men entirely I've decided to lead a celibate life."

Angela swallowed her smile. "Oh, really? Well, that explains the six gallons of ice cream then, doesn't it?"

"I've been hungry, not horny."

"Yes, but not hungry for food, would be my guess. You're hungry for Nick. And I bet horny, too."

"I've been alone before. I can do without."

Eyes filled with concern and compassion, Mia's sister

asked, "Are you sure that's what you want, Mia? Are you sure you're making the right decision?"

"No. I'm not sure of anything anymore."

"But, then, why not give Nick another—?"

Mia shook her head. "It's over. I won't risk being hurt again."

"Nick doesn't think it's over. He's been all over town asking about you."

Though Mia's heart skipped a beat, she shrugged, trying not to sound as interested as she felt. "Who told you that?"

"Mary said he'd been into Mama Sophia's several times for dinner. But the whole time he was there— alone, I might add—he seemed like he was waiting for someone to come in. He's also visited Danny Boy's, Santini's Butcher Shop, Fiorelli's Bakery, Franco's Dry Cleaning . . . I could go on. It's obvious to everyone that he's been hoping to run into you, since you made it quite clear that he wasn't to darken your doorstep again."

"Nick called here a few times and left messages. I didn't return his phone calls."

"How long do you intend to punish him?"

"I'm not punishing him; I'm—"

"Punishing yourself? Because you were taken in, because you felt you should have known better, because you felt betrayed?"

Mia replied with a shrug.

"It's not like Nick didn't have a good reason for deceiving you, Mia. It's not like he had a choice in the matter. I agree that he could have gone about it differently. But I've tried to put myself in his shoes, and I'm not sure I wouldn't have done the same thing.

"This isn't the same as last time, Mia, as much as

you'd like to convince yourself of that. Greg was married, had children, and never had any intention of marrying you. At least Nick's confessed his feelings for you."

Pulling a face, Mia said, "I hate rational people."

Angela smiled, stood and kissed her sister on the cheek. "I'll leave you to clean up the mess."

She didn't elaborate on which mess she meant, but Mia had a pretty good idea.

TWENTY

Nothing is final until you are dead,
and even then I'm sure God negotiates.
Ever After

Nick had spent the last two weeks in hell, and he didn't care who knew it. His coworkers, including SAC Higgins, whom he'd told to "shove it where the sun don't shine" when the guy flayed Nick about being late with his reports, had learned to cut him a wide swath, except for Burt, who had just told him to get over it, or do something the fuck about it.

No matter how hard he'd tried, Nick couldn't make Mia forgive him. He'd written her heart-wrenching letters, pouring out his guts and declaring his love, and she'd returned them unopened. He'd left numerous messages on her answering machine, begging her to call him, and she wouldn't phone him back. He'd taken to practically stalking her, visiting all the places he knew she would normally visit, in the hope of running into her. But he hadn't.

She'd made it quite clear that he was never to visit her apartment again. She hated him that much.

He was in hell.

And he didn't know what to do about it.

Nick was determined to win Mia back. He'd grovel, if

need be. He'd already set aside his pride, figuring if he had to crawl on bended knees and beg her forgiveness, he would.

But she never gave him the chance.

Damn stubborn woman!

Mia had ignored him. Totally blown him off. Refused to have anything more to do with him. He'd become nonexistent to her, persona non grata, and it just didn't set very well. He wasn't used to being rejected by females; he'd always been the first to cut bait and run.

Nick liked things organized, and loving Mia had disrupted his entire existence. Things didn't fall into place anymore. The fact that he'd left his dirty socks on the floor for two days running hadn't even fazed him; he had no interest whatsoever in playing the stock market—how could he, when Mia wasn't there to advise or nibble on his ear? All the fun had gone out of it; and he'd grown so inattentive while driving, absorbed as he was in what to do about the woman, that he'd had his first car accident—a fender bender that was going to set him back close to one thousand dollars in repairs, thanks to his high insurance deductible.

Oh, he was definitely in hell. There was no doubt about it.

And he didn't know to whom he should turn for help.

Not only had he messed up his relationship with Mia, he had ruined the close ties he'd made with the DeNeros and Russos. They had embraced him into their families, trusted him, been kind, and treated him like one of their own.

They'd been the family he'd never had. And now they were lost to him. They might acknowledge his existence, say all was forgiven, but things would never be the same again. Gone was the easy camaraderie, along with the friendships he'd treasured.

He couldn't turn to Burt for help. The man was hopeless. Since he and Muriel had found each other again, and he was having sex on a regular basis, he didn't care to discuss Nick's love life. He had bigger fish to fry. In fact, Burt was thinking about asking Muriel to remarry him. It seemed the man had never fallen out of love with his ex-wife and had finally come to realize that she was *the* one.

Burt's newfound happiness made Nick even more depressed. Misery loved company, and he felt more alone than ever.

So when Nick happened upon Angela at Mama Sophia's one evening he got his courage up and decided to speak to her about Mia, ask her advice about what to do; providing, of course, she was still speaking to him. He'd been told that women tended to hold grudges, and Angela, being Mia's only sister, could be holding a whopper of one.

On the other hand, Angela was a lawyer, so perhaps she would look at things a bit more logically and calmly than Mia. He hoped so. His options were dwindling, as was his optimism.

"Sit down, Nick," Angela said. "I only have a few minutes. I'm meeting John, and he's not a big fan of yours, at the moment, so it would probably be best if he didn't find you here."

"I understand. I know this may sound strange, considering the present circumstances, but I was hoping you might be able to help me."

"With a legal matter?"

MAD ABOUT MIA   303

Nick shook his head, looking more miserable than any man should look. "I need some advice, about Mia."

"I see. This puts me in a rather awkward position, Nick, since Mia is my sister and you've broken her heart."

"I love her, Angela. I want to get her back. My life is nothing without her. I'll do anything."

Angela's brow arched, and she smiled a secretive smile. "Anything?"

"I'm desperate. I've tried everything I know, calling, writing, leaving messages on her machine, but Mia refuses to have anything more to do with me. I'm at the end of my rope."

"Well, we can't have you hanging yourself, so come to my apartment tomorrow morning, around ten. John will be gone by then." She handed him her business card. "We'll talk there, where we won't be disturbed. I have a feeling this discussion could take a while, and I'd rather not be interrupted."

Breathing a sigh of relief, Nick smiled gratefully. "I will. And thanks, Angela."

"Don't thank me yet. I haven't come up with any earth-shattering ideas. I may have to bring in my consultants."

"Consultants?"

"Annie and Mary. Between the three of us, we may just be able to straighten out this mess you've gotten yourself into with my little sister."

"I don't know what I would have done, if you hadn't decided to take me up on my job offer, Dad. We've got more business than we can handle right now. I'm not sure we should take on any more clients."

Concern filled Mia's eyes as she flipped through the pile of protection requests and shook her head. She was elated by the amount of work they had before them, but also scared that it was too much too fast. She didn't want to shortchange anyone by giving the customers shoddy service. That wouldn't be fair, or good for her fledgling reputation, which had been considerably enhanced by the media coverage she'd received during the Palumbo-Calzone arrest.

Sam grinned, flicking imaginary specs of dust off his red velvet jacket. He had agreed to forego his female attire unless a specific case warranted it. "I'm happy to be working again. It gives me a chance to expand my wardrobe. And if you get too many clients, you might need to hire someone else, in addition to me. It's not good to turn down work. It's too hard to come by. And businesswise, these are difficult times."

Mia thought her father looked like a pimp in the red velvet suit, but didn't want to hurt his feelings by saying so. She thumbed through the pile of papers and finally found the form she'd been looking for, pulling it out. "I guess you should take Mrs. Fabrizi's case, Dad. She wants protection from her dead husband's family until after his will is read, and I don't have a lot of patience with old people."

"Should I wear sequins or suits?"

"I think a suit would be more appropriate, don't you?"

Sam looked disappointed, but didn't argue, asking instead, "It's not a sleepover, is it? Your mother wouldn't like that." He winked. "Though I might not mind. Mrs. Frabrizi is quite a looker."

Mia rolled her eyes. "Dad! She's in her seventies. I think she's a bit too old for you. And she's got more wrinkles than a shar-pei."

Seated in the blue damask wing chair in front of Mia's new oak desk—Sam and Rosalie had donated a few pieces of furniture for Mia's office—Sam locked his hands over his belly and studied his daughter. "I owe you an apology, Mia. I never thought you would make a go of this business, and you are."

She smiled. "With your help, Dad."

"I haven't been here long enough to make a difference. No, you've done this on your own. You're gaining new clients every day from referrals and building a very solid reputation."

"Some of our clients are fruitcakes." Mia thought of Angela's client, Mrs. Mattuci, who had paid Mia one thousand dollars to baby-sit her dog, Hector, for six days, so no harm would come to him while she was out of town.

When Mia had suggested that she might want to put the dog in a kennel instead, that it might be less expensive and more practical, the woman had gotten hysterical and started crying, so Mia had relented, and now wished she hadn't.

The spoiled pooch had eaten four pair of shoes, including her Nikes, so she wouldn't be jogging for a while, and had demolished one of the end tables in her living room. She intended to ask Mrs. Mattuci to reimburse her for the damage her dog had caused.

Animal customers, Mia decided, were out.

"True, but they're paying fruitcakes, and that's all that matters. You're doing a good job. I want you to know how proud I am of you. I know you probably won't believe this, after all the negative things I've said to you over the years, but I've always been proud of you, Mia, even when I didn't come right out and say so."

Mia arched a disbelieving brow, but was thrilled to finally hear the approval she'd longed for. As childish as it seemed, she had yearned for her dad's good opinion her whole life. "Even when I worked on the bulldozing crew?" she asked.

"Well, maybe not then." Sam looked somewhat chagrined. "But I was impressed that you had learned to operate such a big piece of machinery. Though it frightened your mother and me to have you doing that kind of physical work. You could have been hurt."

"I've been hurt as a bodyguard, and might be again, and you haven't been all that vocal about it."

"I guess because I've seen how competent you've become with your martial arts and your use of a weapon. And don't forget, I've also seen you in action with Nick."

Mia felt her face flush, but knowing her father hadn't meant it the way it sounded, she smiled. "I saved the bastard's ass and look what I got in return—the rug pulled out from under me."

"Nick's a good guy, Mia. I like him, and so does your mother. You could do a lot worse."

"Please, Dad, don't you start, too. Mom's been on my case for weeks about Nick. Why don't I call him? Why don't I invite him for dinner?"

"Well, why don't you? Any idiot can see that you love the guy. And it's plain as a horse's ass that he loves you, too. Seems to me when two people love each other they should be together."

Drumming a pencil in staccato rhythm on her desktop, Mia heaved a frustrated sigh and knew she had to stop her parents' harrassment about Nick, once and for all. "Remember when you agreed to come to work here and I laid down the rules, so we wouldn't step on each other's toes and get hurt feelings?" Sam nodded, looking rather uncomfortable. "You promised me then, Dad, that you wouldn't browbeat me about Nick? Well, I'm holding you to that promise. He's not to be a topic of discussion, now or ever. Is that clear?"

"So my daughter is pulling rank on me, huh? Okay, you're the boss. I was out of line and I apologize."

Mia came around the desk and gave her father a hug. "Don't ever apologize for being my dad. I know you care about me. Maybe I had to grow up a bit before I realized where your motivation was coming from,"—she shrugged—"I don't know. But what I do know is that your heart is in the right place, and I love you."

Kissing his daughter's cheek, Sam asked, "Nick who?" and then grinned.

Mia smiled, but it never quite reached her eyes. She might be able to avoid talking about Nick, but she hadn't been able to stop thinking about him.

Coming back to her office swamped her with memories of their first encounter. It should have made her angry, realizing how badly he had duped her, but she looked back on it with mixed feelings of sadness and joy.

They'd had some great times together. She doubted she would ever play the stock market again. It just wouldn't be the same without Nick there to offer suggestions and guidance.

Dammit, Nick! she cursed silently. *You should have stayed a geek.*

Setting a cup of hot coffee down on the kitchen table before Nick, Angela seated herself next to him, with Annie and Mary seated on the other side.

"Would you care for a doughnut, Nick? We pregnant

women find solace in food." She pushed the plate toward him, but Mary reached across the table and pulled it back before he could get to it.

"Wait! I want one of the chocolate ones."

Nick grinned at the woman's panicked look. "I'm not very hungry, so you can have mine, Mary."

"Hey, thanks! And you needn't frown at me, Annie. I've been pretty good these past few days, considering I could eat paint off the walls."

"I'm sure Angela's told you why I'm here," Nick said to the two women seated across from him.

"Because you want Mia back," they replied in unison.

"Yes. I've made a mess of everything. Mia hates me."

"Do you blame her? You lied to everyone. Mia feels betrayed. I'm not sure you deserve her," Mary said, and Annie nodded in agreement.

"You played her for a fool, Nick. You should be ashamed," Annie said.

Nick hung his head like a chastised schoolboy. "I probably don't deserve her. But I love Mia so much. I can't see spending the rest of my life without her. I was so alone before I met her. Now that I've found her I just can't let her go. I want to marry her, have babies with her, make a life with her."

The three women exchanged satisfied looks, then Annie said, "Good. That's what we wanted to hear. Have you told Mia how you feel?"

"I tried, but she won't listen." He related his many failed attempts to talk to her. "Mia's very stubborn."

"There are things about Mia that you don't know, Nick. She's insecure, doubts herself in many things," Angela said, reaching out to touch his arm. "She's like a wounded hummingbird behind her brash demeanor."

"But Mia's smart and resourceful. I've told her that many times. I would never have been able to get the goods on Palumbo and Calzone without her help."

"Mia's always lived in the shadow of her older sister. Isn't that right, Angela?" Annie tossed out, staring meaningfully at her friend before pouring herself more coffee.

"Yes, I'm afraid that's true. My father tended to dote on me. He didn't love Mia any less, but it seemed that way to her. She was always trying to please him, and she never felt that she succeeded."

"But I don't see what that has to do with my . . . our relationship. I've told Mia that I love her."

"Men have always let my sister down, Nick. You are not the first man to deceive her. Mia fell in love with her college professor when she was twenty. He fed her a line, and she believed him, actually thought he'd marry her. Problem was, the bastard was already married with a couple of kids. The betrayal devastated my sister."

Nick paled, then ran impatient fingers through his hair. "Jesus Christ! No wonder she hates me. She probably thinks history has repeated itself. But I love Mia. I do want to marry her. I swear I'm not like that other guy."

"But Greg Farris told her that, too. And then she found out the truth. He used her, just as you used her, Nick. Can you blame her for wanting to protect herself?"

Nick clutched his head between his hands, and heaved a sigh. "No."

"All's not lost, Nick," Mary said. "We've all been in difficult relationships, which is why Angela thought we might be able to help you. Things worked out for us, and they can work out for you, too. But I don't think it will be easy. Mia will have to be convinced of your sincerity, and your love."

"I told Angela that I'd do anything to get her back, and I mean it."

"What most men don't understand, Nick," Annie began, "is that women want romance. They want to feel special, loved in a way that's totally their own."

"So what you're saying is that I need to woo Mia? That I've been going about things all wrong?"

"Women want to be swept off their feet," Mary said. "You made a mistake, and I think in time Mia will forgive you. But first, you have to earn her respect all over again. You have to show her that she's the most important woman in the world, in your life. And you have to paint her a picture of what your life will be like together." Mary paused to take a bite of her second doughnut, then wiped her lips with a napkin. "That's my advice. You can take it or leave it."

"Mine, too," Angela agreed. "You've got to pull out all the stops. If you're willing to listen, we can make some suggestions that may help."

"I'm listening. Should I take notes?"

"It couldn't hurt," Annie said with a grin, shoving a pad and pen in front of him. "But just don't let Mia know that you spoke to us. That would defeat the purpose. And besides, we're only going to make suggestions. The real ideas have to come from your heart."

TWENTY-ONE

The greatest thing you'll ever learn
is just to love and be loved in return.
Moulin Rouge

Perched precariously on a decrepit wooden stepladder that she'd borrowed from Mrs. Foragi and had hauled three blocks to her office, Mia was attempting to hang on the wall a rather large landscape painting that she'd purchased yesterday afternoon from the "Starving Artist" sale at the Marriott Hotel.

Her father had recently painted the walls a muted gray color, as part of their joint decision to spruce the place up a bit. Rosalie had helped by hanging burgundy drapes at the window, which hid, for the most part, the bent-out-of-shape venetian blinds, and had donated a colorful oriental rug that she no longer needed for the floor.

The Guardian Angel was beginning to look like a reputable place of business, if Mia said so herself.

The buzzer that Sam had installed on the front door went off, and Mia, thinking he was back from the deli, shouted over her shoulder, "I'm glad you're back, Dad. I'm starving. Did you get my meatball sub?"

"I don't have a meatball sub, Mia, but I did bring you these."

Mia turned so quickly that she almost fell off the ladder,

311

but managed to right herself, just in the *nick*—no pun intended—of time.

"Nick!" Her heart started thumping at the sight of him, like Crusader Rabbit on a mission, and she wondered if she would always react the same way, no matter how much time had passed. "What are you doing here?"

And why are you holding that enormous, beautiful bouquet of flowers?

"I figured since the mountain wouldn't come to Mohammed . . ." He shrugged, smiling sadly. "I've missed you, Mia. I know you told me never to bother you again, but I just had to come by and see how you were doing." He glanced around the room, eyes widening in appreciation. "Looks like you're doing well. I'm glad. The office looks very nice, much better than it did the first time I visited."

Yeah, and she didn't have any banana smeared on her nose, either.

"Thank you. Um. Are those flowers you're holding for me, or are you on your way to a funeral?"

He thrust them at her, looking almost embarrassed, which, of course, Mia found endearing. "This is my way of saying I'm sorry that I screwed up everything. Please forgive me."

She felt a lump rise to her throat and sighed deeply. "Oh, Nick."

Don't you dare cry, Mia DeNero!

He held up his hand to forestall the argument he thought would be forthcoming. "Please, don't say anything, Mia. I'm not going to stay. I just wanted you to have these. I want you to know that I love you, and I always will."

Before she had a chance to respond, to thank him for

the sweet gesture, Nick turned on his heel and hurried out the door.

Mia clutched the pink baby roses, stephanotis, and baby's breath to her chest, then burst into tears.

Which is how her father found her a few moments later.

"Was that Nick I saw racing to his car?" He set the paper bags that held their lunch on the desk. "Never mind. I can see by those tears that it was."

"He brought me flowers." She sniffed loudly. "Wasn't that nice?"

Sam shrugged. "I'm not saying a word."

But three days later, when six more arrangements of flowers arrived, Sam finally did say something.

"This place is starting to look and smell like Buffano's Funeral Parlor. I think you should tell Nick to stop sending those damn flowers. I feel like I'm ready to be laid out in a coffin. You're going to scare the customers."

Inhaling the cloying scent of gardenias, Mia smiled. "Three of my female clients happened to remark just yesterday on how beautiful they were."

"Women!" Sam grabbed *The Baltimore Sun* off the table, took a seat behind the newly installed reception desk, and decided to keep his mouth shut, knowing that where women were concerned, you were damned either way.

Mia was tired when she arrived home later that evening. Not so much physically as emotionally drained. Notes had accompanied each of the flower arrangements she'd received from Nick, professing his love and desire to see her again. And each time she read one, her spirits soared to the heavens, then came crashing back down to

earth. She was riding an emotional roller coaster with no
way to get off.

Nick had even had a singing telegram delivered to her
office the other day. Sam had answered the summons,
to find a man dressed in a furry white rabbit costume.
When the rabbit suddenly burst into song, performing
an off-key rendition of "Some Bunny Loves You" Sam
reached for his gun, and the rabbit impersonator took
off down the street. Mia had nearly wet her pants, she'd
been laughing so hard.

After hanging her coat on the rack, she headed into the
kitchen and opened the refrigerator, eyes widening when
she found a bottle of iced champagne, sitting in a silver
bucket. "What the—?" Next to it was a plate of Godiva
chocolate truffles, with a card that read: "You're far
sweeter and taste much better than these truffles. I love
you! Nick."

Thrilled all the way down to her toes, Mia reached for
the plate of chocolates at the same time the disturbing
thought formed that Nick still had a key to her apartment. She'd forgotten to ask for it back.

Expecting to feel violated, or at the very least creeped
out that someone had been in her apartment while she
wasn't there, Mia was surprised that she didn't. Instead,
Nick made her feel . . . well, cherished and special.

Dammit! She wasn't supposed to feel that way. Not after everything that had happened.

She was supposed to hate him, Mia decided, popping a
truffle into her mouth, then letting the chocolate melt on
her tongue and caress it.

Damn, but it was hard to hate a man whose taste in
chocolate was this good!

Opening the champagne, which exploded over most

of the kitchen, Mia filled a crystal flute with what was left of the bubbly liquid, and took it into the bedroom with her. She decided she would relax in a hot bubble bath, drink champagne, eat truffles and feel sinfully decadent. Cleaning up the mess she'd made in the kitchen could wait.

Upon entering the bathroom, she found a heart-shaped note taped to the mirror over the sink, which read, "Behold the most beautiful woman in the world!" and her eyes filled with tears.

"Dammit, Nick! You are making it very hard to hate you. Now, stop this at once! You are not playing fair."

Setting the champagne and chocolates down on the vanity, she pulled back the shower curtain to find that her bathtub had been filled with rose petals, hundreds and hundreds of fragrant petals, in various colors. She found another note taped to the tile: "Your skin is much softer than the petals of a rose, your body far more perfect, your face even lovelier. Please forgive me, and let me make it up to you." It was signed Nick.

No surprise there.

The surprise was that the man had the soul of a poet, or else he had found some really good how-to book at the mall and was following its advice on romancing a woman into submission.

And damn if it wasn't working, because Mia felt very weak and submissive at the moment.

Should she call and invite him over?

To forgive was divine, after all.

Her answering machine showed ten messages, and she hit the button, knowing in advance whom the persistent caller would be. Nick's voice came through the speaker, like warm honey on toast, sending tingles of awareness down her spine.

There were so many *"I love yous"* and *"forgive mes"* and *"I can't live without yous,"* not to mention a very sexy performance of the song "Nobody Does It Better," Mia finally decided she would call Nick back.

If nothing else, she would tell him to return her key.

Yeah, right!

Mia had agreed to a date.

Okay, so she was easy. The chocolates and champagne had done their work. And Nick had been at his most charming on the phone last night when he'd talked her into meeting him.

He'd told her to dress warmly for their date, and so she had donned a navy wool pantsuit with a red cashmere sweater. It was dressy enough for dinner, or casual enough for just walking around the mall. Nick hadn't bothered to tell her where he was taking her, so she had to cover all the bases.

He said it was a surprise.

She hated surprises.

And now, while she waited for Nick to pick her up at the appointed time of ten o'clock—she glanced at her watch. Who went on a date so early in the morning?—Mia wondered if she had done the right thing. If she was ready to forgive him, to trust him with her heart again. She just didn't know.

And she still didn't know an hour later as the Volvo sped down the interstate, radio blasting, with Nick singing "Bridge Over Troubled Water" at the top of his lungs, doing a fairly decent impersonation of Art Garfunkel.

Who knew the man could sing?

And then Mia realized that there were a lot of things about FBI Agent Caruso that she didn't know, like what kind of songs he liked, or what his favorite ice cream was. Did he butter his English muffin, use jam, or just eat it plain?

She knew he slept naked, and that was important. But did he really iron his underwear, or did he use a laundry to get them looking so crisp? She swore he had them starched.

These might seem like unimportant questions to the average person, but to someone in a relationship, or contemplating a relationship, they were significant.

And was she contemplating a relationship with Nick?

"So where are we going?" she asked when the song finally ended, something like eighteen minutes later. Simon and Garfunkel were quite long-winded, not that she minded. She loved the duo.

"If I tell you, you have to promise that you won't be mad."

"Just tell me that we're not going to see any type of sporting event. I don't think I could deal with that."

"We're not. It's much better than that."

"Are you kidnapping me? Because there are laws against that sort of thing, as you well know, being an FBI guy, and my parents will be worried."

"It's only a kidnapping if you don't consent, and I think you will once you learn where we're headed. And I've already spoken to your parents. Your mother was very helpful."

Mia snorted her disdain. "I bet. So are you going to tell me our destination, or do I have to jump out of the car and call for help?"

"New York City."

Mia's mouth dropped open. "New York City! Are you crazy? That's a three-hour drive, at least. And why are we going to New York City? That seems like a long way to go for a date. Couldn't we just have one in Baltimore? I like The Cheesecake Factory."

Nick laughed. "I wanted to do something special for you, Mia. It was supposed to be a surprise."

"I'm not sure anything you could do from here on out would surprise me, Nick. You managed that a few weeks back. And I doubt very much you can top it."

Nick turned off the radio, his voice filled with remorse. "You'll never know how sorry I am about involving you in my stupid investigation, Mia. I've cursed myself a thousand times for using you like that. I should have found another way. It was selfish of me. And I'm sorry. I don't know what else to say."

Mia sighed. "I guess you were doing what you thought was best at the time. And as it turned out, my involvement with your investigation helped my business a great deal, so I'm grateful for that."

"I never meant to hurt you. I never meant to fall in love with you. I still love you, Mia, very much. And if you can find it in your heart to forgive me . . . Never mind. I'll leave the rest of that speech for later."

"Later?" But she was dying of curiosity now.

"I'd like you to take the next few hours to think about all that's happened between us, to see if you might still have feelings for me. If, by the end of the evening, you decide that you're unable to forgive me, I'll take you home and never bother you again. Deal?"

Mia, who was too choked with emotion to speak, merely nodded her acquiescence.

*   *   *

Mia awoke to find that they'd arrived in New York City. Honking horns and shouts of invective blared from impatient, angry drivers, people bustled along crowded sidewalks, obviously in a hurry to reach their destination, and the air crackled with excitement that only a vibrant city like New York could produce.

The sun was still shining and Mia glanced at the clock on the dash to find that it was only one-thirty in the afternoon. She thought it would be much later. It seemed as if they'd been driving forever. Like an impatient child, she'd been tempted to shout several times, "Are we there yet?" but had the good sense to refrain. Nick was the kind of driver who didn't stop for bathroom breaks, she'd discovered.

Nick stopped the car in front of the Plaza Hotel and cut the engine.

"We're staying here?" she asked, taking in the massive ornate building, the flags flying proudly at the entrance, and was rendered momentarily speechless.

"I hope you like it. I wanted to do something extra special, so I reserved a two-bedroom suite. You'll have your own room. I'm not trying to pull anything funny, so don't worry about that."

Sex was the least of Mia's worries. She had more important things to think about. "But I didn't bring any toiletries or fancy clothes for dinner. I'm going to look like a country mouse. I'll be mortified among all these sophisticated people."

Nick grinned. "Not to worry. Angela packed an overnight bag for you. It's in the trunk."

"Angela was in on this, too?" Mia could hardly believe that her own sister, the woman she hero-worshipped, had participated in this. Her mother she could believe. But Angela?

"How many people have keys to your apartment, anyway?" Nick asked.

"Too many, apparently. And I'll be asking for yours back."

"But not until after tonight, correct?"

It took her a moment to answer. "All right."

"I can't believe you actually got tickets for a private tour of the Stock Exchange. It was the most thrilling experience of my life. I won't ever forget it."

"Should I be insulted by that?" Nick quipped, as they walked down Fifth Avenue toward their hotel.

Mia grinned, knocked Nick's arm playfully, then said seriously, "Thank you, Nick. You shouldn't have gone to so much trouble. I can't believe that you arranged for me to ring the closing bell. I thought that was reserved for dignitaries and really important people. I felt so honored.

"And from now on I'm going to invest my money seriously, no more pretend. I feel confident I can make money at investing."

"You won't have much more investing to do, Mia. I opened an account in both our names. The stocks you picked for me to invest in have done extremely well, for both of us. You have a nice little nest egg put away, Miss DeNero."

Staring wide-eyed, Mia's mouth dropped open. "You did that for me? But why? I was choosing the stocks for you."

Stopping in the middle of the sidewalk, Nick grabbed Mia gently by her arms and turned her toward him.

"Don't you know, Mia? Search your heart and ask yourself why I would care."

Mia had never fallen out of love with Nick, and the realization that he might really love her hit her smack between the eyes. But she intended to proceed cautiously. Men had lied to her before; Nick had lied to her before.

"Thank you again. I don't know what to say."

"Well, if you can't say you love me, at least you can tell me that you forgive me."

"I do forgive you, Nick. I'm not saying that things will change between us. I need more time to think about whether or not we, as a couple, will work. But I hope that we can remain friends. I want that more than anything."

Nick prayed Mia didn't take too much longer to make up her mind because he had plans for later—later today—plans that could change both of their lives forever. He'd waited long enough—his whole life—for a woman like Mia to complete him, and he didn't intend to wait one moment longer than he had to.

They dined at a romantic French restaurant on 48th Street. Mia stuffed herself on onion soup gratinée, duck à l'orange, and crème brulée, and listened while Nick delivered his thoughts on love, marriage, and child-rearing.

She liked the idea that he was opening up to her, and had revealed more about his childhood, college years, and his work with the FBI. She was finally getting to know the real Nick Caruso, and she found that she liked him, in addition to loving him.

There was a big difference between like and love. You had to genuinely like someone before you could contemplate having a relationship with that person. You had to establish a friendship, for without friendship, nothing worked.

And yes, she was contemplating having a relationship with Nick. And it had nothing to do with the half bottle of Bordeaux she had polished off over dinner, although that had helped.

When they returned to the hotel, Mia turned toward the steps to go in, but Nick clasped her arm, saying, "Don't be in such a hurry for the night to end," then escorted her to one of the waiting carriages that was parked near the hotel and paid the driver to take them on a ride through Central Park.

Mia, who was beyond thrilled, squealed in excitement. "I have been wanting to do this since I saw *Barefoot in the Park* with Robert Redford and Jane Fonda. How did you know?"

"It's one of my favorite movies."

"Really?" She smiled happily. "Then that means you have excellent taste, Mr. Caruso."

"I'm addicted to you, Miss DeNero, so I guess that's true."

A soft blush filled Mia's cheeks, and she reached for his hand as the horse began clip-clopping along at a slow speed, oblivious to the cars passing by. "You're kind of growing on me, too," she admitted.

He kissed her cheek. "Good. That's my plan."

When they entered the park, it was as if no one else in the world existed but them. It was quiet, considering they were in the middle of a huge metropolitan area, and very, very romantic.

"You were probably wondering why I brought up the topic of marriage and family over dinner," Nick said, squeezing Mia's hand.

"I did. But I'm happy to know your thoughts on every subject. I feel like I know you so much better now. And that's important to me."

"I want you to spend the rest of your life getting to know me, Mia. I want to marry you. I know you don't want children right now, and I can live with that, in the hope that someday you might change your mind."

"You're proposing to me?" Mia choked out over the large lump in her throat. Her heart was beating a thousand beats a second, or so it seemed, and her eyes grew moist with tears of joy.

Nick reached into his coat pocket and produced a small velvet ring box with the Tiffany's label on it, handing it to her. "I love you, Mia DeNero. I want to spend the rest of my life with you, grow old with you, argue with you, laugh with you, fight with you, make up with you. I'm asking you to be my wife and love me, as I love you."

Mia began crying as she gazed upon the perfect diamond solitaire ring, and Nick grew alarmed. "You can pick out something else, if you don't like this one. I want you to be happy."

"No, it's beautiful. I love it."

"It pales next to you, sweetheart."

"Oh, Nick, I'm so confused."

"I know you wanted longer to think about us, Mia, but I can't wait any longer. I want you too badly. I want us to start our life together, now, this very minute. The only thing I need to know is whether or not you love me."

"I do love you, Nick. I've never stopped loving you, though I tried really hard." Nick released the breath he'd been holding. "But I'm not sure I'm ready to take this step right now. It's an important decision to make, and I'm scared."

"But you proposed to me once."

"I know. It's just . . ."

"That you don't trust me."

"I've been hurt before, Nick, by a man who professed to love me." She explained about her involvement with Greg Farris. "And then after what happened between us . . . well, I'm not sure that . . ."

He squeezed her hand. "You'll never know how sorry I am that I hurt you, Mia. I promise if you say yes and marry me, I'll spend the rest of my life making it up to you. I have no life without you. You are my life."

Mia swallowed the lump in her throat, knowing in that moment what her answer would be. "Yes, I'll marry you, Nick. And I'll even have your children. But I want to be knocked out before delivery, so I don't know what's going on. You have to promise me that. And I'm going to keep my bodyguard business. I've worked too hard to give it up."

"Whatever you want is fine with me, as long as we're together. That's the only thing that matters."

"You mean I could have asked for more?"

With a grin, he placed the ring on the finger of her left hand, and she threw her arms about him. "I love you, Nick, and I'm hoping this carriage ride is about over, because I feel the need to test out that humongous king-size bed in our suite. It's been a while, if you know what I mean."

"No one is more anxious than me. I've missed holding you in my arms."

"Oh, I can hardly wait to plan our wedding. Angela, of course, will be my matron of honor, and I want Mary and Annie to be bridesmaids. And do you think we should ask Sophia and Mrs. Foragi to be flower girls? That would spice things up a bit. Weddings can be so dull, don't you think? And Grandma Flora could be the ring bearer. What do you think, Nick?"

He groaned. "I think maybe we should just elope."

"What? And spoil all the fun."

"You have a warped sense of humor, Mrs. Caruso."

"*Oooh,* I like that. Say it again."

He drew her into his arms and kissed her passionately. "I intend to say it every day for the rest of our lives, right after I say 'I love you.' "